The Duke Don't Dance

by

R I C H A R D S H A R P

ISBN: 1467949167
ISBN-13: 9781467949163

626 Shelton Street
Charlotte, NC 28270
rgsva@aol.com

To Lillian, Ari, Fran, Beth and Inga, whoever you were

CHAPTER 1

Annapolis, 2011

It was a breathtaking view. A garden of red roses and carnations lay ahead along a path of snow-white gladioli and ferns. On the left, an array of fragrant lavender and pink roses, pink snapdragons and chrysanthemums; on the right, pungent yellow jasmines, orange orchids, pink roses, and red gladioli, all striving to dominate scent and sight. The visual and olfactory overload silenced the soft nautical sounds of Spa Creek in the distance.

Frank presided over this landscape in a resplendent dress uniform acquired for the next day's military honors, an image of strength and stoicism, nonjudgmental, set in his position but not rigid, unemotional and at peace, as suits an honoree. He was imposing, albeit uncommonly liveried, as no one present—not even his wife, Lillian—could recall having seen him in dress blues. Yet despite having abandoned such trappings of military authority long ago, Frank was perfectly attired for the occasion in his one-time rank as a United States Air Force major, comfortably assured, if not fully deserving of credit for his elegance, a beneficiary of the mortuary director's assistance. Regrettably, he had no choice in the matter.

Those assembled on that Annapolis afternoon were mostly retirees, once young, impressionable readers of Orwell who had feared the arrival of 1984 right up through Reagan's reelection. They populated a generation to whom the collapse of the Soviet Union was inconceivable, to whom China remained the land of little red books, who had loved Dylan when he knew which way the wind blew or hated him in a time it was acceptable to do so. It was a menagerie of men who tolerated Sinatra but thought his daughter had nice legs, women who once wore her boots and knew they weren't made for walking, women who despised the '50s for beating down their mothers, and men who loved the '60s as those women rebelled against their mothers. Compressed between legions of the self-assured emboldened by victories over Japan and Germany and the swarming plague of their entitled progeny, they entered, endured, and were now departing a world they could not control, but messed with as much as it did them.

Frank had outlived his childhood friends or lost track of them, so only his mother and two surviving sisters were there to remember his childhood days in Colorado before entering the new Air Force Academy in 1957. A few former cadets from the academy appeared, but only those who later served with Frank in FAC units in Nam and Isan. Those from Vietnam, forward air controllers stationed with Frank mainly in Bien Hoa, paid respects to a brash lieutenant in unlaundered fatigues; those later engaged in the Secret War honored a seasoned and cynical black ops flyer in dusty jeans and a *Spy vs. Spy* tee shirt. Though the swashbuckling of early tours yielded to Spartan warrior fatalism, the FACs all shared much in common. They chain-smoked tobacco and weed as available, drank heavily with little discrimination, cursed LBJ and Nixon incessantly and interchangeably, and set aside thoughts of remote wives and girlfriends to carry Zippo lighters inscribed "If you want sex, smile when you return me." As a rule, they had been pigs in those days and those who let that era define them mostly still were.

The ex-military guests were outnumbered by those from a lobbying firm in D.C. that Frank joined in desperation a few unemployed years after the fall of Saigon. A brief crossroad on divergent paths, the place served as a virtual rehabilitation center where survivors of the war abroad and '60s at home recovered from the first half of their lives and began the second. Ted Stein, then the firm's publicity director, took to calling the place Ward 22, or simply the Ward, in reference to the Joseph Heller novel everyone had to read in college in those days, and the name stuck. Being in the Ward was, appropriately enough, everyone's second choice, but the diversity of the firm's clients, who solicited the government for favors or relief, provided decent preparation for a high-tech world to become increasingly preoccupied with personal computers, video games, cellular phones, SUVs, ATMs, PDAs, Windows, Macs, mice, music downloads, and Internet porn.

Those interned there needed the Ward. The coming world challenged the most fundamental beliefs of Frank's generation; faith in the superiority of the TEAC reel-to-reel recorder, the unparalleled fidelity of the Shure V15 Type VMR cartridge, universal Ma Bell telephone service, the IBM Selectric and Whiteout, its faithful sidekick. Beyond the material, their old faith encompassed certitude in the immunity of heterosexuals from the gay plague, the contentment of female employees to serve secretarial and clerical roles, the fundamental sameness of American political parties, and the sanctity of the separation of religious belief and secular behavior, hypocrisy be damned.

They struggled to change, but in those days there was no app for that, and they were tempted by false gods. The Ward, in fact, proselytized many of them, making the case for BETA's superiority over VHS, increased frequency allocations to citizens' band radio, mainframe time-sharing advantages over so-called personal computers, and the necessity of adopting Japanese business practices to compete with that nation's inevitable global economic domination. In that transitional place and time, Frank had been the lone conservative, the sports-coat-attired everyman in meetings of three-piece navy blue suits, the canary in a liberal mineshaft. After Reagan's easy reelection, he realized that his unchanged views had become left of center, tired of this fickle civilian world, and left the Ward by the close of that Orwellian year.

There were just a few of Frank's post-1984 colleagues present: some associated with the shadowy world abroad to which he returned after domestic life soured at home and in the office, some contemporaries, some junior, some mutual friends from his marriage to Lillian, all less consequential than earlier acquaintances, as views became more fixed and predictable, journeys less mutual, interactions more commercial or more trivial. Some of Lillian's intimates of both sexes also attended, individuals Frank didn't know, didn't care to know, or regretted knowing, there to support Lillian, not caring any more about Frank than he cared about them.

And lastly there were a gaggle of spouses and significant others dragged unwillingly to the event, a few disinterested observers present to assist or otherwise accompany the infirm, and the normal quota of well- and ill-behaved children; that is, the typical disarray on such occasions.

At her assigned post at the entrance, Isabella, the assistant to the funeral director, one Dr. Welch, welcomed Frank's contemporaries. They were cute, especially the old men. Hardly one under seventy, she judged. The women were nice, but a bit stiff and uncomfortable, even irritable, perhaps concerned about appearances after so much time, wary of how certain male arrivals would react or, more importantly, how they might be ranked by the other women. On the other hand, when she stepped out to greet them, the men were all so sweet, hobbling along as best they could, many clad in long-unworn ill-fitting suits, standing a little straighter than seemed natural, attempting to be lighthearted, offering flattering compliments. They were trying, she surmised, to show one another that they each remained youthful in spirit. It was a forgivable misjudgment. Sweet young women with attractive figures typically do not recognize flirting by elderly men or the annoyance of spouses for whom such provocations once were an actual concern, not simply absurd.

Those entering the Sunrise Funeral Home were indeed taken with the elemental extravagance of the floral setting. It appeared, actually, as though some animal had worked his way into a garden shop, eaten into the seed packs and scattered the seeds in all directions on topsoil excessively infused with horse manure, allowing nature to take its course. Delivered that morning, the eclectic choices of sprays, vases, and baskets created a floral kaleidoscope devoid of lamentation, a splatter of some gay Jackson Pollock on amphetamines. The discordance of color was buttressed by the continuous cycling of an instrumental recording of "Sunrise, Sunset," adding to the sensual cacophony. It arguably related to the name and function of the funeral home, but…really? Frank would have preferred "Light My Fire," and everyone knew it.

Few entering were true mourners. Most had survived the deaths of closer intimates, and many had not seen Frank in two decades

4

or more; they had responded to Lillian's invitation as a kind of reunion, knowing Frank's utter contempt for bereavement, a form of self-abuse in his opinion. It was more an alumni party with a corpse in attendance than a memorial service.

To the extent they really knew him, most present had liked Frank, a few greatly and unreservedly, some setting aside envy, others with a degree of condescension. Those who knew him best were aware that he could be a bone-headed son of a bitch, but did not hold that or other grievances against him, with the exception of Beth, Inga, and, to a lesser extent, Ted, and maybe one or two others. A Western farm boy stranded among effete East Coast urbanites, Frank had been blunt, intelligent with no intellectual pretenses, free to admit that his youthful follies continued well into adulthood, conservative by nature and liberal by experience, with no greater respect for right than left, fundamentalists than atheists. He did as he pleased, didn't give a rat's ass about what anyone thought about it. He had no time for people's affectations or sympathies.

Lillian had arranged a separate private service for Frank's Colorado sisters and ancient mother next morning, prior to the military ceremony in Arlington Cemetery, providing a somber outlet for those dedicated grievers who didn't quite accept Frank's irreverence, whose memories of his innocent childhood caused them to believe him to be different from the man he had become. His sisters could exercise their sentimental authority and play the whole soundtrack of *Fiddler on the Roof* tomorrow if they chose to do so, but this, the present occasion, would be more a wake than a memorial. Someone thankfully killed Tevye in favor of the sounds of silence, allowing the hard of hearing a fighting chance to understand each other.

The youngsters below retirement age soon faded away from the lobby and Repose Room, where the casket lay, to the adjacent Meditation Room, where a free bar was set out, and they could drink to the deceased or to themselves and play with their iPhones, iPads, and other instruments of modern solipsist contemplation. In the Meditation Room the young and middle-aged would stay, clustered among their contemporaries, texting or gaming in

5

mutual isolation, dreading an outbreak of inappropriate behavior by their particular elders, bored at the thought of enduring more chatter over aches, pains, and other symptoms, and fearful of embarrassing remarks about themselves or their children.

Those in the Meditation Room wouldn't admit it, and knew it was irrational, but at some level the elderly seemed sprung from an alternate sepia-tinted universe of the conventional and uninspiring, a static world portrayed in carousels of faded 35 mm slides abandoned in countless attics, images the elderly created themselves, never relating tales of escapades to their children, not admitting to getting drunk or smoking pot, committing adultery, getting busted, engaging in adventurous and acrobatic sex in cars, closets, elevators, swimming pools or more inappropriate venues. The idea that they might have done so, or might do so now if they were physically able, was disgusting, appalling, and in violation of known laws of nature. Only the exceptional nature of the present occasion permitted glimpses into the past reality and then only among the subjects of those faded transparencies.

With youthful deference to the wisdom of the elders merely an abstract fantasy, the young and middle-aged abandoned the old at the wake, as is usually the case in the absence of familial bonds, childhood memories, pity, financial considerations, or the need for responsible babysitters. That suited the senior generation just fine; there are only so many times persons born before 1946 can hear the word "awesome" without throwing up.

There were, nonetheless, a few exceptions to the young shunning the old. Dom, Lillian's oldest daughter by her first marriage, eventually took over her mother's greeting duties, once Lillian became preoccupied with the gaggle of Frank's old male friends, drawn to her like moths to the brightest candle in the room. Dom's younger sister had had a few drinks, allowed herself to be introduced to the elderly and left early. Having been estranged from her mother for at least twenty-five years prior to Lillian's third and final marriage, she had had little contact with Frank. Frank's son, Rick, an accomplished popular musician, attempted to entertain the crowd with a few of his father's favorite tunes from the '60s and '70s, alternating acoustic guitar versions of Doors classics with

Joplin, Cash, Willie, and a riff on Chuck Berry. Rick's sister Nancy cruised back and forth between the senior set, the even older Colorado relatives, and their mother from Frank's first marriage. A girl in her twenties named Triana hovered around the fringe of old folks, Rick, and the bar. Others occasionally checked on whether their charges were ready to leave or needed help to the toilets.

Lillian was "holding up beautifully," Frank's sisters would say reservedly, having never approved of the liaison. She greeted each arrival until Dom relieved her, acknowledging condolences pleasantly, accepting the future assurances proffered on such occasions, and betraying only the slightest touch of irony in a half-amused, canary-consuming smile that most of the assembled company had not seen in years. Her trim figure and still-shiny black hair, now tinted with gray, conveyed a resilience that few expected, considering the days of her addictions and self-destruction, not recognizing that beauty can be preserved by sheer vanity, Lillian's greatest curse and asset.

It was a subdued vanity now. Lillian certainly felt sorrowful; because of Frank, she eventually had lost the need to confirm her attractiveness to men through a succession of ill-conceived seductions. She had been tolerably faithful, sober, and in control over the many years of the marriage, even before age killed most of the temptations. A wise woman had advised Frank after his own failed first union that he needed to look within himself to discover his minimal conditions for a relationship to be successful and then find a partner who shared those values. For him, that consisted merely of respect in private and avoiding embarrassment in public. Many thought that Frank had the patience of a saint with this difficult woman, but in truth he was not patient at all. In keeping with the fatalism of his rural heritage, he simply had accepted their vows as final, convinced that even if things were done right, the marriage, like a crop in a bad year, might fail anyway. That revelation came to Frank in his later life: to see the person as tangible but evolving and the relationship as an ephemeral and transitory process one could not control beyond a certain point. That he might undramatically accept the collapse of their union if it became an embarrassment made Lillian more determined to make it work; and she did. Those mutually acceptable conditions made it easy.

Lillian's mood that day was sustained with the knowledge that her failures as a wife, lover, or caregiver did not contribute to Frank's death. Frank had not died in despair or in a long struggle to survive, but in a sudden, fatal accident. She stood near the casket, proud of him in life and in death. Like a loyal graduate, she remained true to her school, faithful, a once-failing delinquent graduated and restored to society. Well, that describes one view of Lillian. To others, she was just a crazy old lady with over two hundred pairs of shoes. That alone probably was enough to drive Frank into the river.

Out of all those present, a small clutch of those from the Ward dominated Lillian's attention: Sam, Fran, Ben, Rafi, Beth, and Ted.

Sam arrived for the gathering early with his wife, Francesca, who begrudgingly responded to Fran after years of fierce resistance to such familiarity. They were both taciturn, their passivity driven primarily by conflict avoidance necessitated by their radical politics and unreserved atheism, or, as they termed it, common sense. Uncompromising in these beliefs, unwilling to be activists in everyday encounters, endeavoring also not to be seen as condescending, and preferring not to argue with the supercilious, they were not easily lured into the minefield of polite conversation.

Among those present, Sam had known Lillian the longest, as they had attended the same northern Virginia high school in the 1950s. He had first met Frank during the Vietnam War, almost as long ago as the few pilots present. Now a semi-retired management consultant, ordinary in appearance with an impressive but unspecialized education sufficient only to engage in allegedly technical situations requiring no actual technological knowledge, Sam's true expertise lay in passing for an expert, so as to enable clients to seek help without confessing their own intellectual inadequacies. He viewed this career dispassionately, without personal ego or disparagement of his clients, without cynicism, without exaggeration. Frank once told him that his talent rested on being an unrecognized asset. He didn't object.

Fran had met Frank even before Sam, though their early acquaintance had been quite incidental. She had kept her maiden name of Ghiardelli through two marriages for career reasons and as a bow to her ethnic heritage—and mostly because she loved the chocolate of a similar name. She was reserved, encouraging others to address her formally, the Italian façade being a valuable asset in maintaining distance, her usual preference. Now retired, she was content being a devoted grandmother after a stressful career associated with the Smithsonian Institution Office of International Activities, serving as a coordinator for Special Projects and International Exchanges, a unit with wide-ranging responsibilities for liaison with foreign contacts.

Dealing with remote operations, difficult agents, and fragile assets across her institution's world of art and artifice comprised a challenging career, with the value of her portfolio and the high cost of mistakes demanding precision. Over time, those professional standards extended to her personal attitudes toward matters of language and culture. She became a stickler for grammar, mourning the passing of the subjunctive to the point that "I'd be safe and warm if I was in L.A." ruined "California Dreamin'" for life, and the absurd "Live and Let Die" lyrics of "in this ever-changing world in which we live in" turned her off Paul McCartney forever.

Sam, imprecise and intuitive by nature, needed this counterfoil. Frank, back in the early '80s, had seen that and introduced Francesca to him, as a gesture of friendship and, as it turned out later, as part of an agenda. Sam later reciprocated by arranging for Frank to meet Lillian, then a recently renewed acquaintance, a one-time misadventure from his high school years. Neither man saw these gestures as creating thirty-year commitments for the other. No man wants to take on such responsibilities.

When Sam and Fran arrived, one Herminia J. C. Ng, known inaptly as Inga, waited in a car in the parking lot, talking on her Blackberry. On spotting the couple, she followed them into the building discretely. Having divorced Frank thirty years earlier, the slim Asian woman had never met Lillian, but came to pay her respects to Frank despite there being no love lost between them over the last decades. Except for Rick and Nancy, her children with Frank, closer to him than to her and now helping Lillian with arrangements, she knew only Sam and Fran among the arrivals. Uninvited and unwilling to confront Lillian, Inga planned to acknowledge her children only surreptitiously and, if it came to that, introduce herself simply as a friend of Fran, allowing all to believe she knew the deceased only through that connection. She caught up with Fran just inside the door and, while Sam stood alongside with raised eyebrows, quickly attained her assent to the deception.

Ben and Rafi followed. Ben's wife, Rachel, had declined to attend with a lame excuse cloaking some ancient grievance, making it convenient for Ben to offer his single friend a ride. Rafi, a frail stroke survivor who never married and did not drive, accepted the lift in lieu of a long taxi trip from his posh assisted-living facility in Virginia to the bayside neighborhood where Frank and Lillian had retired. Not buying the story of Rachel's commitment to her book club, Rafi had pestered Ben the entire journey about the real reason for her absence, but to no avail. Perhaps she had had an affair with Ted during the rough spot in his marriage nearly thirty years before and didn't want to open old wounds. Maybe Lillian had once slept with Ben or some other permutation. Rafi, for his part, figured it was merely that Frank once ratted out Ben for eating pounds of bacon on a business trip. That would have been sufficient motivation. For Rachel, corruption came not from breaking the kosher regulations of Halakhic law, but from the exposure of the transgression. Ben was old school; Rachel was Old Testament.

Rafael Valdes, known to all as Rafi, grew up in a Havana orphanage during the 1940s before a Miami family took him in. He supported the Cuban revolution, joined the American civil rights movement and remained an admirer of Che decades after his death. Having witnessed the liberal activism of Ben and Rachel's youth forsaken by them for a crushing social conservatism built on a foundation of family, ethnic, and communal dedication and a wall of taboos forbidding open admission of their own flaws, the shortfalls of their offspring, or the moral fallibility of Israel, Rafi suspected that they were closet Republicans.

Ben had grown thoroughly annoyed with Rafi by the time they arrived at the Sunrise Funeral Home. Being a liberal doesn't require being naïve, he told himself, but Rafi made him feel defensive. Ben understood why his wife had voted for McCain after Obama defeated Hillary, but Rafi would not. Ben felt vindicated in his belief that Obama was just a Chicago politician, not the leftist visionary that Rafi had hoped he would be. God knows how Rafi would react if he ever found out that Ben could not bring himself to vote for McGovern and marked the presidential ballot for Nixon in that old election.

Beth and her new partner next materialized, with Beth betraying a tension more suitable to an audition than a gathering of old friends and her friend the image of a nervous intern. Beth displayed a little too much bling for her modest stature and the occasion, not born of a lack of confidence, but rather as insurance against an indifferent reception to her arrival. Beth Treme, too, had passed through the Ward, and she wouldn't be slighted, despite issues with all the men in the group, including the corpse, who many years ago had taken to calling her Nurse Ratched. Her partner clearly did not belong to the group, barely qualified as suitable under the Golden Rule of Relationships – half your age plus seven years – being forty-three to Beth's seventy.

Beth attended not out of affection, but because she believed it was the right thing to do. The only black person in the building—unless you counted Rafi, which she did not—Beth graded strong on abstract precepts of right and wrong, a true Calvinist at heart despite her Louisiana Southern Baptist upbringing. She was a flawless human being at the macro level. At the micro level, well…the devil was in the details.

Ted entered behind Beth. To some, he emanated the superficial, raunchy glibness that passed for wit and urbanity in the new millennium, but in fact he had come by these attributes honestly back in the '50s and had never let go of them, not filling out like Ben or Sam, either physically or emotionally. Temperamentally the opposite of Sam, he had been a friend and rival from college days and dragged him into the lobbying firm all those years ago. Now over seventy and a recent widower, he personified Dave Barry's mantra that you're only young once, but you can be immature forever. He received a pass from those who knew how he cared for his wife Rebecca during her long illness, while she exploited her condition in a manner that could damn any man to bizarre behavior, and from those who knew his quiet but steadfast commitment to his children, now successful, creative adults. His antics were cute in a way, though combining the sensibilities of a nineteen-year-old with an advertising executive's swagger and seven-figure income was incongruous. Ted seemed harmless and amusing, but how could he be so successful?

Ted had become known for designing popular television ads that sponsors purchased for their inventiveness and positive viewer reception, but left hardly a trace of product recognition. He traded in ads featuring undressed or scantily attired models (woman taking a shower morphing to a shot of the product in a rainstorm or under a waterfall), old popular songs (using a train song to promote a laxative), and sophomoric references (the question of whether a bear shits in the woods being borrowed to sell toilet paper). Sponsors and "viewers like you," especially male, appreciated his naked ladies, clips of nostalgic oldies, and barely concealed references to schoolyard jokes; sponsors enjoyed the hip gloss on their pedestrian products, accepting Ted's assurances that they left some subliminal feel-good vibes for their product, even without conscious awareness, even if the ads portrayed the product's customers as complete idiots. Ted currently was planning a marketing campaign based on a certain "place in France," where the line "where the women wear no pants" might be applied to incontinence diapers so lightweight that the woman wearing them might not even feel them. Now, that might work; a little risqué, a little gross, a little infantile, but there's always an audience for those sorts of things.

Oblivious to any adverse reactions and within ten minutes of arriving, Ted made a blatant pass at Isabella, who, as with the others, completely failed to recognize it; asked Sam to introduce him to the "Chinese chick," a query quashed by the revelation she was Inga, Frank's inconsonantly-named ex-wife; and propositioned Lillian, who advised him to consult with her deceased husband.

It had been at least twenty-five years since Lillian last saw Ted, but she anticipated that he wouldn't have changed much, so didn't find the advance particularly inappropriate; in fact, it pleased Lillian that he still found her attractive.

Then Ted spotted Beth and, in a taunting voice started chanting, "Duke, Duke, Duke, Duke of Earl, Duke, Duke..." Beth did not appear amused, having long had a limited tolerance for Ted's childishness, but she attempted to reply in good spirits. "Ellington was the Duke, you idiot; he *could* dance, he just didn't. Or, hell, maybe it was John Wayne or the baseball player; we all had our favorites. God, I can't believe you would dredge up that illiterate graffiti after all these years."

"Words of the prophets, baby. Words of the prophets. I'm just sayin'."

Sam shrugged and said nothing. Fran went over to greet Beth, asking her to introduce her friend, who turned out to be an accountant named Jennifer, whose work for Beth turned to intimacy after her mentor's divorce. Not sharing the grievances of Beth's former coworkers, Fran eased the tension by seeking out and introducing Inga, also neutral to those old conflicts, the four then drifting off past the coffin and into a quiet corner where they struggled to find benign subjects of common interest. It wasn't easy, but the look of relief on Sam's face, apparent even to Jennifer, made their retirement from the main reunion worthwhile.

Lillian had asked Sam to give a eulogy, an odd choice given his lack of religious sensibilities. He started with the lame joke of many obituaries, stating how he wished Frank could have seen so many of his old friends, mainly because he then would have been alive and made his eulogy unnecessary. He reviewed Frank's contribution to the nation and society through his military career and participation in the war on drugs, then cited the evidence that Frank had died a hero, since according to the police, the absence of skid marks indicated that he had been faced with a choice on an icy road and when unable to stop had swerved into the Potomac, saving the lives of several sledders who suddenly had descended onto the road from the adjacent hillside.

Sam looked around the room and noted that at least half of those present had not seen Frank in more than twenty years, asking rhetorically why they had come, but not waiting for answers nor giving time to ponder the question. Aside from Lillian and a few others, he observed accusingly, not many in the room were experiencing any sense of personal loss from Frank's death. "No, you are not here for mourning or even out of curiosity to see that the son of a bitch is really dead, but because you know he made a difference in your life, directly or through someone important to you. When I started to prepare this, knowing that this wake would be here in Annapolis, I realized that there are dozens of naval metaphors used in eulogies. He was my north star, my compass, my anchor, my sails, the wind beneath my sails. How can you be an anchor, a sail, and a compass all at the same time? Well, thankfully, Frank didn't serve in the navy, so he wasn't so confused in his navigation…No, he prided himself on being a FAC, a forward air controller, with missions of surveillance, directing attacks, assessing damage, and undertaking occasional rescues and avoiding casualties from friendly fire. Frank played that role in his personal life after the war ended. We've all taken some friendly fire over the years, but he helped some of us avoid a lot.

"Frank never believed God was his co-pilot, so he took personal responsibility for his successes and failures. He went about his job honestly, as a colleague or a friend, expecting you to do the same and forcing you to confront your own realities and not go off on a foolhardy quest for some fantasy. He was the guy who would point out, 'Hey, Don Quixote, that windmill over there is just a windmill, not a ferocious giant, put down the lance you stupid motherfucker.' Even if the windmill were the Moulin Rouge, he'd say it's still only a windmill and the dancers are only dancers. Maybe a man might hope to sleep with one, but they were not angels who could save your soul, no matter how much you might want them to be—a sound insight for both dancers and the men in the front row. I like to think we all have had a few less self-inflicted casualties because he shared that insight with us.

"Some here may think Frank too pedestrian, too unimaginative, too readily accepting of his own limitations and ours. If he had been a greater risk-taker, he might have been even more successful, had an even better life, made life still better for others. If so, you did not fully understand the man. Frank took risks on his own account; he just didn't take them on yours. So, I suggest you get over thinking that a newer, better Frank, Version 2.0, might have been a better friend, colleague, partner, or whatever. We all start out as betas and are responsible for our own upgrades. Let's respect the man for what he accomplished for himself and any inspiration that provided for your own evolution."

With that, Sam lifted his glass high in a toast, first in clear acknowledgement to Lillian, then less obviously in the general direction where Inga stood stoically, then with a slight lift toward a hostile Beth as he returned the glass to the table.

"What the fuck were you talking about?" asked Ted.

After the eulogy was finished and once the initial greetings were completed, territorial claims were established and Ward familiars selected a spot just outside the Repose Room where other guests could readily find Lillian on their way to view Frank or to the bar or on arrival and departure. On the way over to that location, Ted pulled Sam aside and said softly that he had brought Ari's daughter, and pointed out Triana. He hadn't told Lillian and thought that for the best. Sam simply nodded, patted Ted on a shoulder, and they joined their old associates.

Sitting in a circle of folding chairs, Sam began relating tales of Frank's idiosyncrasies. "He told me once that he hated his name because the villain in *High Noon* had the same name, Frank Miller. He figured that when people saw or heard his name, they would automatically think of that evil son of a bitch coming in on the noon train—the man who should've been hanged. It kept..."

Beth interrupted. "C'mon. Nobody remembers the name of the outlaw coming in on the train. They only remember Grace Kelley and Gary Cooper and 'Do not forsake me oh my darlin'.'"

"Frank did. He must have been maybe sixteen when he saw that movie and I suspect his pals must have given him a bad time about it."

"Frank didn't let stuff like that bother him."

15

"Sixteen, Beth, maybe fifteen. Besides, Nurse Ratched, you only want to believe Frank insensitive because you left him holding the bag."

"Now, hold on. I asked Frank if he thought I betrayed his trust and he said he didn't like my decision, but wouldn't accuse me of betrayal."

"Exactly. He told you he wouldn't *say* it, but that doesn't mean he didn't *believe* it."

"Don't lay your own feelings on Frank. He's not here to correct them,"

"I have no feelings about you whatsoever, Beth."

"But you think I wounded Frank because he had more of a soft side than I thought, huh?"

"No, because he was smarter than you thought."

Lillian broke off from her conversation with one of Frank's old FAC buddies and slipped in between the two. "Did I hear the song from *High Noon* being sung over here, Beth? I didn't know you did anything but church choir and Motown."

"Sam here told me that Frank felt traumatized by his namesake in *High Noon*."

"Ha. More like a grudge, one of the few he held onto. Usually, he just got pissed for a while and then got over it, and either forgave or wrote off him, her or whatever. But it was not a *stupid* grudge. I benefited greatly from Frank expending his anger on inconsequential things for over twenty-five years and I thought it great for *High Noon* to be one of them. I've come to believe that misdirection of anger sustains successful marriages and almost all relationships, really. Thank God for grudges, peeves, and all forms of annoyances. I owe you a lot, Beth."

The room creaked with the stress of anticipation of Beth's response, when suddenly, like a microburst on a clear day, or perhaps more like a splat of bird poop in the middle of a picnic blanket, Sam turned to Lillian from his folding chair in the corner. "Does Frank still have the hole in his dick?"

Stunned silence.

The room tried to decipher what must have been some kind of bizarre mondegreen. Hearing wasn't what it used to be. Something about holistic? Inga, barely within hearing range, made a choking noise somewhere between suppressing a sneeze and choking on a jalapeño. Beth, shaking her head, slipped away to find Jennifer, who had gone off to the bar with Dom.

At length, Lillian laughed. "Say, what?"

Fran grabbed Sam's arm as if to pull him back from the edge of a cliff, but it was too late. "Does Frank still have the hole in his dick? You know, from back in the day."

"How in hell can you have a hole in your dick?" Ted interjected. Fran winced and was silent.

"Not like a donut, you idiot. Like a piercing for an earring, say. Or a belly button ring or something like that."

"I can assure you that Frank never wore an earring on his penis!" Lillian seemed more amused than shocked. "Not even a stud."

"Never said he did," said Sam, who now seemed to be thoroughly discombobulated. "Shit, he never told you. Frank, you son of a bitch, I'd hide in that casket too if I were you... Well, it must have healed up over time. Forget I said anything."

"Forget? Like that's going to happen," Lillian said. "Zulu, my sweet, I think we need to talk." They had been teenagers together, and Sam had been something of a dork back then, so Lillian adjusted surprisingly easily to his current ineptitude. Sam put his head between his hands and pulled it down to his knee. She had called him Zulu, just as Frank used to do to reprimand him back when, so she was clearly jerking his chain. A barrage of questions followed, but Sam retained his fetal position, quite still except for an occasional shake of the head. *Zulu, Zulu, what an idiot!*

After an eternity Lillian came over, kissed his bald spot and removed him from Fran's clutches, leading him to a corner where they conversed inaudibly for some minutes, Sam at first looking quite abashed and Lillian posturing in a hands-on-hips schoolmarm pose until Sam showed her something, real or imaginary, hanging around his neck and causing her to laugh, the interrogation growing louder. At that point, Ted took it on himself to break the strained silence of would-be eavesdroppers. "The one thing Frank and I had in common is that we both always hated boomers, but I guess all of you knew that. With me, the music annoyed me

17

most. They stole our music. Elvis, the Beach Boys, Beatles, Doors, Janice, Buddy, Ray, Zappa, Hendrix, Tina, Dylan, Clapton, on and on…All of them were *our* generation, not fucking boomers. They think they own the music, just because they listened to it when they were eight years old. Not an ounce of creativity in the whole lot. We invented rock and roll. Go suck an egg, boomers!"

A couple of figures, alerted by Ted's declamation, appeared at the door to the Meditation Room, threw up their hands and disappeared.

"With Frank, though, it had more to do with the war, I guess, and maybe politics. Frank didn't understand how the so-called Greatest Generation could produce such a clusterfuck of overprivileged whiners and losers. 'We lost the war, damn it,' he'd say, 'so get over it. Why should we have been greeted as heroes?'"

One of Frank's fellow officers from the war interrupted from the back. "Yeah, Frank had a case with the draftees who bitched that they weren't showered with roses when they came home, but he hated the military brass and junior officers who bought into it more, shifting the blame for losing the war from military to civilians. Frank and I were in the war one way or another for almost ten years, and knew we didn't lose it because of Kent State or Hanoi Jane or lack of love from the World. And not because some assholes among the grunts abused the locals during the war. Shit happens. We just bet on the wrong horses and didn't know what we were doing half the time… the unwilling led by the incompetent doing the unwanted for the uninterested. That was our motto. Frank hated Oliver Stone the most, I think mostly for providing the fodder for blame-shifting and for conjuring up a portrayal of how sadists and drug addicts corrupted patriotic idealists like Stone saw himself. Frank couldn't stand such self-pity."

Beth returned, pink Cosmo in hand in a plastic wine glass, and interrupted. "Hey, hey, LBJ, how many kids you kill today?"

"You do devour your own, don't you?" The old vet seemed poised to abuse Beth further, but backed off. "Well, Frank also detested both of our draft-dodger presidents, and the chicken hawks as well as pacifists, so he tried to be nonpartisan." Feelings about the war were still raw and unresolved some forty years later.

18

Lillian returned with Sam in tow, chuckling that you learn something new every day, things Frank never told her or his kids. Ted replied that he told his kids absolutely everything, adding, "Lillian, do you remember the Fourth when we got together on the Mall?"

"You didn't!" Lillian flushed.

"I absolutely did. I told them that the Beach Boys are the best Fourth of July band ever. Isn't that what you remember?"

She hugged Sam with her right arm and simultaneously punched Ted in the chest with the palm of her left hand. Ted turned back to the old FAC officer. "Well, yeah, you can say a lot about the boomers, but they did make a damned good market for our artists, and even passed their tastes down to the Xers and Ys," Ted replied. "Can you picture us back in the fifties, listening to music from 1910? God, we thought even the early '50s music was crap, that no real music existed before Elvis and Buddy Holly."

"If you were white," Beth mumbled.

Ted ignored her. "But it's now just as far from the heydays of the Beatles and Stones as our generation was from 1910 and the kids still listen to it."

"I didn't think we had a generation," someone said. "We were just somehow lost between the Greatest Generation and the boomers."

Sam said softly, "Well Tom Brokaw seems to think that; he's about my age, but all he can write about is the Greatest Generation, the boomers or himself. Still, I heard someone say 'Silent Generation.'"

Someone said he had been unfair to Brokaw. "I know and I don't care," Sam replied curtly. Apparently forgiven by Lillian, Sam seemed revived.

The guy in the back of the room must have been a FAC buddy or retired spook. "Who used 'Silent Generation'? You and one other person? How can you be silent and invent rock and roll? Well, Frank wasn't so silent either when he talked to me about boomer women."

That did it, starting a male-dominated round table on the demerits of boomer women, leading to a debate on the relative hotness of Generation X and Generation Y, ending with a near-consensus that women of Generation X, the era of their own daughters, and their sons' girlfriends and spouses, were nearly on a par with the liberated girls of their own day. Candid or not, that was a relatively safe conclusion, as venturing to a preference for Generation Y would have reeked of Heffnerian creepiness, offending all the women present, and the men knew it.

"Ah, back in the day," Ben reminisced, "women saw Bond girls as liberated, the birth control pill came on the market, AIDS remained only the gay plague, and condoms were an unnecessary bother. Those were the days! What went wrong?" Glares from the higher estrogen corner of the room silenced that topic of discussion. Beth observed under her breath that Rachel did not exactly look like a Bond girl on her very best day and Ben did not exactly remind her of Sean Connery either. The men present also knew false bravado when they saw it, just Ben's attempt to be one of the boys, so they cut Beth some slack and agreed with her.

The truce didn't last long. Ted could not help himself from whispering to Sam that he might have ended up married to Lillian himself if Beth hadn't interfered in his love life after she wrote him off as a friend. Sam nodded and admitted that Ted had a point, given his own experience of transitioning in Beth's mind from mentor, to barely tolerated associate, to a career obstacle, to someone she completely abandoned. It formed an annoying progression if you had the self-respect to disagree with Nurse Ratched's diagnosis. With Beth, it might not exactly be her way or the highway, but the men she knew, her business colleagues anyway, were only highways to somewhere else and there were always convenient off-ramps when she decided to exit. Sam considered Beth exceptional in her ability to unilaterally modify the terms of any relationship to her best advantage and hoped maybe she'd change someday, like Lillian. In any case, talking about Beth depressed him and he let Ted's invitation to express his feelings further on that topic go begging.

Thinking of Lillian's response to his earlier injudicious remark and their brief conversation following, Sam felt amazed at how much Lillian had changed and he had come to respect her. Or maybe he'd changed the more. She'd been a slut by anybody's standards back in the day and, in reality, he couldn't really convince himself that if she could have that youthful body again, she'd be any different. But she had adapted well to aging and he had recently come to understand, or think he understood, the causes of her behavior years ago.

Ted tapped Sam's shoulder and whispered, "Obama killed Ari, you know. He owes us. Let's go see Triana." They both glanced around the room for an escape; seeing the young woman by the casket, they wandered over and, looking down at Frank's body, took her hands on each side. After a few hushed words, she nodded, and gestured for them to return to their friends.

Lillian had joined a group of women who were now discussing books and movies, wondering aloud whether the American version of the *Dragon Tattoo* series would hold up to the Swedish films, or the books, which she thought best of all. Overhearing as he left the Repose Room, Sam called, "Whatever, I'm totally in love with Lisbeth Salander."

Lillian laughed. "But Sam, she's a fictional character."

"Not a problem. Every woman I had feelings for before I turned forty turned out to be a fictional character, you included. Mostly of my own making, I admit, but I had my female co-authors. Like you, for example, Lillian."

"That's unfair. We were just kids"

"Well, I didn't say we were publishable, much less a literary classic, but even amateur fiction is still fiction and at least we left it a short story and not a novel."

"More like a tweet," replied Lillian.

Fran started to apologize on Sam's behalf, but Lillian waved her hand. "Men," she offered, "are like underwear."

"Who would know better than you?" Beth said to herself.

Not hearing, Lillian continued, "You know what I mean, Fran. When you run underwear through the wash and dryer, it always comes out inside out. Right? Well, that is because underwear is made inside out, with the ugly side of the seams showing and they are reversed so they'll look pretty. But in the wash, they revert to how they were made. That's men, you can teach them to be discreet and subtle and all that, but it always comes out in the wash that all they think about is sex. Why? They're made that way!"

Ted joined them in time for a contribution. "We also think about fart jokes."

"God," said Beth. "Well, at least they still have more sophomore moments than senior moments."

Fran diverted Beth's attention by defending Ted, giving Sam and Lillian another opportunity for a quiet exchange. "More than fifty years ago," he said softly. "I'm sorry I never understood what you were going through."

"You knew more than you thought, Sammy," she replied. "In those days we couldn't even think about some things, much less say out them aloud. You never despised me, that's what counted... Besides, we were kids. We had a lot of growing up to do."

"Guess we're still working on it. We'll see you tomorrow." Sam held her hand warmly, and sought out Ted again for a brief goodbye before he and Fran left.

It was getting late, and the mortuary needed to close and prepare for the next day. Due to schedules and religious issues, the military ceremony in the morning would not be accompanied by an open-casket service, so Isabella started to circulate, asking those who wanted to say goodbye to Frank to do so now.

A few moments later, Isabella pulled the velvet drapes across the entrance to the Repose Room and dimmed the lights in the reception area. The younger generation left first, except for those waiting in the parking lot to provide transport for the elders, who, after milling around for several minutes in the gloom, slowly and reluctantly trudged to the parking lot exit guided by Isabella. Beth, Ted, Sam, Fran, and Lillian were the last to exit. Beth defiantly hummed "Do Not Forsake Me, Oh My Darlin'" for Sam's benefit as they walked toward their respective cars. Isabella locked the door and returned to close the casket and prepare the flowers to accompany the hearse in the morning. She started to close the lid and drape the purple funeral pall over the casket when she gasped in disbelief. Her shriek drew Director Welch from his office faster than if it had been a fire alarm.

"Dr. Welch, it's terrible! Somebody pulled down Major Miller's pants and shorts!"

———

All but one of them unaware of the emergency inside the mortuary, the dispersing outpatients of the Ward and their intimates departed, pondering the decades leading to their reunion. Frank's late difficulty in keeping his pants on was not unique to him among those present that evening nor hardly the greatest of their individual and collective embarrassments. Many time capsules opened in the minds of those leaving, disinterring other indiscretions, elucidating some.

CHAPTER 2:

Vienna, 1960

S am pounded his fists against the steering wheel of the old '49 Chevy 3100 pickup that his father used to deliver goods from his Vienna hardware store to customers throughout Northern Virginia. Diagonally parked facing the row of shop windows, he harnessed his frustrations to the beat of "Poison Ivy," while cursing the Coasters for their insights, the Chevy for its temptations, and mostly Lillian for coming on like the rose he believed her to be and then transforming herself into the toxin of the song. He was too old and much too young for what had just happened, so he took it out on the steering wheel as he waited for Lillian to emerge from the Ben Franklin. The thought flitted through his head that she was a lot faster last night than this morning, then cursed himself for reacting like such a jerk. It was a problem of his own making, he had to admit that.

It had started off innocently and appropriately enough in chemistry class, where they were thrown together by the teacher's philosophy of pairing good and bad students as lab partners, hoping to avoid acid burns, mercury spills, and excessive asbestos dust from the large heat pads they would subdivide for individual beakers. She was as lively as he was shy and became very much engaged in the assigned experiments, especially those resulting in violent reactions, explosions of color or noxious odors. With that enthusiasm, he couldn't understand how she could be such a horrible student and couldn't believe her locker-room reputation as an easy score. She seemed smart, too smart to do dumb things, with boys or in the chem lab, or so he thought until she instigated a race with a couple of D students to dissolve pennies in Dixie cups filled with nitric and hydrochloric acids in mixtures of their choosing. He couldn't do anything about her risky behavior outside of the lab, but his cautious nature prevented her from overreaching into dangerous territory in the classroom, at least insisting that she perform the experiment with proper glassware. The results thrilled her, so much so that he taught her how to make aqua regia with a precisely measured acid solution and, with his help, she successfully dissolved her father's wedding ring, stolen at home from the bathroom sink, into a tiny pile of orange-brown dirt. He did not report on that particular experiment.

By assuming the roles of instructor and protector, Sam gradually overcame his fear of rejection and worked up the courage to ask Lillian out. A surprise to both, she accepted, the "no" on her lips suppressed by the thought it would be a small payment for the destruction of her father's insincere pledge of fealty to her poor mother. She would later scatter the precipitant in the sink at home and let the bastard flush it down the drain himself. In the meantime, she could enjoy the fun of helping Sam show off to his honor roll friends. What good is a reputation if you don't shock people with it? And at least Sam didn't have zits.

After school that Thursday, they met at the soda fountain in the Rexall drug store, where Lillian made a point of squeezing close to share his milkshake, then went to the JV basketball game, she making sure they were noticed by cheering vigorously for the pathetic sophomore team. After that, they went to a party to celebrate the return of Elvis from Germany. Sam had no expectations that evening of even getting to first base with Lillian, if that meant anything more than being seen with her in the stands or, if a miracle occurred, a peck on the cheek goodnight. To be with her would be enough, letting her shady reputation offset his own as a hopeless dweeb and bookworm, a worthy goal for an eighteen -year -old boy who was, in fact, a hopeless dweeb and bookworm. They fully met his aspirations in the half hour at the soda fountain and exceeded them at the basketball game, but Lillian had not nearly finished Sam's makeover. To put him at ease, she had suggested to him quite explicitly that they would play a flirting game all evening to make his friends jealous and maybe tweak some of the guys who were after her to go out as well. It worked, and although their antics in the stands may have cost the team a couple of free throws from distracted shooters, it certainly felt worth it.

But perhaps Sam's parents were right about Elvis being a bad influence. The dance floor was hot and dimly lit, and by eleven o'clock, it being a school night, the honor roll crowd had disappeared to meet their curfews, but Sam and Lillian stayed on. At their corner table after a slow dance, Lillian pulled from her purse a flask of Canadian whiskey stolen from her dad and poured a generous amount into their root beers. Following more close dancing, Lillian began singing "love me" along with the record. The two soon departed in the pickup with Lillian's girlfriend and her date, each teen pair taking turns necking in the cab or the pickup bed, as they cruised around the neighborhoods, harassing the merchant rent-a-cop, peeling out of stop lights, and throwing toilet paper into selected trees. That, too, contributed to upgrading Sam's Goody Two-shoes reputation. He had a blast.

Sometime after two, Sam dropped off the other couple near their homes and drove toward Lillian's house, expecting to say good night and head home. Near her street, however, she asked him to pull over on an isolated dirt road to listen to the end of a Buddy Holly tribute playing on the radio. As with any proper sport, the game must continue even if it is late in the third overtime and all of the spectators have gone home. And so it did, at first with laughs and observations on the pleasures of the evening, then quieting to the silent pleasures of the moment. With Holly's own pleas of "love me" reinforcing Elvis's earlier demands, the exploratory caressing in the cab intensified, and with inviting blankets already spread in the bed of the pickup, one thing led—or more properly was led—to another.

He should have felt overjoyed by his initiation into manhood. He would later brag about the night to his closest friends, much to his own disgust for adding to Lillian's reputation like the dork he was. But, picking her up again Friday morning, he remained thoroughly embarrassed by his combination of adolescent awkwardness, alcohol-induced coordination disabilities, and complete absence of knowledge. She had much more experience than he and, uninhibited by the alcohol, had placed few demands on his sexual competence, but she more than offset that benefit by laughing at his awkwardness even as he struggled like a drowning man against the tides of excitement.

Their love-making, lubricated as much by alcohol as bodily fluids, felt like remedial instruction, mocking that he—the serious academic, awaiting acceptance letters from prestigious Ivy League schools—would be out drinking before a big test, screwing the school tramp, as she called herself, slumming with a failing student who fully intended to drop out rather than repeat her senior year. And she had mocked his vulnerability to her enticements and his willingness to give up everything for a few minutes excursion into the sordid *Peyton Place* world that Lillian occupied, an excursion that meant far less to her than even the brief shudders she betrayed at the depth of his penetration. It was degrading and she had reveled in his degradation, or so he thought. The bitch.

Waiting outside the store to take her to school, pounding on the steering wheel, he continued to be mad as hell, an anger excusable only by his ignorance. She lived a life closer to the Selena Cross of the book than he could ever have imagined, he having read only the dog-eared passages of sexual encounters passed around by his classmates. He had no idea. He had no idea whatsoever.

Sam removed his hands from the wheel and shut off the radio. From his parking spot he watched Lillian through the five-and-dime window, as she walked past the cashier without stopping. She exited the open door, dragging behind her a wooden duck making a loud "quack, quack, quack" sound with every turn of its wheels. Christ, it looked like the very duck that she had admired twenty minutes earlier, that he had offered to buy and she rejected, along with an instruction for him to wait in the car, an instruction he now very much regretted following, as the purloined waterfowl advanced, with loud protests, to the pickup. *Jesus.* She was trying, he thought, to get him arrested. Had he been that bad a lover? No matter. She jumped into the cab, throwing the duck ahead of her and commanded him to go, which he obliged. Sam strived to be honest, but he was not so stupid as to go back and attempt to return the toy.

Besides, Sam knew something that Lillian didn't. Three colleges had accepted him the previous week, including Harvard, so any sabotage on her part didn't matter. He didn't give a damn about the test. Missing it might kill an A, but slipping a position or two in the class academic hierarchy no longer seemed important. In that moment he decided he would skip school and spend the day with Lillian, knowing she would assent, letting her believe that she was leading him astray and, since her parents were visiting an older sister that evening, hoping to redeem himself later on. Maybe it wouldn't be so bad the second time around. "We're late already and I'm in no shape for the test," he said. "I'm skipping. How about you?" Lillian rolled the duck across her thigh. "Quack, quack, quack," it agreed enthusiastically.

"Damn," he thought, "now she's got the duck mocking me. Did she find out about my acceptances and know I'm allowing her to seduce me again? Who's playing what game now?" He had no answer to that and never would, but felt guilty anyway.

The day passed relatively uneventfully, other than Lillian walking up the street to smash a random parking meter with a brick to get change for their expired meter in front of the movie theater. He cringed, but as with the duck, did nothing about it. The matinee movie was *Suddenly Last Summer,* a second run playing for adults on a school day and of no interest to either except for adding to the heat in some foggy way neither understood. They stopped watching and made out heavily in the appropriate high school fashion reserved for steadies, including the time-honored tradition of consuming licorice from both ends and continuing past the meeting point. Of course, they weren't exactly steadies and never would be, but the theater didn't care and the few patrons probably enjoyed the distraction, certainly one or two classmates also skipping that day, as they would learn later.

Teenage guilt, as it turns out, is a less powerful force than teenage introduction to worldly pleasures. Someone would write later that life is a box of chocolates, that you never know what you might find. Teenage sex is more like a bag of potato chips; you know what it's like after the first, but you just can't stop at one. Starting late that afternoon, with Lillian's parents having left town as she had expected, they spent several hours together in a proper bed. It was better, but he still felt embarrassed by his need to go home by around three o'clock in the morning, before his own parents woke up. She made it clear that she had boyfriends that had no such juvenile obligations and teased him about it unmercifully until he finally got into the pickup truck and headed for home.

Alone, awaiting the dawn, Lillian sat silently on the edge of the bed, smoking a Marlboro, wishing she had been nicer to Sam before he left, feeling unsatisfied, despite the repeated sex that, even with his inexperience and clumsiness and overeagerness, provided a gentle, soothing, and sedating respite, a kind of white noise that silenced the malevolence of the night. Letting the natural physical instincts take control over her emotions and feeling the same in him had a kind of purity about it; a purity that felt good then and gave relief from pain. Yet that escape proved only temporary, not transformative; so, having failed to escape the squalid reality of her life, she insulted Sam in the same manner she had insulted earlier lovers and would their successors—one night stands, husbands, and anything in between. Believing in her powerlessness to resist nature's demands had the effect of sedating the encounters that came before, especially those lying half-buried, too repulsive to entomb completely, the ones that came not from impulse, but betrayal and force. She was not punishing herself, but desensitizing her trauma. It worked, but it left her feeling utterly alone. She lay back and held her old Raggedy Ann doll to her breasts for a very long time.

Boys, she thought, have no insight whatsoever and Sam was worse than most. She knew that she had a terrible and well-deserved reputation throughout the high school and that Sam knew about it, yet he had worked up the courage to ask her out only because she sat next to him in civics class, treated him nicely, and then became his lab partner. It must have made him think that she was smarter than her awful grades would indicate, less tainted than her reputation. At least he treated her like an equal, unlike almost all the other boys. Although she could tell he had become powerfully attracted to her, he had always been restrained before last night and kept their conversation on the most casual level, mostly talking about the class, the football team, their after-school jobs, and the like, not daring to presume anything beyond their being classmates. He took her at face value, a good thing normally, but a face is only a façade. Sometimes you need another to see beyond the façade, but he couldn't or wouldn't.

She seduced him in the vain hope that maybe he could actually see her, even allowing him to call her Lily in the heat of their passion, her childhood name before she was despoiled and a concession she only granted to her mother. Nothing's more pathetic that a wilted lily, with its imputation of ruined innocence and chastity. To allow him to call her that granted him permission to see her as she existed before she became the wicked Lillian, the caricature she now was, to allow him to create an illusion of her that she almost certainly could not sustain, but she would have tried, if only he could have seen the offer behind that the simple acknowledgement of his familiarity.

But, of course, he could not. He would be leaving and an enormous gulf lay between them with no future. She could tell that he already regretted the episode in the pickup and so she had tried to drive him away with taunts and the shoplifting misdemeanor and, when that failed, the minor felony over a handful of nickels. Nothing had worked. Whoever said "accept the things you cannot change" had to be an asshole, she thought. There is nothing more maddening than being accepted for who you are by someone who really doesn't have a clue who you are or how you got there. Maybe Sam couldn't change who she had become and he certainly couldn't change what had happened to her, but at least he could fucking try! Why didn't he at least ask why? How could he just hold her as if she were as innocent as he? Why did he have to call her Lily?

She lay back in the bed, but it had the scent of lovemaking about it and she couldn't sleep. She placed Raggedy Ann carefully on a shelf and stripped the bed. After throwing the sheets in the washing machine, she took a long walk alone in the first light of morning and returned after a couple of hours later to toss everything in the dryer. She was taking her dog out the back door for his own exercise just as her parents arrived at the front. Walking the dog until she knew with certainty her father had left for work, she returned to the house, had a virtually silent breakfast with her mother, made the bed, and slept until mid-afternoon. When she woke up, she felt tempted to call Sam, but she didn't.

Sam got an A-minus on the makeup test the teacher had kindly scheduled for him, accepted a scholarship to Harvard, coasted through the spring semester, and took a summer job at a Greek restaurant in Vienna before heading off to college. Shortly after their time together, he asked Lillian out several times, but she either claimed to be busy and refused, or became unavailable after accepting. He could feel something was wrong and worried about her. He would have continued to pursue her, but began experiencing unpleasant urinary problems and, wisely figuring that no amount of calamine lotion would cure the problem, made a secret appointment with the doctor. Diagnosed with the clap, he abandoned the effort to be with Lillian again in favor of card games with his fellow graduates, contemplating his foolishness while washing down tetracycline tablets with cans of American Beer, Baltimore's finest and least expensive. He swore off girls, rumpled up his unfinished bag of potato chips, so to speak, and tossed it aside. Chips are addictive, however, and it would only be a matter of time before temptation would lead him back to the concession stand, sex being the junk food of the romantic soul.

After a couple of weeks, without breaking his resolution of abstinence, he decided that he at least had to tell Lillian about his condition, as he had heard that girls sometimes didn't know that they were carriers and there could be problems later on. So, on the last day of classes, he overcame his embarrassment and managed to get Lillian alone and tell her the bad news. She reacted by exploding in anger with the convoluted condemnation that if men would wear god-damn condoms or take a little care to be more sanitary, nothing would have happened; so it was all his fault. He reacted by giving her all the cash in his pockets to help her get pills or see a doctor and later feeling like a fool for doing so. He said he was sorry and tromped away, expecting and hoping never to see her again.

Late in the summer, however, Lillian called with an apology for her inappropriate reaction. She had taken antibiotics and her infection had disappeared, so thank you, she said. The emotionally frail sapling that he was then, Sam abandoned his determination not to see her again and suggested dinner at the restaurant where he worked. She accepted.

When he made reservations with his boss, she insisted on providing a free, elegant five-course dinner in thanks for his work and to honor his academic career. He dug into his graduation gifts to pay for wine, sensing correctly that Greek hospitality would be unconstrained by drinking age legislation. And so Sam and Lillian dined over a festive meal highlighted by a delicious leg of lamb and a fine Peloponnese wine, far superior to the Hearty Burgundy both would learn to enjoy in a few years. Sam said nothing more of his adventure with antibiotics and Lillian kept her conflicted emotions to herself. It went well, a quiet evening of unspoken forgiveness, explicit good wishes, and long, hopeful conversations, ending with a kiss goodnight that would satisfy only siblings but somehow seemed appropriate. She would spend the night alone or with some target of opportunity she might meet after midnight at the Green Door, a local tavern named after the old '50s song. She owed Sam enough that she should let him go. He felt relieved as they parted, regrets coming only months later.

———

A year after, Sam came back from college to Vienna for the summer, returning following Kennedy's election with the exciting prospect an internship with a Massachusetts congressman arranged through the university. He couldn't wait to tell Lillian about his freshman year experience, now thinking that their parting hadn't ended badly and perhaps she would be impressed enough to go out with him again. Harvard was a semi-arid desert environment for a boy like Sam and he had thought about her a lot over the year, wiping away the negative reactions experienced earlier. He called and they arranged to meet at a restaurant in DC near a lingerie shop where she worked, this time over a simple lunch.

He arrived to find Lillian already seated. After ordering and talking for about ten minutes he noticed that some things had changed. First, she was smoking Parliament Lights, which she had ridiculed as sissy cigarettes when he had offered her one at the end of their festive meal before he went to college. She then ordered a very light lunch and asked for a Seven-Up. He had thought she would certainly order a drink, since she had reached eighteen and D.C. still resisted demands to raise the drinking age to twenty-one. Just as the food arrived, however, he realized that underneath her unusually loose dress, she had gained weight and had been tightly squeezed into the booth. His dismay betrayed him. "Yes," she whispered as the waitress departed. "I'm about five months pregnant."

Sam asked what he thought were all the right questions. Who was the lucky guy? ("You, I think. But the father is Will Graham; he was a football player over at Oakton High.") Are you going to marry him? ("He's asked.") What does he do? ("Construction. He'll be working on building the new airport, Dulles they'll call it.") You're going to keep the baby? ("Unless I can get the money to go to New York, or maybe you'd be willing to say you raped me so I can get one here legally. I'm not going to that abortion mill in D.C. and it's getting late to do anything.") Lillian was beginning to get annoyed, he could see that. Then she looked down at the table, and told him softly that she didn't want the baby and wasn't at all sure that Will cared enough for her to put up with her, but at least marrying him would get her away from home and that would be worth a lot. She thought that if she could get to a proper clinic in New York, she would tell him she had a miscarriage, but then marry him anyway. If he didn't know what really happened, he would feel sorry for her and promise her that he would make her another baby, wedding her with even greater enthusiasm to prove himself a real man and confirm that her losing the baby could not possibly have been his fault. He was a good man with a kind heart, but a complete idiot. Maybe Sam could help her get to New York.

As compassionately as he could muster, Sam told her that her plan seemed like the dumbest thing he had ever heard. It was too late and too dangerous for her and it bothered him greatly that she would probably be six months along before any possible abortion. Sam was wholly unversed on such matters and he really didn't believe that an actual human being existed from conception, but he did feel it wrong to destroy a fetus after it had all the required body parts and might survive a surgical birth. So he urged her to have the baby and argued that she would be a good mother. Both of them were pretty sure that the latter argument was bullshit, but it was one of those things that had to be said.

They met a few more times that summer, with Lillian eventually acknowledging that she would have the baby and accepting Will's proposal. Lillian invited Sam to the ceremony and reception and he attended, concluding by the end of the evening that he had been correct about Lillian being smart and that she correctly perceived Will to be as dumb as a post. After meeting her parents, he couldn't say why, but he also felt sure of Lillian's conviction that escaping her parent's home was worth everything. By the time his train reached Boston he reconciled himself to Lillian being in his past. Ray Charles had just released "Hit the Road Jack" and it got him through the first semester without excessive grieving, confirming that nothing eases regrets over past discomforts more than singing about them.

CHAPTER 3:

Colorado/DC, 1961

rancesca Ghiardelli was anticipating her graduation from Colorado College when she first met Frank Miller. It happened at a dance to which the college invited a few cadets from the still-unfinished Air Force Academy out of a sense of misplaced charity, it being years before that institution would recruit its own women to sexually harass. A few days earlier a plane crash had killed the members of the US Olympic skating team, virtually all having trained at the Broadmoor Hotel, located near the CC campus, and the town and school were in mourning. The students knew many of those killed, through the skaters attending CC classes, visiting the bookstore, or by students viewing their practice sessions at the training rink, though few could claim they knew the fallen skaters well. That intensified the grief, however, as the skaters were remembered by almost all only as the flawless ice butterflies described in their obituaries, enhanced by the beauty of their sport, and not with the solace that comes from the comfort of a shared, albeit flawed, humanity. The tragedy placed a dark cloud over the previously scheduled dance.

The dance was poorly attended, conflicting with a memorial service for the deceased skaters. Frank and Francesca each were there only due to the insistence of friends, his on the prowl for any companionship qualifying as female, hers seeking to divert Francesca's attention from the dismal prospects received thus far from her employment applications. Frank and Francesca were opposites in almost every way possible. Only the absence of plausible conversation alternatives brought them together.

Frank grew up a farm boy in the West in a family claiming to be Protestant in the superficial manner of those too tied to the harvest to listen to a preacher's claim on ten percent of their incomes. His musical tastes ran to Johnny Cash and Hank Williams and he distrusted the East, the press, politicians, and all sects from Seventh Day Adventists to Unitarians and Roman Catholics—that is, any group of any kind with a claim to superior wisdom. A decent student in his youth despite constantly being in trouble for pranks, fights, unexplained absences, and conflicts involving girls at his or rival schools, he began to attain greater academic achievement after the seventh grade due to a high school ROTC program commanded by a retired Korean War master sergeant, a man tolerating nothing short of peak performance, a man who rewarded outstanding achievement by secretly allowing the elite student to throw live hand grenades at rats in the town dump. He had never lost anyone in that exercise, so it must have been safe.

Frank envisioned himself as a lone wolf unsuited to a life of following orders, but with the John Wayne role model of the master sergeant, anything other than a military career became unthinkable. He applied to the service academies not with the intention of leading a structured life within military codes of conduct, but rather, like his mentor, to be able to bend the rules with sufficient authority to get away with it.

It would be, he thought then, a short career. He would return to the West, buy a ranch or work the land or work his way to the top at Colorado Fuel and Iron or Ideal Cement. He reveled in the space of the hinterland that gave him freedom and, apart from the appeal of a military career with early retirement, would have been content to live in rural Colorado forever. Even downtown Denver gave him claustrophobia.

Francesca, on the other hand, came from the East, if you consider Canonsburg, Pennsylvania, the East, as Frank most certainly did. She was Catholic Italian, brought up to believe in papal infallibility and that Hail Marys could make a difference, long before Roger Staubach proved it. Graduating from a Catholic high school in Pennsylvania, she applied to Loretto Heights College, a small women's Catholic college in Denver organized by the Sisters of

Loretto, a social activist order emphasizing educational and poverty relief missions. After many family arguments and promises to pursue her Catholic faith, her parents allowed her to transfer to CC in her junior year to better pursue her ambition to become a journalist.

Francesca had been unfazed by the frivolity of the Beatles, the shrieks of Little Richard, or the gyrations of Elvis, and hadn't even heard of most of Frank's musical icons, remaining secure in the belief that Perry Como, a local hero, represented the very best in music and only slowly shifting her loyalty to the rising star of Bobby Venton, another product of Canonsburg. As part of the third-generation removed from Tuscan immigrants, bilingual but largely assimilated with Americans of diverse ancestry, she retained the immigrants' fascination with democracy and free speech, determined to build a career in journalism or maybe public service, but terrified that she would fail and be pressured by her father to join an order of nuns, unless she had babies first. In the end, it would have to be one or the other. She could buy time in the workplace until perhaps thirty, but beyond that looming deadline, only motherhood or sisterhood would avoid disgrace.

While, like Frank, Francesca was born into provincial life, she couldn't consider living outside of a world city, a New York, Washington, London, Paris, or Rome. Unlike Frank, she was a romantic in her personal life, and eagerly wished to find the right city and the right man, but experiencing life before domestic life pressed in on her, having determined motherhood to be her only option. She loved babies. Certainly she would not enter a nun's life in some isolated convent just because the men in her family saw that as a means to their own salvation. She had been deeply religious when she transferred to CC and, despite some doubts, remained so, but not now so passively as to be a religious sacrifice on someone else's behalf. Having made that determination, she stood resolute in defense of it, the first step in an irreversible ratchet, each catch in the rack pulling her further from her foundation in the church under a stress that Frank could never imagine, faith to him being little more than the absence of explicit repudiation.

Unlike Frank, moreover, Francesca was a good soldier, rather than a hired gun or buccaneer, as he imagined himself to be. Given an acceptable assignment, she would carry out its requirements in meticulous detail with discipline and precision beyond expectations. She would have informed on the master sergeant if her school honor code required it, but eliminated the rat colony without hesitation and without mercy on acceptance of his proper authority. Catholic girls of that era were not to be underestimated.

Each twenty-one, both Frank and Francesca felt out of place at the dance, albeit for slightly different reasons. He was a skirt chaser, a proclivity that would continue well into mid-life, but women who considered themselves part of the upper class and rejected men with his modest, rural upbringing easily intimidated him. Colorado College, which considered itself the Oberlin College of the West, was a liberal arts college where the well-bred and well-read could receive an excellent education or simply smoke weed and enjoy a Rocky Mountain high among their own kind. Frank decidedly did not belong to that set, and he concluded immediately that all the girls in the room looked down on him, whether they did or not. In his own mind, of course, he felt not so much intimidated by their anticipated perception of him, as unwilling to trouble himself to try to change it. The very thought of having to prove himself to a woman appalled him.

In a minute overlap of disparate personalities, Francesca came to somewhat the same conclusion. She had been lucky enough for her transfer to the school to be accepted and to have barely sufficient resources to attend, but still considered herself part of the immigrant class, not the bourgeois elite, even if the elite were merely the sons or daughters of a banker or well-to-do merchant from a modest Western town. Like Frank, she saw their perceived disdain of her class as superficiality born of undeserved privilege and would not compromise to win their affections. Even though he wasn't her type nor she his, they at least had that certain psychosis in common. So when he breathed "hello walls" sarcastically at some primly attired girl haughtily walking away from his dance invitation, she laughed and a conversation started.

Despite the minimal sexual attraction between them, the two got along well enough for the evening. In addition to the nexus of their underdog mentality, Frank had older sisters, as did Francesca, a common burden to bear through adolescence and one that affected both immeasurably. In his case, it resulted in a clear bifurcation of personality: if he wanted to sleep with a girl, he pursued that end in the most stereotypical manner, caring only about results, not her thought process before or after the accomplished goal; if he did not, he reverted to his sibling mode, becoming quite egalitarian, even deferential, as younger brothers are compelled to be. Francesca had no such bifurcation, beaten down by her older sisters, the one always receiving hand-me-downs and criticisms of her failings, but striving to meet their expectations and achieve their status without much expectation of ever doing so; she deferred and resented it. Frank could understand that, and the conversation inevitably turned to future plans and the burden of reaching them under the tyranny of older sisters and their exaggerated status in the eyes of parents. The academy had been his escape, and the journey to Colorado hers, journeys sufficiently similar to build enough rapport to survive a disappointing evening.

As they talked, Francesca expressed her excitement about Kennedy's election and formation of the Peace Corps expected shortly. Frank was not so sure about either, his family convinced that Nixon had been robbed and his own future apparently headed for war, not peace, but he felt convinced from his own experience at the academy that the papal influence business was a lot of crap; if Kennedy, a military man himself, had anything in common with the Catholics in the cadet corps or the academy faculty, there would be nothing to fear. He figured from the name that she was Catholic, so he made a point of his tolerance in that regard; she tolerated his tolerance, or at least his efforts in that direction.

They discussed the Peace Corps for some time, with him not understanding why she had any interest in it; if she wanted to be a journalist, why not skip being a do-gooder and just get a job here with the *Denver Post* or *Rocky Mountain News*, where her school's recommendation would carry some weight? That probably made sense, she admitted, but she had visited both and wasn't that impressed. She wanted to travel the world, to report on international affairs, and hoped to find a job with that possibility. She failed to mention that there had been no response to her résumé by either paper. She did admit, though, that she would be graduating in four months and had no job offers.

"Oh, hell, maybe I have a name for you," he said. "My uncle went to CC and worked for the *News* until three years or so ago, when he snagged a job with the *Washington Star*. I could send him a note and I'll bet someone on the faculty here remembers him and might recommend you." Francesca saw this as an incredible opportunity. While Washington was not New York and the *Star* was far from the *New York Times*, the *Herald Tribune*, or even the *Post*, at least it was a big city newspaper where international news was important. She thanked him profusely.

They danced and laughed and the evening ended with a polite kiss goodnight, for her at least. Frank and a couple of fellow cadets went over to the Antlers Hotel and tried to pick up girls in the bar. His friends were not successful. Frank was, that being the usual case with girls for whom he had little respect.

A couple of weeks later, Frank called Francesca, asking for a movie date. Feeling sure that he would soon be in Vietnam, he wanted to see *The World of Susie Wong* as a coming attraction to the Oriental companionship he expected to enjoy in a few months, all Asian countries then being the same to him. He judged the movie sentimental enough for Francesca. Besides, he'd found his uncle's address. She accepted and he picked her up at seven.

The movie was more to her tastes than his, apart from his barely repressed fascination with Nancy Kwan's silky long black hair and silky long legs. Afterwards, they stopped by Jay's drive-in across from the campus for a snack, where he gave her his uncle's address. Then, there being no convenient parking near her dorm, she gave him a light kiss good-bye in the car, got out, and walked to her room. Although she thanked him for the reference later on the phone, that would be the last she'd see of him for some five years, and then only briefly.

In the following weeks, Francesca found a professor who did remember Frank's uncle in a positive way and was willing to give her a reference letter, which she enclosed in an envelope with her own note on Frank's recommendation, sent, and awaited a reply. It came in late April. All they could offer might be an internship during the summer, not much more than a clerical job, really, and if she worked out, she might have to join the union, but if she wanted to give it a try they would make it happen. She accepted, and after graduation traveled by Greyhound home to Pennsylvania and thence to the nation's capital.

At the *Star*, Francesca took on the menial tasks typically assigned to interns, especially female interns at a conservative journal where editorial assistance meant little more than typing a male reporter's handwritten notes and participation in staff meetings meant bringing coffee and cleaning up afterwards. But Francesca was a good soldier, doing clerical, secretarial, and janitorial tasks with no sign of resentment and always with a willingness to do a little extra, to provide actual editorial suggestions in a non-threatening manner, to work late when needed, to do background research without being asked, to subtly call her superiors' attention to evidence that their initial interpretation might be incorrect, and to adopt the posture of little sister to the male staff and the few females who had slept their way to greater responsibilities, thus avoiding both sexual harassment and sexual competition. By the end of summer the paper made the job permanent and she wrote Frank again, thanking him profusely.

Frank had never made a contribution to anyone's success before and took great pride in his role in getting Francesca the job. Because of that, she retained a place in his memory well out of proportion to their time together, rapport, or any indicator of friendship. He looked on her as an acolyte, or would have if he had known the word, and his pride in that would again bring them together.

Over the next year Francesca was given increasing responsibilities, albeit without increasing recognition or compensation. That itself posed no problem. She expected the initial stages of her career to be difficult and remained a disciple of her mother's tenet that she must find a man in her workplace so she could retire to be a wife and mother, using her employment experience to help further his career, not her own. She would not forsake her interests but channel them through her husband, funneling them into a woman's traditional role. Excessive female ambition constituted a dysfunctional symptom of mental illness, according to a *Time* magazine article frequently quoted by her mother. Accepting this with resignation, Francesca managed to be relatively content. The *Star* was in most respects a continuing education that in all probability would eventually leave her better prepared for a life with an accomplished husband in, perhaps, publishing, or even better, diplomacy of some sort.

Still, in many ways, Washington and the *Star* were disappointments. For all of its global importance, the city was an unsavory combination of urban ghettos, pockets of ill-concealed southern bigotry stratified by income and a legion of transients on the make. Traversed by U.S. Route 1, a motel-populated, strip-mall-heavy main street catering to all classes and classless, D.C. was a slum, an enclave of the rich and powerful, and a tourist park of monuments and museums with a semi-functional government attached. Gas stations along Route 1 often had two sets of men's and ladies' rooms, one of each betraying signs of where the word "colored" had been removed or painted over, but still invited selection exclusively by the former patrons. A place of double washrooms and double standards, Francesca hated it. She soon found herself longing for the closeness of Canonsburg, with its solid old neighborhood identities, pining for the sense of belonging she found in her Italian heritage, eager for the comforts of home, all absent in a city where everyone was from somewhere else— a somewhere else that they had left behind in favor this place, which they mostly despised and publically disparaged—until she met Gianni Leone.

Gianni, known as Johnny around the office, had been hired by the *Star* as a stringer at the outset of the Kennedy administration, due to the interest in the Vatican associated with Kennedy's Catholicism. A graduate student at American University who had overstayed his visa, he had sold the *Star* on the proposition that he could cover their assignments in Rome, although as a Milanesi he was less familiar with Rome and the Vatican than the average San Franciscan was with Georgetown. The newspaper didn't pay him much, so they could afford to overlook these shortcomings. For Gianni, however, his employment provided the basis for obtaining the coveted Form I-151 alien registration receipt, or green card, a step toward his ultimate goal of U.S. citizenship.

An immediate attraction formed between Francesca and Gianni, hers being his cosmopolitan experience, their common ethnic and linguistic background, his perceived professional status and his old-world charm, and his being that she had sufficient naïveté to be charmed by him, her domestic orientation, her intelligence and better English, her likely more permanent status at the paper, and her American citizenship. She adored little children and he wanted sons that he could claim as his own, so he wanted a wife. He wanted other women, too, but what good Italian man doesn't? It seemed like a perfect match, albeit not a symmetrical one.

The romance proceeded rapidly, cemented by a visit to the New York World's Fair to do a feature on the Vatican exhibit. Overwhelmed by viewing Michelangelo's Pietà, Francesca succumbed to both Gianni and the Catholic teachings on birth control that are so conducive to domestic union and found herself pregnant. That summer they were married in Milan.

The marriage had a good beginning. Gianni's paltry salary at the *Star,* already well below hers, did not afford a luxurious life, but it did come with plane tickets and a generous allowance for accompanying family. Her children would all be born at Sibley Memorial Hospital in D.C., but about half of the next three years would be spent in Europe, either with Gianni's family in Milan, his apartment in Rome, or in Luxembourg, Brussels, and Paris, where Francesca had been able to obtain assignments from the *Star* related to the European Economic Community and its sister institutions. Gianni's family provided ready babysitters for the twin girls born on Christmas Day in 1962, a third girl born in early 1964, and Gianni's long-awaited son, born in 1965. Francesca's passable Italian became fluent, her French passable, and her dreams of combining a cosmopolitan life and traditional family seemed to have been realized. That changed quickly.

———

Having finished his tour in Bien Hoa and awaiting assignment to Thailand, Frank Miller found Francesca at the *Star* in 1966, during a short visit in the few days before his orders were received. He was not particularly surprised by her marriage and motherhood, or by her successes at the newspaper, but felt disappointed that she was not happy.

Apparently, the birth of Gianni's son had somehow signaled to him that Francesca had fulfilled her main role in his life and he had begun to spend more time away and in the company of other women. She had put up with it earlier, being familiar with the proclivities of males in her cultural heritage, but it eventually became excessive and embarrassing. Upon discovering that there were two apartments in Rome, rented as much from her salary as his, she became thoroughly disillusioned. Finally, just before Frank visited, the *Star* terminated Gianni's contract. He had been submitting fewer and fewer usable reports and interest in the Vatican collapsed following the Kennedy assassination. No one wanted to be reminded of the decimated promise of Camelot, and surely not the petty religious prejudices that accompanied it, so the paper could not justify even the low wage offered Gianni. That meant the end of Francesca's European assignments, as well. It was back to domestic reporting at the same low level in the staff hierarchy she had occupied three years before. Three years of maternity leave and work away from the home office were not a recipe for success in a slowly dying publication.

Frank listened to her story and cheered her up as best he could. She would make it through all that, he said, and he believed it. Catholic girls should never be underestimated, especially when annoyed. Feared, yes; underestimated, no.

CHAPTER 4:

Harvard Square, 1964

Ari's New Year began horribly. JFK, her idol, had been assassinated more than a month earlier, and that was only the beginning. On New Year's Eve, her lover proposed, a joyous occasion for most young women, but for her a cause of great trauma that forced her to confront the fact that he was already married with a family in Africa he now promised to leave. She knew that his commitment to her, as much as she desired to accept it, would destroy not only his marriage, but also his political career, making him an exile from his own just-born country.

Capitulating to her Harvard-Radcliffe advisors' warnings that her interracial affair was untenable was excruciatingly humiliating, even though Ari had dissolved the relationship for the greater good, not with any concession of it being morally improper. The guilt of curtailing the relationship with a great lie weighed on her even more heavily, the lie to convince him that she herself shared, buried in dark corners, the hated prejudice they had flouted so righteously and unwisely. It was unbearable.

Still, to extract him from the web they had woven for themselves, she had to kill the great romance; draw and quarter it and burn it to ashes, leaving no ambiguity in his mind and heart as to the existence of contemptible flaws in her nature, fully deserving of his hatred. Even worse, the murder could not be accomplished as with a bullet or the quick slash of a knife, but only by starvation and repeated blows; affection had to be withdrawn and the lies resumed day after day after day, until he could no longer perceive the reservations in her soul. And so a month of bitter accusations and encounters passed, then another, then spring break, allowing avoidance for some weeks, and then bitter confrontations, and finally he gave up, accepted his PhD and returned to his country.

Ari was convinced that her decision truly served the greater good, but tormented herself even with that. Had she flouted convention because she truly repudiated racism in her soul, or merely used that as an excuse to initiate a romance she surely knew to be doomed from the outset? Was she punishing herself for her parents' sins? Did it amount to no more than spitting in her father's face, a spiteful gesture declaring that, if he were oblivious to his racial hatred and fascist complicity and infidelities, she would take the burden of them all on herself? Of what value was that gesture, when her father didn't give a damn what she did, who she loved, or whether she lived or died?

Was she rebuking her mother for her passivity, her penchant for burying the significant in a series of trivial diversions, for allowing others, all except her, to get away with anything by dismissing it as unimportant? The one thing she would never do would be to confess any of her trauma to her mother, but instead would flaunt the affair like a banner of revolt. Try to trivialize that, you bitch. God, how she hated her mother.

In 1964 Ariadne Gavalas was a twenty-eight-year-old graduate student and teaching assistant at Radcliffe, the daughter of Greek immigrants who had fled that country after the war and managed to make it to America. She had been old enough during occupied Greece to remember giving the Nazi salute to passing German troops, later foolishly displaying the same sign for Americans as they passed through the streets of Athens. Her parents' loyalties during the war were uncertain, but she later concluded that her father must have been a collaborator, although his loyalty to any given cause or person was tenuous at best.

For all Ari knew, her father might have been a communist or anarchist as well as a Nazi sympathizer, being capable of entertaining all of those passing fancies simultaneously, an ability reflected in his transitory affairs with women of all those persuasions. Recently, that included Republicans—American Republicans, no less, not those opposing the ascension of Constantine II. There might have been some excuse for that. The woman he picked up the previous year, however, provided the last straw for Ari's mother, who somehow managed the energy to throw out the philanderer. He disappeared with his new companion into the West to campaign for Nixon, until at the Chicago convention his new love caught him with a Nixon Girl no older than Ari herself.

Her father never returned home, which allowed Ari's mother full license to prod her for greater and greater educational achievement and to underscore her disappointment in Ari's failures, failures buried somewhere under an insubstantial dusting of acceptances to the best schools, scholarships, internships, and teaching appointments, failures that only a mother's eye could see clearly beneath the thin coating of attainments praised by others. Sometimes Ari almost wished her father back just to deflect some of her mother's disappointment. Of course, she would be satisfied to avoid them both.

In her second year of graduate studies, Ari had met Suluhu Modise, a Rhodesian from the Ndebele group, tall, dark, and handsomer than any of her European or American boyfriends, full of ardor for the pending liberation yet unburdened by hatred of the colonial oppressors, poised by his education and family connections to play a critical role in the coming nation, kind and gentle, with soft eyes and an understanding smile, easy to fall in love with, easy to come to bed with, simple to forgive for the distortions he made in order to obtain her, a formidable companion in her rebellion against liberal hypocrisy, a man in need of her love to compensate for the burden of his arranged marriage to an ill-tempered second cousin. He was her one great love; that was the one thing that could not be challenged, not by her, not ever.

Yet that conclusion did not put an end to it. She persisted in asking herself all the right questions, some wrong questions, and a host of unanswerable ones. How, if at all, was his infidelity different from her father's? True, the selection of a bride was not his choice. But who can say that one's own youthful preference for a bride is any better than one's elders'? Certainly, she knew of many, many bad marriages borne of the inexperience and stupidity of youth. Was their love sanctioned somehow by the hypocrisy of those who condemned it? Did their humanistic politics justify it? And, again, was she driven to it by her father's racist collaboration? Was she driven by guilt for what her father may have done in the war? Was she spiting her mother for being so ambitious for her and so subservient for herself? Was she cursed in the manner of the protagonists in the Greek tragedies she taught? Was it wrong to have given her love? Was it immoral for her to now abandon her love? Was it perverse to keep her trauma to herself? Was it specious to share her trauma with others? Was she psychologically defective, genetically defective, ethically defective, or worse? Did the mere fact that her love was an emotion, not a logical act, condemn all efforts to determine the right and wrong of it to utter futility?

She explored all of these dark corners of her mind, her soul, her heart, only to find that the corners didn't really exist, but only led into a labyrinth of tunnels, each turn darker than those before, each deeper, each narrower, but with too many choices, vessels becoming smaller arteries then capillaries, so narrow that only the most basic instincts could pass through, breaking down the rationality she cherished into fragments of thought that would emerge, reconstituted into distorted forms of her former convictions. She had absorbed her lover in this circulation, a cell that might help a nation recover from the infection of colonialism, but for him to do so, she had cut the vein to release him for transfusion to a higher purpose. She had bled for his sake and there was nothing to replace her loss.

And then, she decided there could never be. She could not find answers in herself, could not reconcile her own contradictions and could not escape dwelling on them without betraying her love, except as a teacher, as a guide to extracting others from their own intellectual or emotional mazes without reward to herself. She would take no pride in her internal worth, a thing of small value undeserving of happiness, but take great confidence in her counsel to others. That too was a contradiction. She was an immensely effective teacher. The teaching profession was her natural calling, but it only constituted a performance equated to play-acting. She played that role very, very well, but it meant adopting a Jungian persona, not really her but merely an insubstantial image presented to the world. So pursuing success in her profession could not provide a source of pride or ego and, as such, could be merely a fraud, a charade she could carry off easily, but not a talent she desired to expand beyond what came to her naturally from her own exploration of the subject. And so she would remain on her emotional island, ready to receive visitors with her inherent gift of counsel, an obligation of any proper host that would not break faith with her lamentation.

———

Ted and Sam were juniors then, twenty-three and twenty-two, respectively. As with most of the Harvard community, the assassination eviscerated their hopes for a new era of public service, turning them off on all matters political and driving them toward some soothing academic refuge. They didn't know each other when they signed up for the classical literature course, but did so for essentially the same reasons, albeit with somewhat different weights.

For Ted, the first reason beyond avoidance of politics was, well, girls. Harvard remained essentially all male, with the small number of Radcliffe girls crossing to the main campus subject to intense competition among the ten thousand men of Harvard. Moreover, though nominally co-ed, Ted's prior school had been practically a monastery and his dates since high school numbered less than a dozen. He figured that since the course would be held at Radcliffe rather than over on the Harvard campus, the attendees would be largely female, gravitating to convenient classrooms in the center of the women's campus where other girls congregated. Admittedly, the female students were Radcliffe girls, they of tartan wrap-around kilts complimented by dingy men's shirts, mammoth buckles and safety pins, long black leggings, unkempt hair, and dingy green book bags, sometimes clinched in the teeth when biking between classes, or draped over the bike handles, with a Gauloises cigarette from Leavitt & Peirce dangling from the lips like Jean-Paul Belmondo in drag. Still, they were girls.

Ted had been a transfer student from St. John's College in Annapolis, where he had applied because of the Great Books curriculum and absence of tests. Although Ted came from a secular Jewish background and St. John's was non-religious, it had a kind of medieval monasterial ambiance that appealed to him, at least in the applications process, so he turned down a Harvard scholarship in its favor. Once there, however, Ted decided that his teenage vision of enlightenment in scholarly isolation didn't quite work. He found learning Greek and Latin painful and total immersion in a sequence of literary classics coma-inducing, but discovered that he loved the tests that he had eschewed. So, Ted's father agreed to help persuade Harvard admissions to accept a transfer, and there he was, chasing girls and passing tests easily with a thin veneer of knowledge and an impeccable sense of what the testers desired.

For Sam, who had considered himself a serious student of political science with no time for overrated classical literature, the course's attraction was its reputation as a "gut," an introductory class notoriously easy to pass. Sam, like Ted, had to work part-time jobs to cover his expenses and an easy course brought welcome relief to a trying schedule. Moreover, the Brattle Theater sat about midway on the walk from the Cliffe to the Charles on the way to his room in Dunster House, so at the end of the week it would be convenient to stop off at a Bergmann retrospective, Bogart festival, or the like.

The classical literature course at the Cliffe allegedly was taught by Cecilia Rathburn, an aging professor who had become a popular drama consultant on the New York theater scene. In the best tradition of Henry Kissinger and other Harvard faculty with flourishing consultancies, leaving actual classroom instruction to others formed a common practice in those days, the name and course outlines inherited from earlier, leaner, years being contribution enough. Consequently, Dr. Rathburn seldom graced the podium in the lecture hall, instead leaving multiple copies of a typed lesson plan on a seat in the front row and assigning a teaching assistant to the lectern. In 1964, Ari was that assistant.

Both Ted and Sam were immediately attracted to the young woman, slight, dark-haired, sad-eyed, more European in bearing than American, extracting the emotion of Greek tragedy from what they presumed to be the depths of an inherent cultural understanding, not from what had happened just last month. By the time her lectures reached the *Hymn to Aphrodite*, each had convinced himself he had fallen in love, she being the goddess and he the mortal who might seduce or be seduced by her.

Unfortunately for the two undergraduates, Ari was mortal and about six years older at an age when six years is an enormous gulf for the older woman, a gulf made even wider by the experience of war as a child and by the recent end of her youth-shattering affair. Aphrodite—being immortal, eternally young, and fickle—might have amused the youths, whereas Ari, the opposite of fickle, could not, as she was dedicated to the memory of the love she had just put to death, convinced that the apex of her life had passed and that she was facing a future of regret, despair, and loneliness. She knew she would seek male companionship again, probably not far into the future, but it would not be with either of these innocent boys. Ted was too filled with simple urges and confused by an unwarranted belief in some unspoken soul connection, and Sam's idolatry stemmed from his shyness and inexperience. Ari saw right through them.

While Sam merely sat in the class, following Ari's every gesture over the top of volume two of Richmond Lattimore's volume on Greek tragedy, Ted was less restrained. One day, with the lyrics of "I Saw her Standing There" playing back in some corner of his brain, he crossed the room and approached Ari, saying that he simply couldn't understand what the gods were up to in *Iphigenia in Tauris*. He needed some after-class help, and her office hours conflicted with his class schedule. Could he come by her apartment that evening? To his own surprise, Ari accepted.

At seven thirty that evening, after finishing his job cleaning student rooms at Elliot House, Ted appeared at Ari's apartment. She seemed upset and was drinking a glass of white wine. She offered him one, which he eagerly accepted as perhaps a promising start to an adventure. They sat next to each other on a soft sofa, touched glasses, and then, with the text on the coffee table before them, Ari began to explain how *Iphigenia* stood as one of the most carefully developed dramas in Greek theater, that he should appreciate how well the characters are defined and behave plausibly and realistically; how the plot brings out the anticipation of danger, the romance of foreign adventure, the nostalgic yearnings for home and stability; that Ted should particularly focus on the relationship of Orestes and Pylades; that he should note that while Euripides was a poet and dramatist, he was foremost an instructor and social critic, bringing out unpleasant characteristics of Greek culture, not merely being an apologist for them; and that he should observe how Euripides' treatment of Orestes' visions almost anticipates a modern psychological interpretation of the myth of the Furies.

More broadly, she continued intensely, Ted should appreciate how little respect Euripides shows for the honesty and wisdom of the gods; how he allows Athena to enable the Greeks to escape, giving the audience a happy ending if they choose to see it that way, but preserves an atmosphere of man's vulnerability to fate, fate that might not bring salvation to his audience in a last-second miracle. The message of the play was not that the Greeks or any audience are deserving of an uplifting ending but only should consider themselves exceptionally lucky if the Fates give them anything remotely close to that. For life is mostly lost love, death, betrayal and disappointment. These are the true conditions of life. Great sacrifices do not bring great reward or even the satisfaction of making the best decision. No, the burden of the sacrifice always brings mostly regrets, regrets over the joy the more selfish choice might have found, envy of those benefiting from one's own sacrifice, eternal questioning of whether some other path had been possible. Her passion for this interpretation brought tears to her eyes, tears of anger and desperation, tears of frustration with Euripides and his meretricious gods. The true meaning of *Iphigenia in Tauris* lay in its dire portrait of the condition of life, not its momentarily distraction of an improbably favorable accidental outcome, and should leave the discerning with the realization that heroic sacrifice is merely a deceiving chimera. The pain of sacrifice lasts not for the moment, but for eternity.

After two hours of the extended interpretation in this vein and a second bottle of wine nearly gone, Ted excused himself, thanked Ari profusely, and descended the stairs to the exit. He looked up into the night sky. What the...? What the fuck? Sucking in the cool night air, he headed to a bar near Harvard Square, where he watched a highlights broadcast of the last Maple Leafs–Red Wings Stanley Cup final. He didn't give a damn about either team, but at least it wasn't so profoundly serious, or whatever the hell had happened back there. How could anyone get into Greek literature that intensely?

It took a good three weeks of attending lectures and admiring Ari's trim figure before Ted reclaimed the audacity to invite himself to Ari's apartment again. This time, he had a more workable plan, or so he thought. He would have only three or four discrete queries about the translations of certain passages in Aristophanes' *Frogs*, employing the modest Greek reading ability retained from his two years at St. Johns to ask some credible questions. He would bring a very expensive bottle of Greek wine, knowing that with her European sense of propriety, she would insist on sharing it on the spot; then he would turn the conversation to personal matters. No Euripides—anything but that.

Having shared with Sam his painful experience with *Iphigenia,* the two had developed some rapport, so Ted related his plan and asked Sam whether he knew anything about Greek wine. By that time Sam had figured that Ted had no chance in hell with Ari. So, to Ted's surprise, Sam said, "A good choice would be something from the Peloponnese region." Ted was unaware that the week before Sam had had a brief after-class discussion with Ari about his Vienna dining experience and sole exposure to Greek wine. Even though Sam didn't have a chance in hell, either, at least if Ted found the wine, Sam would get credit for it.

Once again, Ari assented to Ted's visit, this time for the following Monday. Ted spent an entire Saturday scouring the greater Boston area for the rare variety Sam had identified. Finally finding it, he purchased two bottles at great expense, one to share with Sam on Sunday to test its worthiness. On Sunday evening, they sat down in Sam's room at Dunster House and sampled the wine with a nice Kasseri cheese Ted purchased in the same specialty shop; both were delighted with the result and the next day's prospects.

Monday evening came and Ted arrived at Ari's apartment at the appointed hour, frog quotations at the ready and bottle in hand. At first, things seemed to go exceedingly well. Ari greeted the bottle of wine with more delight than he had thought possible, clearly amused by his cleverness in uncovering a vintage so obscure to Americans not of Greek ancestry. Ted felt quite proud of himself. They disposed of the few translations quickly and settled on the sofa to sample the rare wine. Ted extended his left hand along the back of the sofa, touching her shoulder. She was vulnerable, he could sense it, and she did not recoil from his touch. He tensed in anticipation as she moved ever so slightly, her left leg now pressed against his knee. Then, placing her glass on the coffee table, she pivoted toward him, his hand slipping from her shoulder, brushing past her breasts as she reached over his arm and behind the sofa, he leaning backwards in confusion as she strained to reach something, her hair touching his lips, the fragrance of May rose and jasmine overpowering, her right knee penetrating his inner thigh as she stretched for something far down behind his back. And then a sudden release as she pulled a briefcase of sorts from a stack of books on the floor between the back of the sofa and the wall, the spell broken. "Would you like to take the Stanford-Binet L-M Test? It'll be fun."

Placing the case carefully between the wine glasses as she shifted away from him, she unlatched the case and opened it, revealing a book, papers, flash cards, and all kinds of props looking like they were intended for kindergarten, dampening Ted's ardor as much as if he had been sprayed with a fire hose. Ari then pulled out the book and read aloud, "In an old graveyard in Spain they have discovered a small skull which they believe to be that of Christopher Columbus when he was about ten years old. What is foolish about that?" Ted, still stunned by the turn of events, "stammered, "I... I... I thought Columbus was born and raised in Italy." She laughed and raised her glass for a toast. "And discovered America when he was how old?"

"Oh..."

A barrage of questions followed, identifying the missing word, completing the sentence, etc. It was not what he had bargained for. Still, he did love tests, and made the best of this unfamiliar form of feminine rejection. He gradually got into it, determined to prove himself to be smarter than he looked, although Ari could have told him that his actions, rather than his appearance, were the source of any misperceptions of that nature. Without using words, she had already done so.

The session lasted longer than Iphigenia, more than three hours, ending with her telling him that she would make a rough estimation that his IQ was around 140. "Yeah, if I were a six-year-old," he reflected silently. Leaving, however, he felt good, his lust transformed to a fondness that he would retain in the ensuing years. It had been an enjoyable evening, actually.

On the way over to Dunster House, he lingered by the new Club 47 on Palmer, thinking that maybe he should ask out Rebecca, a student who sometimes worked there. He had talked with her on several occasions, but always left feeling a little intimidated, discovering her to be the daughter of a well-known Jewish professor who was teaching a class on the existentialist philosophy of Martin Buber. That, coupled with her intellectual and religious background, seemed more than a little challenging, and much too serious.

Nevertheless, the next evening, he dropped by the club, where records were being played while patrons awaited the evening's live act. After some preliminary bantering with Rebecca between strains of "Blue Bayou" and "House of the Rising Sun," he offered her a large slice of cheesecake that he had brought along from Elsie's Deli. Maybe in gratitude she would have coffee with him after work. She agreed. After the live folk performance, less interesting that evening than the recordings, they walked to the Square to share Elsie's cheesecake over coffee and light, inconsequential conversation. They would see each other again, soon and often.

About a week after Ted's IQ test, Ari surprised Sam by stopping him after class to ask him to swing by her apartment that evening; she wanted to talk about his essay on the mid-term. He arrived at her apartment building fifteen minutes early and killed time by checking out the building's security, as he had been trained to do by the Irish grounds crew to which the college had assigned him in order to earn supplemental income. They were Cambridge guys in their thirties who may have done a break-in or two at his age and had trained him well. Thirteen women had been murdered in the Boston area in the last eighteen months and a half-dozen the year before that, the killer dubbed the Boston Strangler by the press. He knew that Ari and every woman on campus had been warned and the grounds crews were extra diligent, but he would check for himself. On close inspection, the building seemed secure enough, but he would warn Ari again that night. When the time finally arrived, he climbed the stairs and knocked on Ari's door, relieved when she looked through the peephole first and then unlocked a deadbolt and removed the door chain to let him in. Before he even began to speak, she pulled a bottle of Peloponnese wine from behind her back. "I knew you bought this for Ted," she smiled. As she opened and poured the wine, he had to explain, not exactly, he had just told Ted and Ted searched for it all over Boston.

As they moved to the sofa, she recalled that Sam had told her he'd enjoyed this wine with a girlfriend; was she Greek? No, not as far as he knew, just a regular American mixture, and she wasn't a girlfriend, she was never a girlfriend; they were just friends who went to a Greek restaurant and the proprietor selected the wine. "An expensive wine to serve a high school student," she observed.

That led to an explanation of how he had worked there while preparing to go off to college, so they were rewarding him; he was close to the girl but they stopped seeing each other after he had given her some bad news; it was kind of an embarrassing situation and he wanted to do something special for her, so he asked for the very best wine the restaurant had. The restaurant had treated him to the meal and a bottle of wine, although they weren't yet of age, and he contributed a little extra for the special vintage out of his high school graduation gifts.

Ari took this all in, smiling, and then summarized, "You worked in the restaurant and were going off to Harvard, so they were rewarding you, including an expensive meal, but you also needed to buy a *very* expensive wine for you and your special date, who was never your girlfriend, but you were once very close to… Ah, Sam, my little puppy, you slept with her!"

Sam turned bright red and almost choked on his wine, but nodded affirmatively. "So you were close to the girl and you slept with her and you wanted to do something special after you had had to tell her something urgent that she didn't like. Hmm, well, you certainly weren't pregnant and wouldn't know if she was, so you must have told her…must have told her… she had given you a social, ah, infirmity! Am I right?" She clapped her hands cheerfully. No answer was really necessary as Sam choked and spilled the glass over the coffee table. Ari laughed and grabbed a towel from the kitchen. "You're a dear, not many boys would have let her know." With that, she leaned down to wipe away the spilled wine with a cloth, and then kissed him gently on the forehead, a mother's kiss.

Their conversation resumed. She asked about Lillian and he found himself unable to hold anything back about his conflicted feelings, his total lack of understanding of Lillian's self–destructive behavior, his anger and concern, and his sense that he had some kind of responsibility toward her that it was too late to do anything about, as she had gotten pregnant and married within a year after that dinner.

"You can't always be the right person to solve another's problems, even if you care about the person a lot." Ari's words were comforting. She surmised that Lillian must have been wounded in some fashion. Perhaps someday, if he ever should see this Lillian again, he should find a gentle way to ask her what is troubling her. He might find her answer painful, but it would be worth it.

They would test the temper of that advice instantly. Midnight approached, and Sam began asking Ari about her own demons. For weeks, Ari had kept her pain to herself, but it was becoming too much to bear. So, with Sam's simple question, her true feelings erupted in a flood of tears. They talked through the night, with Sam trying to understand, to say the most supportive things his young, inexperienced mind could muster. Eventually, he told Ari that he believed in her as much as she believed in her lost love, and that her self-examination and her honesty were acts of courage. He was only an undergraduate, but he did the best that he could.

That night cemented their friendship, and they met a few times for movies, sporting events, and the like. When Ari's teaching assistantship ended at the end of the term and she left Boston, they corresponded for a time. But Ari's despair did not end with her confession; it remained, dominating their correspondence, a widow's cruse of despair that constantly complicated what should have a close and productive friendship. Eventually, she broke off the connection "at least for a time," and he, exhausted, accepted it and made no effort to renew their relationship.

———

Sam, trying to understand this experience, came to believe that he somehow had been allowed behind a secret door where he had no right to be. He concluded that all women, or at least the complicated, independent women he came to be attracted to, must have their secret doors, dark interiors full of emotions that a man had no right to know anything about. What was true for Ari, he thought, must also be true for Lillian and for any other woman worth knowing. Not that they were alike or interchangeable in any way, but they had a depth that a man couldn't properly understand and conflicts that he was unable to solve. His friends, like Ted, might casually label such women difficult or high maintenance, but he could not brush them off that way. Sam had always been physically and emotionally attracted to such women, but after Ari, they scared him to death.

He resumed dating a girl from Boston College whom he had seen a few times casually before his infatuation with Ari. Taking it slowly, they gradually became more intimate. Two years after he entered graduate school, they began talking about getting married or living together. She began to reveal secrets that genuinely surprised him—stuff about reefer and sexual adventures during a semester in Europe. He wasn't so much shocked as he was haunted by the thought that she had seemed so stable compared to Lillian or Ari, and had come from the perfect suburban family, but was simply much more successful at concealing her demons. How could he be so unlucky as to be born in an era when all the women seemed like a compilation of Patsy Cline songs? Crazy, falling to pieces, and all the rest of it.

Nonetheless, he sucked it up. After assurances that it didn't matter and he would always be there for her, he proposed; marriage at the time was the only acceptable option for cohabitation. His prospective fiancée left for a weekend at her parents' cottage on Cape Cod to think it over. Then, on that Sunday, the unthinkable happened: her parents called to say she had gone missing. He drove to the beach and searched for two days. Her body washed ashore a day later. Rip currents, the police surmised. Sam refused to speculate. A grim month later, he accepted a defense department job offer in Thailand that he had put off earlier in anticipation of the marriage. Without that offer he would have volunteered for Vietnam, with the goal of getting as far from New England as physically possible. He would remain single for a very long time.

Ted, frightened off earlier by Iphigenia, had had a more immediate reaction to Ari's departure. He still thought he loved the woman in some way and would continue to correspond with Ari for decades after she left the campus, but his passion required an outlet, and that could not come through her. It didn't take long before his relationship with Rebecca passed from sharing cheesecake to intense, torrid, desperate lovemaking, driven by what he felt must be true love, as she responded as ardently to him as he did to her. There were no inhibitions between them.

Rebecca was not always upbeat, struggling with religious issues stemming from her parent's dismay over his secular—albeit nominally Jewish—background and from having broken up with a boyfriend weeks before they met over his demands on how to run their prospective Orthodox household. But Ted set all that aside as irrelevant; she was the perfect lover and the perfect woman. Being at Harvard, where basketball was a minor sport, he never thought about rebounds. He married Rebecca within days of their graduation, quickly had a son with her and a second son a few years later. "Daddy's little draft deferments," he called them affectionately. He eventually discovered that true love doesn't guarantee much. Sam could have told him that.

CHAPTER 5:

Selma, 1965

B eth Treme descended from a successful African American
family from New Orleans; long ago, a member of her family had married—or at least been involved with—one of the
early French developers of the city, and the family bore his surname. The Tremes were an imperious clan, sometimes claiming
that the Treme neighborhood in the Big Easy was as much a tribute to their own darker branch of the family as to the Frenchman
who had acquired the extensive plantation eventually absorbed
into the city. That was, of course, nonsense, as anyone taking the
time to investigate would soon discover, but still the Tremes were
comparatively well off, active in church and their community, and
very proud of their name, despite the fact that it was always mispro-
nounced, having lost the French diacritical mark along the way.

As a girl, Beth aspired to attend Tulane, but she had graduated high school three years before it desegregated and many
years before a black student's attendance became a reasonable
aspiration for even straight-A applicants. She entered Grambling
with justified resentment, transferred to American University in
her junior year, and two years later entered the George Washington University School of Government, Business, and International
Affairs. There she first became acquainted with the civil rights
movement, after a brief flirtation with Stokely Carmichael following a performance of Brecht's *Three Penny Opera* at Howard University.

Carmichael's Trinidadian background, Pan-African ideas, and
cross-cultural tastes, rather than anything connected with American civil rights, were what caught Beth's attention. She had been

particularly fascinated with Ethiopia as a young girl, absorbing the Christian mythology that surrounded the country, believing that the Ethiopian Queen of Sheba was the equal and lover of Solomon and that their son brought the Ark of the Covenant to Ethiopia, where it resides today. She linked Ethiopia's history of avoiding colonial enslavement to her unsubstantiated belief that slavery never had been part of her direct family background. Consequently, she preferred the red, green, and gold of the Ethiopian flag adopted by a minority of the Pan-African movement to the red, green, and black of the followers of Marcus Garvey. The Ethiopian colors were bolder, more optimistic than those of Garvey and less suggestive of violence than the banner she increasingly associated with the Nation of Islam and Malcolm X—that is, the non-Christian elements of the civil rights movement.

Beth was a good Christian and churchgoer, not casual, but a believer who gave the tenets of the church, as she understood them, precedence over her individual judgment, over her selfish desire to avoid conflict or to allow improprieties to pass for transitory social benefit. Crushed when Cassius Clay changed his name to Mohammed Ali following the Liston fight, she refused to call him Ali for more than a decade, thinking it also a great joke when several years later the basketball player M. L. Carr threatened to change his name to Abdul Automobile in response to Lou Alcindor's similar conceit. Her faith simply did not allow such transgressions to pass in silence. Beth eventually begrudgingly reconciled herself to using the Islamic names black men sometimes adopted for themselves, but never thought the fashion more than a macho affectation that was an insult to their upbringing.

Despite her odd Afrocentric mythology and conservative instincts, after meeting Carmichael she did begin for the first time to give thought to the Montgomery bus boycott and the Greensboro sit-in, events that seemed disorderly and somehow not respectable for someone of her imagined social status. Civil rights demonstrations only became acceptable to her with the great 1963 March on Washington. That is, the movement came to her, and it was no more or less an epiphany to her than to the white congressmen who could no longer ignore it once they were stuck in the traffic it created. The movement was a form of congestion to Beth's aspirations, as well, something perhaps to be put up with as a necessary step toward social progress, but not something that should persist beyond the minimum required for equal legal rights. Beyond that, the individual's own accomplishments and initiatives, guided by one's personal adherence to religious standards, should take precedence over collective social protests. She hated the term "affirmative action," which was just coming into vogue. Beyond one's faith, help should not be necessary; the concept seemed almost blasphemous. She couldn't tolerate that aspect of the movement, but at least the March on Washington had been peaceful and led by a Christian.

Still, in the midst of that mental snarl, Beth found herself in a Selma hotel room, having just returned from the Stars for Freedom concert in Montgomery earlier that night. At twenty-five and recently out of graduate school, she now could claim to be a veteran of the third march on Montgomery, although all she had had to do for the marches was show up. Actual marching was limited by crowd restrictions imposed by the authorities and excess protectiveness by the March leadership, so Beth's modest contribution was being transported by car to be a face in the crowd at a concert in support of the event starring Belafonte, Tony Bennett, Frankie Laine, Peter, Paul and Mary and others.

Though she was put off later by the violence of the summer of '65, Beth had been driven to a degree of activism by the events of Bloody Sunday on the road from Selma and by the urging of fellow graduate students at George Washington. She remained uncomfortable in her newfound militancy that day, social outrage tempered by her parents' views and those of the educated African American elite who felt the Civil Rights Act should put an end to the agitation.

A classmate at GW, Rafael Valdes, had goaded Beth to come to Selma. A Cuban orphan who had immigrated to Florida with his adoptive family long before Castro, Rafi had darker skin than Beth and he had been through Bloody Sunday and worse, but in her mind he was not black enough to be there. Beth, in candid moments, took pride that her African ancestors had intermingled with French merchants, rather than poor white southern farmers, but at her most egotistical she saw herself as simply a better class of African, whereas Rafi was Cuban or Hispanic. It didn't matter that he came from the black/mulatto underclass rather than those Cuban families considering themselves European. What could be more annoying than would-be Cuban revolutionaries elbowing into a cause that was clearly none of their business while ignoring their own? If Rafael were a real revolutionary, he would be with Guevara in Bolivia or wherever Che was now, not being a Stokely groupie and criticizing people like Beth for not being active enough in the movement. Well, Stokely was from the Caribbean also, of course, but Jamaicans and Trinidadians were African and Cubans were, well, Latino or something, whatever their skin color.

Beth described her skin tone as "café au lait," a term then used to describe Dorothy Dandridge. She was no Dandridge, but a modestly attractive, petite woman with a vulnerable Judy Garland manner that rarely left her the target of discrimination, drawing protective instincts from men of all color, at least on first impression. Under that surface, however, resided a temperament more like that of a Bette Davis character, never happy without holding a grudge, as she held now against Rafael. In that Selma hotel room, she found herself disappointed on some level that she was never treated badly by anyone during the Montgomery march, either during the modest actual walks or on the numerous shuttles. It seemed unfair in some nefarious manner, rendered more perverse the next night when a white woman was murdered simply for providing rides for the demonstrators. Despite that event, Rafael and others would accuse her of just going through the motions, blithely ignoring that evidence of personal risk she faced along with everyone else there, as if she were to blame that she didn't wear any battle scars.

But Beth did not brood about that so much on that night in Selma. The more disturbing issue was that the leadership never treated her seriously, including Dr. King himself. On the one occasion she passed him, he acknowledged her presence only through what Beth chose to see as a veiled flirtation, a wisp of ostensible concern for her endurance on the long walk manifested in an embrace that didn't offend others, but seemed to her not fully spiritual. In truth, any slight concession construed as made because of her femininity made Beth cringe visibly. Compelled by peer pressure to be there, she truly wanted to make a contribution and resented not being able to do so because of her gender. While such an aversion was fully justified, she knew it evoked adolescent reactions from the male-dominated movement.

Her pride was further insulted when she was not among the select three hundred permitted to march the full distance, but only would be allowed to be an "extra," one of thousands of faces in panoramic television footage of mass gatherings. It was insulting. Hell, she jogged and raced cross-country and could have halved the time of any of the organizers in a fair race. They were taking her for granted while treating her like she wasn't doing her part; she should have protested loudly. But she had been brought up to be nice, to not complain, and to be pleasantly deferential, at least until people proved themselves to be unredeemable, at which point any commitment on her part became null and void. In her eyes, the men in the civil rights movement were on probation, whether they knew it or not.

At least the concert had been pleasant: the Caribbean rhythms, soft ballads, and, of course, Mary Travers, the unrecognized source of Bob Dylan's success, more of a role model to Beth than Nina Simone, Lena Horne, Mahalia Jackson, or other female black performers at the rally. Beth would leave Selma with the same mixed feelings she had had when she entered, with the concert—not the cause— being the highlight of her journey.

———

The months following Montgomery were insanity to Beth. The Watts riots were a monstrous macho stupidity, as were those that followed, not to mention the ill-timed formation of the Black Panthers, with their stalking-in-the-night symbolism, together setting back the cause for the race and marginalizing equally or more pressing feminist issues. An ardent follower of Alice Rossi and Betty Friedan, Beth concluded that the civil rights movement had become counterproductive, at least for women. When Dr. King was murdered in 1968, followed by Robert Kennedy, the assassinations shattered any remaining scraps of idealism left in the decade and scattered liberal activists in all directions. For Beth, not much of a civil rights idealist even in the beginning, that meant refocusing on her own wellbeing, making better use of her financial and accounting expertise, and abandoning political activism for business, giving the gold of the Ethiopian flag new meaning. Her concession to social activism would be to first seek a position in business development in the black community, it being the most in need of economic pragmatism and a cure for rampant sexism. She found a position in—of all places—Watts.

By the time Beth arrived in Los Angeles in 1969, the National Guard troops called in to suppress the 1965 riots were long gone and LAPD chief William Parker had imposed routine order through his thin blue line of largely white southern officers. Watts still felt a little like an occupied war zone and there was still trouble every day, as Zappa observed, but the gangs had yet to establish their turfs and go to war over them. Beth felt safe. Being raised in New Orleans where there was also trouble every day, it wasn't hard.

Beth reported for work at the Bread Power Foundation as a financial analyst in the spring of 1969. Meant to convey financial self-sufficiency, the name sounded stupid and it wasn't long before she concluded that the executives of the foundation were as stupid as their choice of a corporate identity. By August, Beth became CFO after her predecessor was caught moving bread into his personal checking account rather than providing dough to minority enterprises to open their own bakeries, franchises, and small businesses, the group's mission. She could not but be amazed by the naiveté and incompetence of the foundation's management given its initial success, the foundation having secured federal and state government grants, a substantial kitty of seed money from Hollywood figures, and an equal sum through black athletes and their agents. Beth believed in meritocracy, and it never dawned on her that bureaucrats would hand over cash so readily to a bunch of amateurs whose financial credentials consisted at most of having played Monopoly as children. But the federal money poured in, as far as she could tell, just because some civil servants idolized a black singer, actor, or shortstop who had some lame business idea the foundation supported. The way men would suspend their judgment if they were fans drove her crazy, and she couldn't understand it; a few years later, Ted would explain it to her.

After the first few weeks of disgust and disappointment, Beth realized that her employer's incompetence could be her opportunity. If you were stuck in muddy waters, they said on the bayou, be a catfish. Cream may rise to the top, but nutrients fall to the bottom if you have the stomach to scavenge for them. Beth did. Timely, innocently worded reports to the company president resulted in the dismissal of the financial officer and her accidental discovery of résumé padding eliminated his deputy, the primary competition. Neither of those men deserved the CFO position, so she easily reconciled any subtle contributions to these events on her part with her religious faith; righteousness may be seen in the success of one's works, and there was no better work than weeding out corruption and dishonesty. Beth loved the new office, enjoying the view of 103rd Street and Watts Towers without reservations as to how she got there.

Beth fit in to the Los Angeles environment easily. The foundation attracted a continuous flow of entertainment figures and professional athletes, generating a similar flow of opportunities to participate in the local social scene. Beth had a flair for the dramatic and a moderate talent as a singer, and soon helped form a female group called Soft Salvation, modeled after the Supremes, with a little of the Dixie Cups tossed in. The group achieved modest success locally. With Beth's help, Soft Salvation retained a young agent named Tom Marshall, who had represented a couple of the Bread Foundation's would-be entrepreneurs, but he was unable to translate Salvation's fleeting local fame into anything national. It was only a sideline for Beth, in any case, and it wasn't a great loss, as she would marry Tom within the year.

Tom was the epitome of the clean-cut urban professional, raised in an upper-middle-class neighborhood on the north side of Chicago, where it was acceptable for a black man to be a Cubs fan and get away with it. He was of average height, clean-shaven, and youthful-looking to the extent that he still had his ID checked not only when he first dated Beth at age twenty-four, but ten and fifteen years later. Tom appeared non-threatening, typically mistaken for the client rather than the agent, and was unassuming to the extent that he didn't particularly stand out in a room full of white guys; consequently, he frequently was underestimated. As with Beth, his formula for success rested on that fact, but he didn't resent it nearly as much as she did. To be smart and under the radar was the key to minority advancement in the white-bread business world of that day.

They decided to be married in New Orleans, where Tom would meet Beth's parents, siblings, and extended family, and then take a Caribbean cruise from there for their honeymoon. Her family was impressed by his demeanor and credentials, but remained biased against his northern upbringing and suspected him of marrying Beth because of her superior social status. His parents, pulled up by their bootstraps and patronage through the waste management trade, were equally prejudiced against the pretenses of the Southern black aristocracy and were suspicious of this older woman who stole their son away. In the end, however, the families enacted a marital treaty and three decades would pass before tranquility would be shattered.

It was a match that was very well suited to the couple's flourishing careers. Tom also had a financial background, with an MBA from the Wharton School back East, and an education far beyond Beth's in investment banking. He had established his credentials in the civil rights movement while still an undergraduate, had interned two years with the SEC corporation finance division while at Wharton, and then jumped into financial management for experience in the private sector before pursuing his goal of a career on Wall Street. Like Beth, he refused to think that affirmative action should have anything to do with his personal advancement, and he felt that his services to the foundation had paid his dues to the movement. Neither he nor Beth wanted children. Their personal lives together would be intensely private, unreservedly passionate, palpably sensual, and immune from the envies and resentments of the outer world.

Tom's work managing the finances of African American celebrities was rewarding, but he was hoping to return to the East in the near future, where he could make a greater mark in the world. He offered the suggestion to Beth in a collegial manner, not in the demanding or devious modus operandi of the typical male. They would mutually consider their options and arrive at a concerted plan of action.

Back from the islands, Beth dwelt on that possibility as she left the Watts offices. She wanted to go back to New Orleans, the city she loved, and flaunt her attainments before those who had doubted her, but it wasn't a practical choice, not with the economy in the toilet there, as usual. Beth did not feel quite ready for New York, but a return to D.C. was not out of the question. She was familiar with how the city operated and still had connections there from her university days, and, while he would prefer Manhattan, her husband would find a return to D.C. acceptable as a next career step for many of the same reasons. Of course, the foundation would complain mightily over her departure, but what did she owe them, anyway?

As Beth left the Watt's office, a young man sat sullenly in his blue '66 Mustang, watching her warily as she approached, but relaxing once he realized that she couldn't be a cop. The Four Tops were singing "Walk Away Renee" on the car radio as Beth walked past, but the lyrics meant nothing to her, metaphorically or otherwise.

CHAPTER 6:

New Haven, 1967

S hortly after Lillian married Will in 1961, she gave birth to a healthy baby girl. She blamed Sam's bad advice for that mistake for years, wishing that she had gone to New York or even a back-alley D.C. clinic. She named her Dominetta, after the girl in the novel *Thunderball* who survived torture to save Bond and exact revenge on the villain by shooting him through the neck with a spear gun, rewarded for her troubles with great sex. It reflected Lillian's fantasies at the time, picturing herself as the beauty that might transform herself from femme fatale to heroine, if only the right man would come along, but it was a stupid name and a stupid dream to boot. She gave birth to a second girl, conceived at the Newport Folk Festival in 1963, giving her a more frivolous name, Tikki, in the spirit of the Beatles and the emerging hippie culture. Lillian thereafter devoted greater attention to birth control.

Lillian's delayed enlightenment in pregnancy prevention and sudden entry into motherhood were, as she told her mother, her very own Bay of Pigs, with her husband Will being the chief swine and their rented apartment certainly a sty, the air constantly saturated with the smell of baby poop. Will was of no help with the babies, that being purely a woman's work, and while Lillian was obsessed with cleanliness, she was even more appalled by the thought of washing diapers by hand, even to the minimum required for transfer to a diaper service. If disposable diapers had not become available in the market the year Dominetta was born, both infants might have found themselves on a church doorstep. Even with that invention, the confined apartment's lack of space and facilities to care for the girls properly and conveniently dispose of cleanup items made the place less than a home. It was impossible to entertain even a solitary guest, except for the occasional stop-by of one of Will's drinking buddies; entertainment of other couples was completely out of the question.

Only seventeen when she married, Lillian held the view that a woman should not waste her youth on children and the squalid living conditions reinforced that view hourly. A devoted Joan Baez fan, Lillian felt that she should have been with the beatniks and flower children in San Francisco, not confined to the role of a housewife. While remaining technically faithful to Will until she conceived Tikki, Lillian had not forgotten the power she could hold over men as a free woman. Upon learning she was again, as her father crudely put it, "knocked up," she soon returned to the one source of solace that she knew would take away the pain of her burden, at least for the moment. She would trade babysitting nights with a couple of loyal girlfriends, usually freeing her from the apartment once or twice a week. After that it was easy, just entering a bar during a slow period, taking a stool or booth surrounded by empty places, ignoring the room through reading or quiet contemplation, and waiting for the men to come to her.

Lillian rarely left a bar alone. She thrived on being compared to movie stars, on being called magnificent, hot, or whatever else a guy could think up, but flattery would afford the supplicant only a visual inspection. She, not the man, would choose who, when, and where, and most importantly, when it was time to go home; one and done, that worked for her. She was not exactly a seductress, as seduction required effort. Lillian had that rare attribute of unadulterated sensuality; beautiful, yes, but a beauty subordinated to a Darwinian imperative of natural selection that excused any flaws in her physical appearance, dismissed any prior tastes in a woman's form or bearing, and sang a siren's song that the man must seek to reproduce himself through her. That evolutionary endowment required her to be proficient in coping with the male gender, which sadly emerged only after the abuse of her youth and then was mastered too well.

Despite Lillian's innate skills through all phases of the mating process, she played a dangerous game, risking aberrant behavior from her encounters and detection at home. But it didn't seem that way at the time. The 1960s were the era of peace, love, cultural change, and optimism. Times were good, despite war, racial conflict, political assassinations, and the threat of nuclear annihilation. They were good if you just willed them to be good and put the rest into the background, if you lived in the moment. For Lillian, sexual adventures were not so much exciting as they were calming; they took away her anxiety, reduced her tension, eased her insomnia, and quelled her panic attacks. They were as much mother's little helpers as the pills praised by Mick Jagger and, in fact, Lillian emerged a much better mother each day after her evening enterprises. They signaled that the girls were only a part of her young life, not the end of it, and the care they demanded became tolerable.

While Will's absences on booming construction projects throughout the region provided opportunities for Lillian's dalliances, his schedule was unpredictable, and he would often return to find her absent. Her sympathetic female friends provided alibis, and the deception worked well for a long time. Will trusted Lillian's girlfriends, as he had known most of them since high school, and, for the most part, he accepted her excuses as plausible. But, over time, her constant protests that she was not home because she had been spending time with other women led him to one conclusion: Lillian had become a lesbian.

That was too much for a man to bear. Will accused her loudly and often, and her denials were unconvincing, with inadequate explanations for the nature of a friend's illness or why a shopping trip to Baltimore took two days and not one. Moreover, he knew from the day she started to wear pants that Lillian's most frequent companion must be a lesbian. Accusations alternated with fierce lovemaking, reflecting his conviction that a real man's attentions would reconcile a woman with her heterosexuality. This eventually led to a profound silence to underscore his revulsion with her deviant behavior, and, finally, to physical brutality borne of his frustration that nothing had changed.

Lillian, more prejudiced against homosexuality than her husband, could only offer honest denials. She took pleasure in each of Will's efforts to tame her and even in the batterings, as they were victories for her: he was not a truly violent man, and the beatings were rare and bearable, signaled his defeat, and were a tolerable punishment for her prior misadventures. She despised what she was doing in the daylight hours, but the beatings freed her of all debts to him, wiping the slate clean.

Shortly after the RFK assassination, when Lillian reacted by disappearing for four days, leaving Will with the girls, he responded by filing for divorce. Lillian found a competent lawyer to argue for alimony and child support and received both in acceptable quantities. She spent the initial lump-sum payment on preparation for civil service exams, and obtained a clerical job at the U.S. Department of Labor. She hired babysitters or left the babies with girlfriends or her mother, trolled for lovers more frequently, and within two years had found a suitable candidate for a second husband. He also worked in construction, at far-flung military facilities that sometimes left him on the road for months, which suited her inclinations as a natural woman. Her periodic dalliances accelerated to an unwise pace as her girls became more self-sufficient, her inhibitions lessened by marijuana and occasionally cocaine.

Lillian was becoming too well recognized at local establishments, and it began to get dangerous. She needed to broaden her range. And so she did, securing a position within the labor department involving data exchanges with state offices in the mid-Atlantic. It offered ample opportunities for misadventures in new environments by night, while allowing her to accumulate professional experience by day. Lillian had become expert in compartmentalizing and managing her addictions in a manner that did not threaten her career advancement. In the office, she gained a reputation for being dependable and easy to work with, a harmless flirt who teased her male colleagues, but never followed up on it, earning the acceptance of female colleagues who were more actively interested in the same males and occasionally benefitted from the desires that Lillian brought to the surface. She was a good and constant friend to those female colleagues, and a lively distraction to the men in the office, making them happy to begin the day and willing to work late as needed, but never allowing for any possibility of office romance.

By night, however, she materialized as a vision at the end of the bar, a Lorelei who sometimes called herself that, a prospective once-in-a-lifetime sexual experience, taking whatever she could get from men, from the mildest of libations to more perilous narcotics. She did, however, practice moderation; there was never a second rendezvous, nor a return to the same tavern, never the same drink or the same drug in the same month or more, never an indulgence before a critical work day, never ever a visit to her home, though her second husband had a decent house more amenable to that possibility than her apartment with Will. She never exposed her daughters to her encounters. While they would suffer from her absences, compounded by those of her second husband, she at least prepared them to be self-reliant, and sought, as much as she afford, to compensate for their loneliness with educational or social activities, little comfort for them or their mother, but at least insulation from Lillian's inexorable compulsions.

Lillian lived on the edge, but it was never the same edge, the cliff scaled before, too familiar, so that she lost all cautiousness. She fed on the thrill of danger, but she punished herself no more or less than she had as a teenager, only seeking the oblivion of the moment, not the oblivion of eternity. And she was better at that than she had been as a girl. She would revel in the thought that her partner was lost in her, that he would never again experience that night, that moment, and might dream of her forever. The risk was acceptable, the escape worth everything. Or so she thought.

In December 1967, Lillian finished her presentation at the labor seminar in Hartford on a Friday and checked out the local newspaper for entertainment over the weekend before she returned to D.C. She had explored the town earlier in the week and was unimpressed. An article about a Doors concert in New Haven the next day, however, intrigued her. Priding herself on still being asked to show her ID and finding the eagerness of college boys a nice indulgence, she vowed to drive to New Haven the next day and return in time for her Sunday flight.

Entering the New Haven Arena that night, Lillian did not realize that she was about to witness an historic event. Some sort of hubbub had occurred backstage, delaying the concert by about an hour, and Lillian took the time to befriend the young man next to her, an unemployed musician from the town, not a Yalie. He was not quite her type, a little too intense for her tastes, but still a possibility. By the time the first set began, the man felt convinced he had a conquest, but halfway through the set, Morrison launched into a profane diatribe to the audience, accusing the New Haven police of interrupting him and a female fan in the shower and providing a few appropriate words for his feelings about that. The police responded by arresting him, dragging him offstage, ending the concert, and starting a riot that spilled out onto the streets.

Lillian's latest companion grew as angry at the police action as anyone and threw an empty pint of Old Granddad in their direction, pulling Lillian with him through the crowd as they surged forward and out into the street. He had been popping bennies in the arena, and she declined to join him but accepted a drink. Lillian had her standards and did not do speed, not seeking the electric shock of sustained power and euphoria it produced and its unpredictable consequences of irritability, paranoia or blackout, but rather the more gentle stardust rush that fades quickly, leaving a controllable descent that might be readily moderated by grass or other antidotes. She was afraid of him but afraid to let go, with trash being thrown everywhere and her eyes burning from mace, tear gas, or whatever had been sprayed into the cold night air. After making their way through the unruly crowd, she led him to her car, where he took the keys, moved her over to the passenger seat and drove to his apartment. She consented readily. She had only drank half a pint of whiskey and still felt in control, her eyes feeling better and his rage subsiding. His alertness reassured her, and his sense of humor emerged. He promised to finish the concert for her with his guitar when they arrived at his apartment. They picked up a bottle of wine on the way, and took the elevator to his rooms with much kissing and caressing. There sat on the sofa and put on the Doors' first album, which he accompanied.

But not for long. Before opening the wine, he suddenly lifted her to her feet and pushed her to the bedroom, not unexpectedly, just a little abruptly. At the foot of the bed, she laughed and started to unbutton her blouse. That's when he hit her, pushing her onto the bed and putting both hands around her neck, choking her until she momentarily passed out. He then removed her clothes and his, hitting her again if she moved a fraction without his controlling hand. Then he came onto her and into her violently, his hand over her mouth, the torture easing only slightly and then being repeated. She faded again into half consciousness, but he instructed her to stay there, calling her a bitch, and snarling that she had asked for it. Then, barely aware, she heard the sliding door to the balcony open, and he was gone.

Some moments passed and Lillian remained on the bed, naked and cold as ice. She wanted to put on her clothes, or even slide under the covers in that horrible place, but she remembered his threat and remained still, afraid to move. The cold, however, soon changed that and awakened her. Cautiously, she moved so that she could see through the open balcony door. He was sitting naked on a lawn chair on the balcony, resting his head alongside a plastic table, a bottle, and a scattering of pills, motionless, apparently asleep. She gathered enough courage to rise from the bed, slipped over to the sliding door, and locked it. Then, just as quietly, Lillian picked up the articles of her tattered clothing, placing his out of the way on the covers, and edged her way into the living area, easing the door closed behind her. With the cartridge of the player clicking on the inner track of the Doors' side one, she placed her ruined clothes in the bag that still contained the unopened bottle, put on her shoes, threw on her coat over her freezing body, and opened the outer door to leave.

She had pushed the elevator button when an impulse came over her. Reentering through the open door, she flipped the record over and set the machine to play, quickly exiting, the door automatically locking behind her just as the elevator arrived. As it began to descend, "Back Door Man" started to play on the stereo and she thought she heard a muffled cry of "bitch" in the distance.

On the drive to her hotel, Lillian discarded the bag, bottle, and all of her clothes except the coat and shoes she was wearing in an alley. Upon arriving at the hotel, she went directly to her room, showered twice, put on clean clothes from her suitcase, checked out, and drove back to Hartford. She was badly bruised around her neck and thighs, but had no visible cuts. She hurt, but not so much as the day a decade before when Lily was disassembled and became Lillian. She vowed it would never happen again. Having kept her room in Hartford, her colleagues were unaware she had gone to New Haven. They met over breakfast, talked about work, and were off to the airport to fly back to D.C. She didn't flirt with the guys as much as usual, but it had been a long week and no one seemed to notice.

———

Back three weeks later for a follow-up training session in Hartford, Lillian pored over the local papers covering the period since her last visit. There were numerous articles and opinion columns on the riots in New Haven, which she reviewed soberly, but deep in the New Haven Register rested a small police report. A young man's nude body had been found on his apartment balcony. He had died of exposure, his corpse containing high traces of alcohol and amphetamines. He had apparently stepped out for air while preparing for bed and managed to lock himself outside accidentally. Frustrated by his inability to get in, he must have drunk and drugged himself into a stupor. Identification awaited notice of next of kin.

CHAPTER 7:

Naked Fanny, 1969

The Doors were more popular in Isan than they were in New Haven. Long before he reached the door, Sam could hear the strains of "Love Me Two Times" coming from the dim interior of the Civilized Bar, the sound emanating from a scratchy LP purchased at the Bangkok PX by a regular patron and drifting into the dusty streets of Nakhorn Phanom. There, a day after the Apollo 11 moon landing, Sam first encountered Frank and it was not going well. Now three years into his self-imposed exile from America's domestic troubles and troubled females, Sam had been up all night in Bangkok watching ghostly images of the landing sometime after oh-three-hundred, then flying in a daze to NKP with Air America. Frank greeted him unsympathetically, annoyed with the disruption of his routine by some groggy civilian and caring less about events back in the World, even if they were out of this world. In addition to the common Cessna Bird Dogs, Frank Miller was then also piloting a specially outfitted surveillance aircraft set up to fly lima-lima, low level above the tree tops, to take exaggerated 3-D images of the jungle floor. Sam wanted access to that aircraft, but the initial efforts at small talk were not progressing rapidly toward that end. The fog of war, in this case, proved mostly physiological.

Frank was one of only a few forward air controllers comfortable with piloting the lumbering special surveillance craft on missions over Laos; much like taking a six-oxen covered wagon through Indian territory—too big to miss, too slow to run—but such flights were in demand, despite the risk. On the mission, a spotter would view the passing terrain through a kind of inverted periscope and direct any deviations from a pre-planned grid. It could be exciting in a war zone, but dangerous as hell. Analysts later would view the images on what amounted to an old-fashioned stereopticon, on which trees stood out as if over a hundred yards tall and any squat manmade structures underneath the canopy were elevated enough to have a greater chance of being betrayed by their straight lines or other unnatural aspects.

The town and province of Nakhorn Phanom in Northeast Thailand was one of those curious backwaters of the war in Vietnam and the not-so-secret secret war in Laos. The small airbase situated there, a few clicks from town, was in Sam's mind not a real airbase like those in Udonthani, Ubon Rachatani, or Satahip, but a sort of beagle base compared to the big dogs of the air war. Known to those stationed there as NKP or "Naked Fanny," it reminded one of the World War I air war, or rather a cartoon version thereof. Diminutive Thai and, rumor had it, Laotian pilots strode about with long purple scarves, envisioning themselves as Red Barons, but coming off more like so many Snoopys.

Special Ops American pilots in jet-black came and went between their vans, tents, or makeshift barracks, their unmarked A26 bombers destined for so-called armed reconnaissance missions in Laos, supposedly at the request of the Laotian government, in an attempt to interdict Victor Charlie's infiltration over the Ho Chi Minh trail. The Ravens, quasi-civilian forward air controllers who had abandoned their uniforms back in Nam for the current charade, went almost unnoticed in their dirty tee shirts, jeans and cowboy hats, looking like ranch hands about to drive off in their battered Chevy half-ton pick-ups. That seemed appropriate, since their low-flying surveillance aircraft, Bird Dogs and whatever Air America could scare up for the decommissioned Air Force types who flew them, were pretty much the used Chevys and Fords of the war. Then, of course, there were the out-and-out spooks who had been there before the military buildup and still conducted various operations through Air America and other guises. It was common knowledge that the spooks ran a lot of things, but not much acknowledged for even the internal records, out of deference to Thai government sensitivities. Between Raven FAC and spook, depending on when and whom you asked, Frank was either, neither or both. Not that it mattered much, the high casualty rates over Laos not being great respecters of unit affiliation.

Sam had arrived in Thailand as a green civilian contract analyst working with some military-consulting office in Bangkok, but now had far more experience than the average expat, mostly in Isan, the northeast region of the country. His assignments had morphed from studying the effectiveness of village development programs to assessing what events or ideas inspired a growing number if Isan men to get caught up in the spillover of insurgency into Thailand. He arrived in NKP to argue the need for deploying a surveillance aircraft for runs in Isan, not just over the PDJ or elsewhere in Laos and the Special Assistant to the Ambassador had backed him up. Frank was not pleased, even though, or perhaps because, the proposed mission would be far less risky than flying over Laos. Frank had a bit of gunrunner madness going for him in those days. Having now seen the beast that he would ride along in, Sam wasn't so enthusiastic either, even though he had asked for it.

Sam had arrived disillusioned by women and the failed promise of Camelot, but remained an academic with an abstract faith in America's role in the world and a pocketful of paradigms as to how to win the cold war. Thailand had seemed like a great opportunity to study the roots of revolution and "internal war," as the professors antiseptically called it, and to develop a framework for redirecting those impulses toward nonviolent democratic progress. So, he naively joined a consulting firm contracted to a joint Thai-US government think tank in Bangkok and was assigned to assist an arm of the Royal Thai Army called the Communist Suppression Operations Command, or CSOC. That assignment quickly displaced Sam's framework of academic abstractions with established military doctrine then favored by spooks and the Pentagon and largely adopted by America's Thai allies. In expectation that his results would affirm existing strategies, Sam was assigned to report on interrogations of villagers detained by police and military authorities on charges of sympathy or involvement with the Viet Cong and local Thai guerilla groups. Some wags at the Embassy took to calling such unfortunates Tango Charlie in imitation of the Victor

Charlie of Vietnam. To Sam, the name sounded like a gay lounge dancer. The two comparisons proved equally inappropriate.

At first, Sam bought into the prevailing notions that Communist insurgents had hit on an ideological mystique and brilliant organizational structure, almost guaranteeing success unless confronted by progressive governments that were both perfectly democratic and ruthlessly draconian. "WHAMOP," some called it: "winning the hearts and minds of the people," but with the option to wham as well as cajole. Then it struck him that the strategy was such an oxymoron that all the dominos already would have fallen if the communists were so brilliant and efficient. The insurgency problem and the proposed counterinsurgency responses were, he concluded, based on assumptions of competency that were invalid on both sides. The academics and military needed to understand that what was happening in Southeast Asia required a good deal less understanding of Karl Marx and more appreciation of Groucho Marx.

"Tonight's secret word is WHAMOP, winning the hearts of the people." Yeah, you bet. Military guys in backwaters of the war like NKP understood that; they were a good antidote to the TDY types from RAND and the other think tanks who showed up at the embassy to display their superior knowledge on how to make the villagers love you through health services and intimidation.

Frank could be a potential ally to help Sam influence the embassy toward a more pragmatic view of what passed for insurgency in Isan, but he seemed committed to being a hard-ass. While Frank had long been as skeptical as anyone about the wisdom of Westy and Abrams and any other officer in the theater above major, he distrusted civilian advisors even more, especially those who were younger than him. Consequently, he had taken Sam for being purely a newbie and questioned him intensely. Sam's claim to know Thai well enough to personally interview Isan prisoners set Frank off initially, since the language was wholly incomprehensible to him beyond the basics of bargirl negotiation. "So, then show me what you've got, Harvard," he'd said.

Sam smiled and replied easily in Thai, with a philosophical wave of the hand as if brushing away smoke, "สิบปากว่าไม่เท่าตาเห็น. สิบตาเห็น ไม่เท่ามือคลำ"

"Fuck you," Frank responded insightfully.

It was late in the afternoon and, having heard the *Strange Days* for the third time, even Side B on which you thought you'd scream with the butterfly before the end, they decided to go over to Johnny's place alongside the Mekong, for a snack and a bottle or two of Mekong, the river's namesake rice whiskey. The food wasn't great, but the atmosphere was, decorated by posters of Joe Namath that made you believe anything was possible and reminded the boys of home. The Isan girls at the bar were a little less aggressive than those at the Civilized and the music was softer, allowing for conversation. Phu Thai ladies, Sam figured. In those days, there wasn't any possibility whatsoever that a female who didn't wish to leave alone would have to and the lasses from that tribal group occupying the nearby hills seemed particularly aware that the *farang*, as they called foreigners, would come to them in due time, most of the boys being half in love or wanting to be, and generous with bright red hundred baht notes, not so much in payment for sex as in gratitude for its availability.

Sam asked for a bottle of ginger ale for a mixer and three large Mekongs for inspection. With his back to the setting sun, he peered through each bottle in turn, scanning the back of each label. "Two months!" He set down the selected bottle in front of Frank and waved the others away.

Frank laughed. "I see you've discovered it ages in the bottle. Took me over a year before I realized they actually dated the thing under the label. You're right. Two months is a rare vintage. Must be our lucky day."

"My guys look out for me, Frank," Sam nodded at his interview team, drinking with some provincial police a couple of tables over.

"By the way," Frank said abruptly and a bit maliciously, "before we continue on business, I'll have to see your ID." Despite the language, which could have been Navaho as far as Frank knew, he still thought it obvious that his companion was a newbie and it might be amusing to blow a little smoke up his ass.

"You've got to be kidding. No, I guess not. OK, what do you want? Embassy pass? CSOC ID? Capture and detention card? I've got two of those, of course."

"Now *you're* kidding! You actually carry those piece-of-shit non-combatant cards with you? Lemme see."

Sam fiddled in his vest jacket pockets until he came up with both copies; the one he should give to the enemy if captured and the one they would kindly let him retain for some future use, maybe if he escaped and got captured again. As if your Asian insurgent had ever heard of the Geneva Convention. It was a load of crap, but then crap seemed to be the cargo always in supply in that conflict.

Frank started reading the card aloud: "Samuel Thomas Zeigler, OSD Analyst, twenty-eight years old now. Well, as I live and breathe, it does look like you." He flipped it over. "What the hell? If captured, you are to be treated as a U.S. Army lieutenant colonel? A lieutenant colonel? And you were, what, twenty-five when they gave you that? Your military friends in Bangkok must have shit their pants when they saw that! Brown hair, brown eyes, O-positive blood type. I won't test that. I can check the fingerprints, though."

With that, he took Sam's right hand and elevated the index finger, ostensibly checking the finger whorls against the print on the noncombatant card. "Yes, yes, it matches." He displayed the finger proudly to the women at the bar, to whom it appeared a familiar obscene gesture. They all tittered like innocent maidens and some returned the gesture. "Yes, it's true. Sierra Zulu, now you can claim to be a bird colonel."

To Sam's great relief, Frank released his hand and pushed a straight Mekong across the table. "Drink up, my friend. Maybe you can use the capture and detention card to get the proper treatment from one of those Isan chicks."

"Sierra Zulu?" Sam diluted the drink with the warm ginger ale.

"That's your initials, moron. I'll never remember your last name. German, right?"

"Yeah. OK, you can call me Zulu if you want."

The afternoon slid into evening, and the evening into midnight and then the wee hours, the tables merging and dividing like cell cultures in a petri dish, with the conversations ranging from Frank's war stories, to the powers of the various amulets worn by members of Sam's team, to flirtations in a smattering of languages and dialects, to attempts to identify fermented, fiery or occasionally edible food products arriving in identical bowls, to serious talk of insurgency, poverty and corruption and the stupidity of the American or Thai or Lao politicians or military officers or police or spooks, to fleeting efforts at cultural understanding, to excuses to go pee or barf in the laterite streets, in other words, the normal range of conversation in the proximity of war, the edge of the universe and the middle of nowhere.

Mekong had the effect of suppressing inhibitions and good judgment without completely shutting down motor skills, consciousness, or sexual instincts. Around midnight, Frank became engaged in deep conversation with Pracha, the senior member of Sam's team, concerning the power of Pracha's amulet to help him please the local ladies. Frank appeared intent on buying the amulet, more out his alpha male instinct than any real faith that a Buddhist monk would devise an amulet for the stated purpose, and the bargaining grew loud enough to attract an audience.

With the negotiations heading toward an impasse, one of the provincial officers stepped forward and identified himself as Nang-Klao, the chief medical officer of Nong Khai, an adjacent province. He expressed his confidence in the miraculous attributes of Pracha's amulet and concurred in his wise decision not to sell it, but informed Frank that he had become aware of an effective alternative. In Nong Khai, he said, men found that attaching a tassel of horsehair near the tip of their private parts would drive a woman to sheer ecstasy. He, in fact, had done it himself and dropped his pants to prove it, to the delight of the mixed crowd of Thai and American men and tittering bargirls. As a medical man he could testify as to the efficacy of the treatment and could perform the minor, painless surgery, no more than an earring puncture, really. Well, what could Frank do and not lose face? By oh-one-hundred he disappeared with Nang-Klao, reappearing an hour later and flashing the crowd before seating himself gingerly behind a full bottle of vintage Mekong.

Sam had had enough of this entertainment. He stumbled down the dusty street to his hotel, stripped off his clothing, and fell asleep instantly on top of the dingy sheets, sweating profusely in the sweltering heat. Awakening the following morning bathed in a thick red fluid that Polanski could've used in *Rosemary's Baby*, he cheerfully showered off the liquefied laterite dust and went off in search of Pracha and the team for interviews that day in Na Kae district in the southern part of the province, where the most serious guerilla incidents recently occurred. Finding Pracha sober, but in need of a cash infusion after a less solitary conclusion to the previous night's festivities, Sam replaced the lost gas money, packed the team into the Land Rover, and headed south.

On the road, Pracha freely admitted that he had somewhat embellished the magic of his performance enhancement amulet, actually a common charm for protection against natural disasters that Pracha once lifted from a flood victim. He'd hand it over to Sam for the low price of two hundred baht. The deal completed, Sam hung the trophy on his neck, where it would stay for the next day's flight plan meeting with Frank and every day of their surveillance for the next two weeks. Pracha would then encourage the Isan ladies at Johnny's to be especially attentive to Sam during the end-of-day entertainments. It was a transparent fraud and adolescent taunt to Frank, but would contribute to a sort of semi-functional relationship built on bullshit and the mutual recognition thereof, not exactly a brotherhood, but maybe a kind of step-brotherhood that develops on the margins of conflict. The relative prowess of the tuft of horsehair and the bogus amulet never underwent rigorous comparative testing.

The long day in Na Kae was like many of the others, an interview with four young men held at a local police outpost, discussions with the police and the team's CSOC escort, a late-afternoon meal with the headman of the prisoners' home village—made less appetizing by the headman's wife continuously spitting bright red betel juice through the gaps in her teeth and the floor—and, finally, a table of free flowing Mekong, with anyone other than the prisoners apt to randomly turn up. In these sessions, where CSOC oversight became lost among diverse preoccupations, the truth of local events often could be uncovered.

That proved true in Na Kae. Two of the four boys had confessed to some connection with the Pathet Lao and a weapon had been discovered, a homemade pistol that fired a single shotgun shell. The police branded all of them members of a communist guerilla cell, part of a larger plot to attack the NKP airbase, a theory strengthened by a shotgun blast fired at a U.S. military supply vehicle the week before. As the evening progressed, however, a young policeman, a local youth well lubricated with Mekong, quietly gave his opinion that the one prisoner he knew, the one with the gun, was upset that his former girlfriend was working in a bar in NKP. He most likely had fired at the truck in retaliation. About the planned attack, he believed that the police chief, new to the area and abusing his position, had just told CSOC what they wanted to hear. As far as he could tell, the only evidence that the men were part of a cell was that they all knew one another, there were only four of them, and they couldn't detail any larger plot, even after confessing, so they must be a cell.

Sam and Pracha had heard similar stories before. In prior expeditions they had run across a few VC and Pathet Lao wannabees, like the group who sewed a red star on a Thai flag and harassed border crossing guards with it, but Sam could remember hanging "Down with Bautista" signs out the high school men's room window, so he was not quite sure how seriously to take the threat.

Having heard false arrest stories a hundred times more often than serious incidents, Sam had made the surveillance aircraft arrangements under false pretenses, not actually with the hope to confirm a growing guerilla presence in Isan, but rather with the expectation that Frank's 3-D images would come up empty. He had convinced the special assistant to make the investment and had made progress in convincing Frank there might be a near and present danger. Frank wouldn't do it if he didn't think the risks were reasonably equal to those faced by friends who never made it back from Laos, so that was the way he had to do it. You can't send cowboys on a roundup if there they didn't believe there were cattle, only sheep and goats.

Back in Naked Fanny, Frank lay in his hooch, feigning a groin pull, soothing his wounded organ and listening to Jim Morrison. Whether or not love me two times would became a routine accomplishment with his penile enhancement, Frank had diverted from country music to get seriously into The Doors from the date their debut 1967 album made it to Isan. They were a comfort now. Although they were part of "The World," not the underworld of the Southeast Asian conflict, the Doors were a better companion to the disaffected combatants than to suburbanites and college students back in the corporeal universe. The band members were more into the hard drugs and reckless sexual behavior of the warrior than the mellow weed and gentle promiscuity of the home front and, above all, shared the hard-learned fatalism of the FACs and grunts mired in the struggle. A band taking its name from a line in William Blake's poem on heaven and hell, singing songs from Bertolt Brecht, drawing lyrics from the Oedipus tragedy, drifting into nothingness through the interminable strains of *The End*, the Doors were in tune with the psyche of the war, the alienated pilot barely making it back from Laos, the platoon leader who had lost only two men on the last patrol, men remembered only in the phrase "it don't mean nothin'." For Frank that morning the Doors album was his only friend.

As the Secret War dragged on and the Isan insurgency flickered tentatively, Frank and Zulu developed a workable collaboration, if not exactly a fast friendship. Frank was the more decisive, with extensive contacts among the military and civilian operatives with so-called "on-the-ground" experience, and only got them shot at twice. Sam was the better analyst, and was familiar with the men in white soundproof suites with meaningless titles on doors deep within the American Embassy in Bangkok. Both men were assets to certain circles and were assets to one another in securing that status. The dozen young Thai men who Sam had assembled for his "interview project" included at least three who were closely attuned to the shadowy side of Thai military operations and the boundaries of the permissible, so the mutual benefits traversed national and cultural boundaries.

After their introduction in NKP, Frank and Sam were to take many flights together, either in the photo-recon aircraft or in a battered, open-doored Huey to remote landing spots where Sam and his team would work. However, their collaboration was not confined to up-country, as there were reports to be made to the special assistant, permissions to be sought from the Thai operations command, meetings to be held in the plastic cocoon of the embassy safe room, and many occasions for Frank to escape Naked Fanny for the fantasy of Bangkok, an existential wormhole between the War and the World.

On his arrival for the assignment, Sam had rented a guesthouse in the compound of a wealthy Thai-Chinese woman, a single-floor building with two bedrooms, a kitchen, a bathroom, and a sizeable living-dining area wrapped around a bamboo bar and a stack of stereo equipment and LPs. Like virtually all expats and wealthy Thais in Bangkok at the time, Sam had a cook, a "number two girl," and a driver, but they all left for their nearby homes by mid-evening. Populated only by Sam overnight, aside from a thriving colony of chinchooks, small Thai lizards with a habit of falling off the ceiling into food and drink, and passing feral cats in pursuit of the lizards. Sam had plenty of room for Frank, who became a frequent guest.

After a late embassy meeting one evening, Sam and Frank settled in to ponder the meaning of the Stones' *Let it Bleed* album over a bottle of mediocre scotch picked up at the PX and then crashed. A typical Thai house, with heavy shutters to deter would-be thieves, the place was as dark as a coalmine with the lights out, and the two slept well until there came a sudden and insistent pounding on the door. Frank, in the bedroom near the door, got there first, with Sam not far behind. He opened the door in an explosion of light, revealing Sam's landlady in a red Chinese dressing gown silhouetted against the morning sun, the very image of the Dragon Lady from *Terry and the Pirates*. She was angry and demanded immediate action from the two men. Pointing to Sam, she shouted, "Your driver took my number two and sold her to the Lotus Flower! Do something!"

"What the hell...," Sam began, when Frank interrupted with the information that the Lotus Flower was a massage parlor in a seedy section near the Chao Phraya River, not all that far from the old Oriental Hotel, actually a Chinese whore house, but with massage facilities on the ground floor and five floors of private rooms upstairs. Sam looked at Frank enquiringly. "...or that's what I've heard," said Frank.

91

"You must fire your driver. Go get her. Go get her." Sam stared blankly into the image in the sun. "Go get her. She works tonight. Go ask for the new girl. Go to the room and come down fire escape. I wait in your car."

Sam threw his hands up, so Frank took over the discussion, advising the landlady that an alley next to one of the most notorious brothels in Bangkok was not the place for a lady. No, he would go with Sam to the Lotus Flower, and Sam could go in and ask for the new girl. Trying to ignore Sam, who was shaking his head violently, he hesitated; no, he would go fetch the number two and Sam could wait in the car. The landlady cried out with pleasure and hugged them both. Sam was stuck.

Later in the morning, Sam fired his driver despite the man's protest that the girl made him take her there, that he only made sure that she got to the Lotus Flower safely and that the owners did not take advantage of her beyond the usual arrangements; he certainly did not seduce her or kidnap her or anything of the kind. Sam would have none of it and the driver disappeared by noon, having washed the car thoroughly and reclaimed his possessions from the trunk.

The rest of the day passed slowly, but evening eventually came and they headed toward the Lotus Flower. Darkness fell as Frank parked near the front of the unpaved alley alongside the building, the fire escape landing about 150 feet to the rear. Sam moved into the driver's seat and Frank, standing beside the car, told him to be patient, it would probably be a half hour before he could request the new girl, affirm he found the right one with the information the landlady provided, pay the management, find the room, talk to the girl, and find his way to the fire escape when the hall was empty. There would be guards inside with knives and guns and he didn't want anything to do with them. With that, Frank disappeared around the corner and into the building.

Sam sat in the Mustang, watching the freelance hookers plying the street, young soldiers on R&R from Nam accosting prostitutes, female street vendors, and any other women passing by, glancing in the rear view mirror for any action near the fire escape, observing Thai and GI alike come into the alley to pee or barf somewhere behind the car, or in some cases on the car, checking the mirror, watching a fight, watching the Thai police break up a fight, hearing a commotion around the corner and a shot or backfire in the distance, checking the mirror, showing his impressive military ID to a curious Thai policemen who though him a pimp until he approached closely, watching the hookers plying the street. A half hour passed, with no sign of Frank; then an hour, and then an hour and a half. Finally, he heard the rattling of metal behind him; in the mirror he saw Frank drop from the fire escape, then reach up to assist the diminutive number two. As Sam started the engine, they approached the Mustang and the girl squeezed into the tight rear seat, Frank waiting beside the car. "Where the hell have you been? I was convinced you were bleeding to death in a hall somewhere!"

"We had to have sex first," Frank explained. "They made me pay for an hour in advance and she insisted."

Sam gunned the engine and the car lurched forward, leaving Frank standing in the alley. Swearing all the way to his house, he figured Frank would stay overnight at the military hotel he often used, but that he'd have to put the girl in the spare bedroom given the late hour. He calmed her down, ascertained that she called herself Lalana, an Isan girl from Kalasin, and assured her that she would be safe in his house that night. Arriving home, he showed her the room, finished the bottle of scotch from the previous night, and went to bed. In the morning, he awoke to the warm feel of Lalana's nude body beside him, caressing him gently awake. "Your driver take me back to Lotus Flower today?"

"Oh, shit," he said aloud. "I'm going to have to apologize to the son of a bitch." Later that morning, he placed Lalana in the hands of the Dragon Lady, rehired his driver, and called Frank to apologize. It took Frank about two weeks to nudge his nose back in joint, but Frank didn't hold grudges for long. He admitted that his, say, impulsive behavior might have been offensive despite the consensual nature of the activity. Soon, he was again transporting Sam and his team to remote villages, jails and military camps without the slightest recriminations.

In addition to the young Thai men on Sam's team, two women worked in his office: Kuhn Tao ("Miss Turtle," a nickname for her unpronounceable formal name), who was in her early twenties and well connected to the Thai elite, and Herminia J. C. Ng. The former was directly recruited by Sam's firm, but the latter, some five to ten years older, was assigned by the Thai counterinsurgency office on the nomination of the American Embassy. Frank found both women appealing and found reason to spend considerable time in Sam's office whenever he arrived in Bangkok from up-country.

Kuhn Tao turned out to be an untouchable flower, protected by an aura of disarming cuteness that made men view her as their younger sister and condemned any lewd impulses as incestuous, an impulse reinforced by the realization that her influential family could easily have you killed. Even Frank eventually became cautioned by that and admired her only in the fashion that a man who has always purchased Whitman's Samplers will peruse a locked display of Belgian chocolates, pleasing to the eye and no doubt delicious, but too dear and too much trouble and probably not really to his tastes anyway.

Inga was not untouchable, however. When introduced to everyone, Ms. Ng had explained that her surname was to be pronounced like Inga without the "i" or the "a," a feat well beyond the capabilities of the *farang* staff. And so they called her Inga, or Madam Inga to those who remembered the exotic Madam Nhu, the so-called first lady of South Vietnam before her exile. Herminia loved the shock of the name on the newly introduced, most having assumed she surely must be Swedish, so adopted it for her own.

Madam Inga did not engage in the Siamese *wai* greeting that charmed farangs as a combination of a prayer for acceptance and deferential curtsey, but rather stood straight, shoulders back to emphasize her modest cleavage, and extended her hand as if expecting it to be kissed rather than simply shaken. A man could tell instantly that she was his peer or better, her attitude implying an openness to experimentation. She had arrived at the joint Thai-

U.S. facility accompanied by top-secret-level security clearances from both nations, which was baffling given that she was born in Macao of mixed Chinese-Portuguese ancestry and more fluent in both languages than either Thai or English. She admitted to being the daughter of a high official of STDM, the mysterious organization that controlled all Macau casinos, her father somehow involved in China's decision not to retrieve the tiny "overseas province" from Portugal. Inga seemed to have direct access to the Special Assistant, so everyone assumed she was a spook reporting to CAS, CIA's covert in-country section, a rumor she embraced by silence.

This formidable woman impressed Sam, but he was not interested romantically, having just begun a relationship with the English expat divorcee who had walked out of her marriage to a former Thai colleague, yearning for home. Sam had invited the lonely and depressed woman to a dance at the American officers' club merely to cheer her up, but while dancing closely with her as the band transitioned to "Yesterday," he realized she had nothing on under the soft silky dress. For all of Sam's well-cultivated sensitivity to the fairer sex, sometimes a woman had to hit him between the eyes with a two-by-four to convey her needs. The distraction only lasted a few months before the woman left for England, but it left his connection to Inga strictly professional.

Not so Frank. He read her body language accurately the day they met and realized that this would not be one of his casual conquests, but did not retreat from the field as he was prone to do with confident women. There was something about the long, black, silken hair, the long, silken legs. He wouldn't admit to himself that he had some childish movie star obsession, though he had seen *Suzy Wong* three times, *Flower Drum Song* twice, *The Wild Affair,* and three or four others.

Inga didn't look that much like Nancy Kwan anyway. Well, maybe a little.

The affair proceeded fitfully, rapidly consummated at the outset, but interrupted for long periods by Frank's duties at NKP and Madam Inga's whims and unexplained absences. He was decidedly not in control of the relationship and it troubled him greatly, making him more determined to pursue her until some day, in some way, she would succumb to him emotionally.

But then, in July 1971, some months before Sam was to return to the States at the end of his project, Jim Morrison was found dead in a Paris hotel room. Frank showed up at Sam's house with a case of Jack Daniels from the PX. He spent three days getting drunk, playing Doors albums continuously, and complaining that he hated Inga because she was a spy. On the fourth day, Frank did the only logical thing: he proposed to Inga. She accepted on one condition and he removed the horsehair a day before the ceremony. Sam served as best man.

CHAPTER 8:

Fenway/RFK, 1971

Another lame season for the Red Sox staggered toward a close, the team coming off a long, awful road trip on the West Coast and down to a mere five games over five hundred. With Yaz having a bad year, the Orioles were out of reach, but still drew a big crowd when they arrived in Fenway at the end of August. Ted observed the proceedings from well down the right field line with his young son, witnessing the Sox squander a 3–0 first inning lead, off Jim Palmer no less, to be tied 3–3 in the fifth. The pitching settled down but the game moved on at a glacial pace.

Despite his addiction to Fenway, Ted was annoyed. Rebecca had chased him and their four-year-old from the house while she prepared to receive a dozen friends for a baby shower for their second child. It seemed a reasonable demand, but the boy was too young for the game and getting cranky, and Ted's body screamed in rebellion against yet another attempt to give up smoking, the cold sensation of nicotine draining from his veins like a victim of Dracula, making the fuss and the game all the more annoying. By the top of the eighth inning he had packed up and left, only to hear on the car radio that the Sox pulled the game out in the ninth. It figured. It was that kind of a year.

He didn't care that much really, just another lost season. Things were not going all that well at home, either. The baby shower was taking place at his house rather than in some posh restaurant because of Rebecca's poor health. She complained constantly of being exhausted, and her doctors found this to be the result of anemia, but were unable to determine the cause or find an effective treatment. Whether due to the anemia or other reasons, she had quickly changed from the carefree girl he had married to a constant worrier and faultfinder, always concerned that they, meaning he, were not living up to the standards set by her parents and her accomplished siblings. Empathy gradually eroded and their life transformed into a sequence of long days spent separately at work and home, quiet dinners at the kitchen table, where they broke silence mainly to respond to the boy's incessant questions, boring evenings of watching television, and early retirements to bed, where, for the most part, they ignored one another.

Professionally, things weren't much better; he had to grant Rebecca that. While Sam had gone on to graduate school and then took some secretive defense job in Southeast Asia, Ted had joined the creative department of a Scandinavian furniture chain headquartered in the Boston area directly out of college. Already married with a baby on the way, he had felt relatively secure from the threat of the draft and anticipated steady career advancement in a growing economy, a steady accumulation of success to be uninterrupted by the dirty little war. However, the position didn't pay particularly well at the outset and his salary had not increased as rapidly as he had anticipated.

The enterprise was a high-end contemporary furniture retailer, enjoying some success at the time Ted joined the company and built a reputation as an "up-and-comer" through his advertising campaigns, the most successful featuring a blond Swedish-looking model in a white mini-skirt, lounging on stark white furniture below the single word "Basics;" images coming within an inch of anticipating Sharon Stone by twenty years. However, it was not long before cheap competitors, culminating in IKEA, began to decimate the higher-end competition by undercutting prices. Almost overnight they undermined any visions that European furniture might be proper settings for erotic liaisons with unattainable beauties, and replaced them with images of self-assembly, bad directions and missing bolts. Nothing could kill romance like self-assembly, that is, until shrink-wrap came along decades later. Ted had not allowed for the franchising and outsourcing of America when he took the job and paid the price for this oversight. He vowed to never again sucker himself into thinking that product quality had anything whatsoever to do with marketing success. Perhaps that conclusion wasn't altogether true, but at the very least, Ted concluded, people who purchased products based on research, reviews and technical specifications were unlikely to respond strongly to his specialty, the "splash and dash," making a visceral visual or aural impression that sends them running to the store for an instant buy. He had picked the wrong product for building a career on that technique.

On the drive home from Fenway, Ted decided that, as devoted as he was to it, he must divert his attention from impulse marketing, his strong suit, and simply take a higher-paying job. He had learned through a local headhunting firm that a company in D.C. was expanding its portfolio of clients lobbying for reduced transport rates, deregulation of telephones and other public utilities, and accelerated commercial application of defense technology. Ted considered lobbying likely to be as boring as planting seeds for the purpose of watching grass grow—grass that you didn't intend to smoke later. But the salary offered was high, and if he could sell corporate bullshit to congressmen, he could sell anything. He had almost talked himself into believing that the move would be a positive thing, but was not yet quite that good in merchandising.

Still, money talks, and despite Ted's doubts, he tried to persuade Rebecca on a move to Washington, a more difficult marketing task than anything he anticipated in the new job, given that in her eyes Boston was home, culture, education, tradition, and anything else of significance. In the end, however, Rebecca agreed to the move, despite her civic arrogance, reluctance to move away from her parents, pending baby, and doubts secretly amplified by private second thoughts about the marriage and whether she had made the right choices. Still, she had to agree that the change would be very positive financially and Ted was devoted to his son, so divorce was not an option, even without her mother's Orthodox traditions that would require Ted to initiate such a process.

Ted wasn't Orthodox or even Jewish in a strictly religious sense, and he suspected that Rebecca's father wasn't either, since if you immerse yourself deeply enough in Martin Buber you can reconcile virtually anything to Jewish theology, employing the panentheist dodge that God is in everything. The mother was a different story; it was because of her that he had gone through the charade of an elaborate Hassidic wedding. And the woman would never approve of a divorce without irrefutable proof of Ted's irresponsibility, abuse, insufferable burdens, adultery, refusal to engage in conjugal sex, or probably all of these things together, definitively proven through elaborate culturally sanctioned procedures. Rebecca could accuse Ted of none of these infractions, and his being a jerk with excessive frequency was not sufficient. Therefore, she reluctantly agreed to the move.

Their baby, another boy, was born after sunset on September 28, the auspicious date of Yom Kippur that year, tainted only by the Red Sox losing a double-header in Baltimore and closing the season with a final loss the following day. By late October, Ted had acquired a modest house in Silver Spring and they were ready to move. Rebecca remained filled with suppressed reservations, annoyed with Ted for seeming concerned only with the fact that the Senators were moving to Texas the following year and he couldn't watch his beloved Red Sox so often. It didn't help to remind him that the Orioles were only an hour's drive away. Finishing eighteen games back can affect a man's judgment on such matters.

On the other hand, the Redskins were getting better and the new firm had box seats, while the Patriots had finished last in 1970, moving to Foxboro and cutting Boston out of the team name. While he lived and died baseball, Ted could deal with RFK in the fall. That cheered him up to a modest extent.

By mid-November, the household goods were received at the new home, the furniture arranged, the baby room painted, and Ted welcomed by his new boss, J. Ward Barrington, a man who had served as a congressional staffer, deputy department head, and assistant to the chairman of a particularly musty federal commission. He had a PhD in economics and a law degree without having practiced in either field, his primary qualifications to be a lobbyist being not what he knew but who he knew, the proper endowment of the successful influence peddler. That had sufficed to establish the firm, but some technical expertise was necessary to make it flourish.

There were initially only three senior staff members: the president himself, his deputy Ben Samuelson, who had worked with the firm's president in government and came over with him as a transportation expert, and Rafael Valdes, who in the years after marching with Beth in Selma had emerged as a Vietnam veteran with technical education in telecommunications and military training, and agency experience in that field. Ted would head the creative department, which would entail developing media initiatives for those clients not relying solely on either the old boy political network or regulatory judgments. They were still looking for a research department head and financial officer.

Ted immediately liked Rafi, as everyone called him. The two shared a kind of impiety toward convention, an irreverence Ted applied widely to everyday life, but Rafi directed mostly to politics. Growing up in a pre-Castro Miami community of Cuban immigrants that had then encompassed a broad spectrum of political beliefs, Rafi had been encouraged to think for himself and, being a romantic, came down on the pro-Che, pro-Fidel side, just as the community was turning virulently in the other direction. After graduate school he had forsaken the draft shelters of education, marriage, children, or dubiously essential federal employment for civil rights activism and being drafted for his troubles, his presence at Selma no more appreciated by his local draft board than by Beth.

Ted admired Rafi's contrarian personality. Rafi would be a natural ally in the Watergate discussions that would dominate office lunch hours over the next three years, but would also learn to redirect his fervor over Watergate and social injustice to outrage over clients' unfair treatment, an outrage when combined with Ted's manufactured disdain for the clients' oppressors, whoever they might be, were powerful lobbying tools. He and Ted worked well together, and it didn't hurt that Rafi also was a rabid baseball fan.

Ted was less fond of Ben, who nevertheless took him under his wing. Ben was precise, methodical, and quick to grasp whatever perspective that Barringer wanted to adopt in a given context and to execute position papers containing absolutely no deviation from the preferred strategy. Rafi sometimes compared Ben to a sponge, soaking up Barrington's ideas, but was more a human manifestation of carbon paper, reproducing the president's thought processes exactly—perhaps a little smudged, but accurate. After falling afoul of the company line on a couple of occasions, Ted learned that Ben was his road map to staying in good graces. Ben set out the technical specifications, that is, the facts as Barringer defined them; then, having in hand the pre-set path to the pre-set destination, Ted described why it was the best of all possible routes.

At the first company social event involving spouses, Ben's wife Rachel met Rebecca, and in Ben's eyes, at least, the couples became best friends, the relationship principally cemented by their shared religion. That made Rebecca happy, so Ted let Ben's assumption take its course for that reason, taking the existentialist view that it was of no real concern whether Ben ascribed him with religious attributes; God is in everything. From a non-existential perspective, Ted was as religious as a tree stump, no more, no less... assuming tree stumps are Red Sox fans.

July 1972 came, with the East Coast just beginning to clean up from the devastation of Hurricane Agnes, the investigation just beginning of five guys breaking into Democratic headquarters at the Watergate, and Jane Fonda gracing the front pages of the newspapers posing with North Vietnamese anti-aircraft guns in Hanoi. A few days after Independence Day, Ted received a letter from Ari, forwarded from his old Boston address, basically asking what was going on in America and whether he had heard anything from Sam.

Ari had split the last eight years between teaching in the California university system and affiliated programs in Europe and was writing from Brussels. She had exchanged correspondence with Ted perhaps a half-dozen times over those years, mostly in the aftermath of some short-lived relationship that had just fallen apart. At first Ted wanted to believe that that betrayed some spark of romantic interest from the Harvard days, but soon realized it did not; only platonic nostalgic affection and pure curiosity. She always inquired about Sam and he would forward her message, but to his knowledge Sam never wrote back to her, only replying with a friendly but terse note to him, providing a brief summary of recent events in his life that Ted could pass along if he so chose. There was nothing bitter or mean-spirited about Sam's letters, just an implication that he had closed the doors on the past as if locking away some deranged lover. It was as though Sam were Rochester and Ari the mad Bertha from his days in the wild Sargasso Seas. Of course, Ted had an active imagination and it was nothing like that at all.

At that time, Ted had not written to or heard from Sam in at least three years, and concluded he was probably an undercover agent or something of the sort. He wrote a short note and enclosed Ari's letter in an envelope he sent to Sam's APO address. There was no reply for over two months, when at last Ted received Sam's letter, postmarked Alexandria, Virginia. He was back and hadn't called, the bastard.

Ted dialed the enclosed phone number and the two got together the next day, with Sam claiming to have returned and set up an apartment only a little over a week ago. In any case, Sam insisted the letter sent to the APO had just caught up to him. There was plausibility in that latter claim, Ted supposed.

Like the vast majority of conversations in the '60s and early '70s between men who considered themselves friends, the reunion touched on nothing of psychic importance, that being the formula for how men then became and remained close friends. Sam mildly exaggerated his adventures in Thailand and Ted inflated his successes in Boston. Romantic affairs in Siam were implied, anything other than marital bliss in D.C. denied. They discussed how the photos of Hanoi Jane made Ted want to see *Barbarella* again and talked about sports. Women of the era had a superficial understanding of such communions, a misapprehension comparable to Plato's unenlightened individual viewing the shadows on the back of the cave. They simply could not comprehend how the boundaries voluntarily set between men affirmed their well-being and the preoccupation with trivia reassured each of them of an unremorseful future. The silent generation of males did not need shoulders to lean on, a boomer affliction that spread only after the fall of Saigon when contrition became more socially acceptable among the stronger sex.

For Sam and Ted, the meeting was a satisfactory renewal of their friendship. Sam was pleased to learn Ari was well and promised to send her a note, a dubious assurance that Ted let slide. Ted had described his new firm and its lucrative salary structure and let Sam know that he could probably bring him into the staff if he were so inclined. Just returned, Sam was not ready for such an offer, still feeling obligated to his consulting group following his long Thailand tour. He had no idea what his job would be like in the next several months and he wanted to find out before making any big decisions, but he would let Ted know. The meeting, however, gave him the confidence to reassess his options.

On the way back to his apartment, Sam decided he would write Ari. Not right then, but soon.

CHAPTER 9:

Watts/Maputo, 1973

Sam ended his tour in Thailand in 1972, returning to the home office of his consulting firm in McLean, Virginia. As he told Ted when they met in July, his future as a consultant was a bit unsettled. Funding for his type of work rapidly dried up as the Vietnam War and its offshoots in Isan and Laos slid down the slope of national commitment like a mudslide into oblivion.

The so-called "beltway bandits," deprived of their defense contracts associated with the war, retrenched. Sam's firm reacted like all the rest and he retained his employment only through his skills in responding to the dwindling number of solicitations appearing in the *Commerce Business Daily*, the bible for government contractors, generating more prayers than the King James Version and answering more also. After months of deconstructing each CBD entry, submitting proposals to federal and state agencies on every subject conceivable, and seeking subcontracts from private enterprises, the firm secured a project to conduct a performance audit of a minority business-development foundation based in the Watts section of Los Angeles, flowing from cold-warrior research to equal-opportunity facilitators with the ease of a stream diverting its course when blocked by debris.

In a way, it was refreshing. The minority foundation was a nest of young black entrepreneurs on the make who promoted everything from prefab housing modules supposedly designed to appeal particularly to the rising black middle class to minor league hockey franchises. The leadership of the firm came to McLean and attempted to communicate the unique minority segment appeal of their proposed investments to the uptight white researchers in their white dress shirts, narrow ties and pocket protectors, most of whom had never worked for an entity other than the Defense Department. The would-be entrepreneurs accompanied their day-long presentation by playing Marvin Gaye records as background for socioeconomic commentary as to "what's goin' on" in minority enterprise, a futile effort to create sympathetic honorary brothers for the duration of the evaluation. It was the funniest and most racially awkward thing Sam would see until Jeff Goldblum tried to dance to a Temptations tune some ten years later.

On his initial trip to Watts, Sam met Beth Treme for the first time. He found Beth impressive, albeit in a less than conventional fashion. Wearing unnaturally long fingernails extending a good two inches beyond her fingertips to signal that she didn't type, her diminutive form draped in a flowing black robe, a headscarf in the red, gold, and green color of the Ethiopian imperial flag dominating her sepia complexion, always carrying a black ledger labeled with her title as the foundation's chief financial officer, and bearing an intimidating HP-35 calculator keyed with the back end of a gold engraved Sheaffer Triumph Imperial mechanical pencil, she was, in want of a better word, scary. It was her Rastafarian Revivalist do-gooder financial whiz-kid phase. She was still true to her African American roots in a compartmentalized way that did not conflict with her main-stream ambitions, but she would get over it.

Whereas most of the men in the foundation espoused whatever bright ideas were suggested by its clientele seeking seed money, largely celebrities from the sports and entertainment world, Beth was tough. She didn't hesitate to put down any project that she thought crackpot, whether espoused by a twenty-point-per-game shooter, a three-twenty hitter, or a Billboard top-fifty singer. As Sam discovered later, it helped that her husband was a whiz-kid agent with a major contract management firm. In industries sensitive to spousal and other liaisons, in which indiscretions are constant topics in the press, locker rooms, and backstage, Beth knew that even stars are reluctant to offend the mates of possible future agents. She could take a shot at her colleagues without fear of retaliation and often did so.

Beth proved an unexpected ally to Sam in his performance audit of the foundation. For a CFO, she demonstrated much less of a penchant for financial moonshine than most corporate officers in that position. She described the successes of the foundation modestly and illustrated their limitations with detailed and concise references to the books. Her evaluations of proposals pending before the foundation board of directors were at least as harsh as his own, often more so. She would never explicitly criticize the management, except for a joke or two about "Bread Power," but made it easy for him to do so. She proved to be precise, accurate, and honest in her spreadsheet computations and he knew he could trust every calculation in the ledgers. Due to Beth's diligence and insights, Sam's analysis proceeded systematically and wrapped up after about five months from the start, his confidential report to the funding agency turning out to be more negative than he had anticipated. The woman was judgmental, to be sure, but she was absolutely right about the weaknesses of the foundation and he admired her objectivity in the face of intense pressure to look the other way in the interest of racial progress. The foundation could easily have become just another federal money-pit without the continuous auditing Sam recommended along with a more modest level of support than sought by the organization. He thanked Beth extensively for her contributions.

As the wrap-up party in a club near the Watts office wound down, Beth took Sam to a corner and in a hushed voice let him know that her husband was moving to Washington. She would accompany him and would be looking for a job. Could Sam help her out in any way? He said, he'd think about it. She had a chip on her shoulder, certainly, but her talents were undervalued at the foundation, meriting her disillusionment. If he moved to Ted's firm, she definitely could be a candidate for the open financial position there.

The three months of minority enterprise consulting in Los Angeles were interesting to Sam but involved a little too much of walking the fine line between political correctness and objective assessment for his taste. Consequently, Sam was delighted to get a call from Madam Inga on his return to McLean. She explained that she and Frank were still in Thailand, she having given birth to twins, a boy and a girl, but they would be leaving for the States soon, which she was eagerly awaiting. But she had called not just to update Sam, but because she had become aware of a small project for USAID in southern Africa that he might be interested in. She could help win a sole-source contract due to her fluency in both Portuguese and Chinese. He knew right away it was CIA business. It hadn't required Frank's drunken confessions to figure out Inga's affiliation.

The project was an evaluation of railway networks in southern Africa linked to ports in the Portuguese colony of Mozambique. Lines from South Africa, Rhodesia, Malawi, Swaziland, and inland connections flowed to Mozambique ports, or would if they were operational. Formally termed a long-term AID/USIA network planning study, an unclassified policy evaluation of the competitive efficiency of these routes was justifiable but not especially exciting. Sam, however, knowing that this had everything to do with Inga's CIA connections, agreed to his firm sending an expression of interest. It did, and two weeks later a contract arrived listing Sam as the team leader and one Herminia J. C. Ng as the Mozambique expert.

Given the expectation that the Portuguese government could collapse and the liberation revolution explode in Mozambique at any time, the viability of these routes and their geopolitical implications were both concerns. For Madam Inga, the latter issue was clearly most important. It was beginning to become clear that the PRC was unwilling to allow the Soviets and Americans to divide Africa between them. China wanted influence in the region and involvement in railways could be part of that. The Chinese were already heavily involved in the development of a railway line from the Zambian copper mines to Dar es Salaam in Tanzania, with thousands of Chinese workers engaged in the ongoing construction, and there were rumors of Chinese collaboration with Canada to build a second line to Nacala in the north of Mozambique. In the wake of Nixon's opening to China, there was potential for both cooperative and competing initiatives in the region. Chinese participation in regional transport was certainly preferable to Soviet domination, but Chinese control of all key outlets would not be desirable either.

Inga, Sam discovered, was mostly interested in the role in these developments, if any, of the Chinese CIA equivalent, the Central Investigation Department. The CID was more of an intelligence-gathering agency than an espionage unit, but some were beginning to suspect CID agents of complicity in some recent violence within leftist groups of railway workers. Before Inga's telephone call, Sam possessed only a vague awareness that the independence movement in Mozambique was well underway, with the Salazar dictatorship's efforts to incorporate Mozambique and other possessions into Portugal having been rejected. He had not known any of the details she shared concerning the leftist Front for the Liberation of Mozambique, called Frelimo, or the emerging Mozambican National Resistance group called Renamo, the latter seen by many as a creature of the Rhodesian and South African intelligence services, as well as the CIA. He did some quick research and on that basis had a few second thoughts even before departing for South Africa; at that point, he was unsure about whether he would be working for the good, the bad or the ugly.

His uncertainty faded away as Sam pondered his assignment on the long, smoke-filled flights to South Africa; in the cat-and-mouse business of intelligence and foreign affairs generally, it was always the ugly. Nothing reflected Nietzsche's philosophy of the future more than the shadowy side of global affairs, beyond good and evil, terrain traversed only with imagination, assertion of will, acceptance of danger, and the adaption of values to meet the requirements of the hour. The dance between CIA, KGB, CID, and South Africa's Bureau for State Security was merely a manifestation of that philosophy and Sam would help delineate facts, leaving the moral reconciliations to Inga and her superiors.

Two days after his departure and an hour after his arrival, Sam sat alone in his Johannesburg hotel listening to a radio broadcast of the adventures of Sergeant William Preston of the North-West Mounted Police and his lead dog, Yukon King, fighting evildoers somewhere in the Northern Canada wilderness. He had discovered that South Africa's Afrikaner-dominated government viewed television as a potential threat to its control of communications, given the international dominance of English-language programming and the lack of Afrikaner resources to develop local programming. The reluctant acceptance of this threatening medium was still months away, so radio remained for the source of home entertainment. Sam remembered with some nostalgia sitting with his parents as maybe a twelve-year-old listening to the same series, maybe even the very same broadcast, sometime in the early 1950s. In Sam's experience, the enticing fare of foreign assignments frequently was washed down with calming brew of such nostalgia in lonely hotel rooms.

Soon after his arrival, Sam headed to Botswana and then Swaziland a couple of days later, while waiting for Inga to arrive and accompany him to Lourenço Marques, soon to become Maputo. He was in South Africa with only a laissez-passer, a document allowing him only three days to cross the country overland to one of the adjacent African jurisdictions, Botswana and Swaziland, still-Portuguese Mozambique and Rhodesia.

The project description he carried with his papers read benignly enough, but in those days text often departed from reality and perceptions of text often departed from both text and reality, sometimes with fatal consequence. So, Sam was careful, resorting to the Zulu persona he had adopted with Frank's tutelage back in Isan. He would be a listener, not a talker, and keep his political opinions strictly to himself. Influenced by Ari's confidences a decade earlier, as well as his experience in Isan, he remained unconvinced that the liberation movements throughout the region were all led by communists, communist sympathizers, or Soviet puppets. He couldn't believe that she could have fallen in love with anyone who came even close to being a Soviet totalitarian or a Maoist.

Sam was, himself, influenced by Orwell and Hemingway, a supporter of the Spanish Republican cause, hostile to Franco and Salazar, and even an admirer of Che. Eventually, he thought, America would need to adopt a friendlier attitude to the liberation movements, not simply treat them all as Soviet pawns. He would consent to be used as some kind of CIA asset and allow Inga to be his handler, but he would not compromise his findings to meet her biases, any more than he had in Isan.

It didn't take Sam long to realize that he was being watched and that the driver he had engaged was carrying out some instructions from the authorities. The driver avoided autoroutes that would take him through poorer areas and black population centers and disrupted his appointments in South Africa and across the borders, due to alleged traffic delays, bad directions or other issues. He eventually resorted to taxis or arranging rendezvous at his hotels, until Inga's arrival finally eased that situation. If it was the Bureau of State Security on his case, they would simply replace a ride with a tail, but at least he would not inconvenience his hosts.

Madam Inga, he thought when he met her at the airport, was amazing. Now the mother of two and in her mid-thirties, she still could look like either an Asian Mata Hari or a fifteen-year-old waitress in a posh Chinese restaurant, the one who would bring water and tea because she was not deemed sufficiently experienced to carry out higher duties. When she disembarked from the plane without makeup but in proper business attire, she appeared neither of those, but a nondescript civil servant, her trace of Portuguese blood adding to her anonymity, her slightly unfocused profile appropriate to one carrying the workpapers for some deputy minister. Still, it took no more than five minutes of conversation to recognize that she was much more than that. She had a thorough command of the situation, including key political connections, not only in Mozambique but across the region. She even knew of Ari's old lover, at present his country's transport minister, and, to Sam's delight, considered him apolitical on matters of interest to their investigation. As far as he knew, Inga had not previously worked in Africa, so her case officer or whoever briefed her must have been extraordinary, although less so than Inga herself with her total recall. Then Inga made a point of showing him, "just in case," that she was armed with a Walther P38. Nothing fascinates a man more than a pretty woman bearing illegal firearms, particularly when he has no concept of what "just in case" might entail.

As the trip unfolded, with dashes back and forth across South Africa, Sam began to reach several conclusions. The smaller countries—Swaziland, Botswana, and Lesotho—were so dependent on South Africa that their politics should be of little interest to Inga's employer or to the CID. A casino in a Holiday Inn just across the border from South Africa seemed to be the chief economic activity of each country, low-budget versions of Monte Carlo, Vegas, and Reno, respectively. The hotels hosted gamblers, Anglophone South African families who came to watch TV in their rooms, and patrons of interracial prostitution. It reminded him a lot of U.S. inner cities: they might be filled with poverty, crime, and corruption and have all sorts of local issues, but they were incapable of dominating national politics, just as the smaller countries in southern Africa were unlikely to influence the course of cold war in the region.

Of the bigger players—South Africa, Tanzania, Mozambique, and the descendants of Rhodesia—Sam was especially optimistic about South Africa. He knew a lot less about the ANC and Mandela than Inga, but he could see that the many rifts between the English and Afrikaners opened the opportunity for compromise between the colonialists and liberation movements, whereas the unity of the colonial government in other cases focused the independence movements, uniting regions and ethnic groups in an "us-versus-them," confrontation.

The optimism in South Africa was not reflected in Mozambique, where the war of independence was entering its final phase and the ensuing civil war was well in preparation. Sam and Inga, still with her weapon, flew in a private plane to the capital city, a stronghold of the colonial administration. Soviet leaning leftists had attained firm control of Frelimo and the war was raging in the north, while the city was still attempting to retain the image of a seaside resort. With the departure of Portuguese nationals, however, it was progressively bearing a greater resemblance to the Fort Apache it would become in subsequent years. That would greatly accelerate the following year, when the collapse of the Salazar regime in Portugal would bring about the rapid withdrawal of colonial forces and mass exodus of whites, despite efforts to stall emigration. On the edge of this transformation, the city was a nest of misinformation and flat-out ignorance of what was happening.

Sam and Inga flew north to Beira and then to Dar es Salaam to seek out Frelimo in exile and any evidence of CID presence.

After that, it was on to Lusaka to attend a railway forum of already independent nations and aspiring liberation movements, mostly espousing ambitious pan-African future plans overlaid with promotion of ambitious projects mostly benefitting their home countries, home provinces or particular commercial endeavors. The conference presentations and its delegates were surprisingly candid and provided confirmation that CID was certainly involved in the developments in Tanzania and Zambia, but not Mozambique, where it was widely expected that the rail lines might be out of service for decades anyway. That was a positive result as far as Inga was concerned.

The last day of the forum, Sam was able to meet Suluhu Modise. Remembering Ted's insistence that he should write to Ari, he thought he would discuss business first and then mention he knew Ari a decade earlier; that way, he could pass any good wishes on to her in his letter. The interview went well, confirming many of the attributes she had described. He was bright, levelheaded, and well spoken with kind eyes and a charming smile, and was open and precise about foreign interest in railway projects in the region, contributing further to the pending report. Then, Sam mentioned that he once knew a teaching assistant named Ari at Harvard who had mentioned she had been a friend of his. The smile froze; the eyes darkened. For a moment the minister said nothing. Then, tersely, he said he was sorry to hear that; she was a dishonest woman who never should have received the appointment, but it had taken him a year to realize that. He hoped Sam had not had a similar experience. Hearing Sam's reply that he had had no bad experiences, the minister said, quite simply, "Good. It is best to forget her name, like I have."

Ari had achieved her goal, just as she had planned to do. Her sacrifice had worked perfectly and enduringly. Too perfect, too enduring. Sam, on returning to McLean would write Ari, but he would not mention the meeting, much less its contents. The interview did not happen, the meeting did not exist.

Arriving home, Sam wrote Ari as promised, with a short description of his work with minority enterprise—which Ari would surely like—and nothing about Africa. He then called Ted asking whether the job offer still stood and, if so, whether Barrington also would consider hiring a financial analyst he'd met in California. Ted responded positively to both questions, so Sam called Beth, described Barrington Associates, and asked if she would like to come out for an interview. She'd have to clip her fingernails and lose the Dashiki robes. She agreed, and appeared a week later looking like a tanned Rhoda Morgenstern from the Mary Tyler Moore Show, wearing solid, bold colors in a suitably conservative style. Both were hired and asked to begin as soon as possible. Sam started his new job a little over a month later and Beth, despite the unpleasant surprise of finding that Rafi worked there, followed about a month after that.

CHAPTER 10:

Langley/the Castle, 1975

After the Paris Peace Accords in 1973 and the dismantling of Air America thereafter, Frank had had no choice but to return to CONUS. The only thing left to be done in Laos was the search for MIA/KIAs, a job that basically entailed a forensic effort to recover and identify body parts, and that was enmeshed in bureaucracy on all sides. Air support had become little more than a taxi service. True, his old aircraft and its 3-D imaging was of some value in locating crash sites, but there was newer technology now and specialists to operate it. Frank was becoming obsolete.

Inga was eager to move to America and acquire U.S. citizenship for herself and her children. Frank had hopes of continuing an adventurous life around the world that could mesh nicely with her ambitions, but it would be essential that all of them hold U.S. passports. Frank expected his children to be Americans, insisting on naming the boy Rick, after the heroic American in Casablanca, and the girl Nancy, after some Asian-American actress, but nothing was guaranteed until Frank brought them to his country. Life was not always easy for Eurasian children in Inga's part of the world, as she knew from personal experience, and whatever happened in the future, she wanted their American citizenship secured. Moreover, while her position with the Company was solid, and far more significant than Frank's own indirect affiliation, she had bigger ambitions beyond the mysterious Madam Inga's corner of intrigue on the borders of the People's Republic. Those goals were only achievable after naturalization as a US citizen and with advancement through positions at Langley.

By the end of spring, Saigon had fallen and Mozambique had become independent from Portugal, with the former ending Frank's career in Southeast Asia and the latter offering a greater opportunity for Inga in the newly critical region of sub-Saharan Africa. It was time to leave, and Inga pressed Frank to make it happen. Before the end of the year, they were living in an apartment in McLean, Virginia, not far from where Sam had worked. She became enmeshed in the complex orientation process at Langley and he spent time looking for work, babysitting his young children, and seeking out old friends and colleagues who were working in the area. Among those he planned to contact were air force and Air America pals who might have a line on pilot opportunities, his uncle at the *Star,* and perhaps even Francesca Ghiardelli, if she were still with the paper. Sam had become too close a friend to seek out for employment assistance.

When Frank approached his uncle at the *Star* he already knew that the newspaper was in trouble. Two years earlier, according to Inga, the South African apartheid government attempted to acquire secret control of the conservative paper to use as a propaganda outlet for the whites-only regime. While the Company held conflicting views on South Africa given its utility as a Cold War ally, it could not condone the takeover. The Administration quashed the maneuver, but the paper was consequently acquired by US based conservative interests not that far removed from Afrikaner political views. Frank's uncle had had no problem with these developments, being well to the right of Frank, and was fearful only of the paper's declining circulation. He was focused on hanging on to his job until the bitter end and certainly had no insight into employment opportunities Frank might explore.

Francesca, Frank found, had had no such loyalty to the paper. The internship of 1961 had turned into a midlevel editorial and domestic reporting job without either satisfaction or promise, only temporarily interrupted by her marriage, pregnancies, and opportune assignments in Europe. After the paper terminated her husband, it reassigned Francesca to local reporting, she detesting it as the most difficult area of news in which to get at the truth and the least consequential when truth was finally uncovered. The fact that the Post had the resources to scoop most of the bigger stories didn't help either. Journalism was not the exiting career she once anticipated.

By 1965, Francesca had shed her Catholic upbringing sufficiently to join the millions of women flocking to the pill to prevent further pregnancies. By 1970, she had shed her Catholic faith altogether, and in 1974, then a thirty-five-year-old single mother of four, she shed both the paper and her partner. Frank's uncle hadn't seen Francesca in over a year, but had heard she had taken an editorial position at the Smithsonian that had opened up in connection with the national Bicentennial Celebration.

Frank, when he was not with his children lusting for Emmy Jo on the *New Zoo Review,* filled his days with painful searches for employment opportunities and disappointing interviews. Experienced Vietnam War pilots were met with considerable caution in civilian enterprise for their carousing reputations and for the general revulsion to the war and its inglorious outcome. Frank had returned late from the war into the worst economy since the Great Depression, carrying the especially poor repute of those associated with those shadowy missions on the fringes of the conflict. Navy flyers seemed to get all the available jobs, he thought, seawater perhaps washing away the stink of the war. Finding no opportunities through the *Star,* Frank did not think of Francesca again until he read of the pending establishment of the new air and space museum on the mall. It was a long shot, but perhaps there might be something, anything, that he could apply for. Maybe Francesca could point him to someone who could help; so, he looked her up.

It had been fourteen years since Colorado Springs but she didn't look much different, unlike Frank, with his additional twenty pounds and prematurely graying hair. He recognized her immediately when she came out to meet him in front of the Smithsonian castle to take him to the dining room reserved for staff lunches with outside visitors. It didn't take long to exchange pleasantries about Colorado, given that their past acquaintance numbered only hours, not weeks or years.

Frank's job search questions didn't take much longer. Francesca had edited enough press on the new museum's development to know that the air and space activity was overloaded with experts and technicians. The Smithsonian had all but ceased hiring and innumerable applicants chased any rare position that might arise, false opportunities to those who didn't already know someone inside, civil service rules be damned.

That left little to talk about. Frank's last ten years and his wife's activities were veiled in secrecy and Francesca's occupation of such little interest to him as to have the same effect. She did not want to discuss her marriage and divorce. Nonetheless, something good did come of the reunion. The one thing they could talk about was children. Francesca loved children and Frank and Inga certainly needed an occasional evening babysitter if they were ever to spend any time together. So Francesca suggested that Frank introduce her to Inga and maybe they could work something out. The two women met and a friendship developed.

Francesca's new employer recognized the value of skills she had developed during the difficult years spent at the *Star*. After a few weeks, the purely editorial functions initially assigned gave way to more creative responsibilities for the Smithsonian Institution's numerous publications and publicity materials. Then, out of the blue, the Smithsonian transferred her to an office titled Special Projects and International Exchanges, a section claiming responsibilities for liaison with foreign partners in exchanges and nominally covering such diverse concerns as what objects to display, their care and documentation, proper packing for transport, the suitability at foreign exhibition sites, and exhibition security in cooperation with foreign institutions and authorities. Almost all of these activities that were under the museum's direct control, however, were actually undertaken by the Smithsonian's traveling exhibition service or delegated to pre-qualified U.S. agents and contractors. Francesca's purview would deal with situations where Smithsonian assets were unavailable or undesired, and where the Institution did not control the exchange. For a single mother, it would be a formidable leap in authority and accountability. Despite having many relevant attributes, Francesca lacked confidence and experience in key technical skills, so at age thirty-five, she entered a rigorous six-month training program reserved normally for persons a decade younger.

A four-step process, known jocularly in her new specialty as MICE, guided successful exchanges based on unaffiliated foreign human resources, rather than Smithsonian employees or its contractors. The "M," of course, stood for money. King Tut may have been buried with treasure but he wasn't about to use any of it to display his riches to the world, especially the wealthiest nation on Earth. Pride alone was not a sufficient motivating force to share a nation's bounty with the Americans; completing arrangements typically required financing from U.S. sources and part of Francesca's job would include identifying those financial sources and ensuring a proper transaction that would not create embarrassment or adversely impact Smithsonian-controlled programs.

The "I" stood for the idea, the ideology, the rationale for the exchange. Though Francesca's assignments were initiated outside of the institution, their success, like any Smithsonian exhibition, rested on an attractive, convincing story. There must be a hook to bring in the fish; bureaucratic dullness was not acceptable. The "C" was for compromise, as no exchange could achieve everything the proposer wanted. And the "E" represented ego, since across all of the arts satisfying the ego is the driving force for creativity and successful implementation. Francesca was trained to abide by these principles with Catholic certainty, albeit a certainty not guided by faith, but by intelligence.

Training under this rubric prepared Francesca for the delicate task of coordinating with international parties involved in the assignments to her office. This entailed mollifying and flattering the often-difficult individuals on the foreign side of the undertakings, not to mention the American sponsors. Such people and the institutions they represented indeed tended to have large egos, were sometimes crackpots, often knew little about security, and had other weaknesses that were not tolerated at the Smithsonian or any other U.S. agency, but they typically resented interference, requiring at least the illusion of being in control themselves. Francesca's experience as an interviewer and reporter helped her with the diplomatic task of managing relationships with these parties in a low-profile manner, so resisting the natural tendency of American experts to take over everything or to press cooperating individuals faster than their willingness to proceed. The thorough and challenging training regimen, extended to such technical areas as physical security and proper methods of packing, complemented those assets, leading to a more stimulating career path than she ever had deemed possible.

———

While Fran thrived in her position on the mall and Inga in hers at Langley, Frank fell into a deep funk. He had been able to obtain only part-time work since his return home months earlier, as he was under-qualified for technical work in the vast government-focused research community surrounding D.C., overqualified for most of the positions the Pentagon listed for Vietnam veterans, and unable to exploit his indirect connection with the Company without jeopardizing Inga's prospects for advancement. He also was utterly unsuited to being a househusband.

"When we went to Nam," he told the friends he'd meet at the Irish Times, "we were young men with a future. Now we're just middle-aged men with no past." He would toast to that good-heartedly with a Bushmills held high, making light of their mutual quandaries, not admitting that his unemployment was not just a temporary condition. The Irish Times and other watering holes provided temptations, unemployment offered opportunities and Frank retained many of the inclinations inscribed on his own old Zippo. "But when they lay me in my grave, no more nookie will I crave." Time did not weigh heavily on the side of the marriage.

The situation seriously affected Inga, as well. When she first met Frank in Bangkok, she was impressed by his swagger, aroused by his persistence, charmed by his wicked sense of humor, challenged by his understated intellect, and drawn into commitment by the passage he offered to a better life. Having reached her golden destination, all of those attractions now slipped away; swagger became more of a stagger, romantic persistence became distance, his humor went from wicked to weakened, his intellect from understated to underused, and the entrance to America threatened to become a black hole that would suck the energy from her and crush her aspirations.

Back in Thailand, she had had no idea that the financial inducements he enjoyed as payment for risking his life in the Secret War would simply disappear overnight. In her world, wealth persisted, poverty persisted, and status persisted, high or low, through generations. Inga believed that while everything in the universe might seem to be changing, a persistent principle that does not vary with space and time guides everything. The sudden change in Frank's fortunes could only come about through a catastrophic failure in *wu wei,* his instincts for how to act or not to act, a weakness that somehow had been hidden from her. Inga then concluded that it fell to her to correct for this fundamental flaw by making his decisions for him. This did not sit well with Frank.

One of the decisions Inga pressed on Frank was to see Sam about a possible job. He had been reluctant to do so, since he had built up an image that he, Frank, was the mentor and Sam the acolyte, Sam being younger, less experienced in the world and less grounded in practicality, notwithstanding his Ivy League education, high pay grade and ridiculous military rank equivalency. Inga, however, argued Sam's reports in Thailand and his work with her in southern Africa impressed her. Yes, he was a bit of an academic, but he was a valuable asset to her and to the agency and he might have something positive to offer. In any case, she said, she would love to find a way to use Sam on a freelance basis sometime in the future, so approaching Sam would be doing her a favor also; it would not simply be a job opportunity. It took three years, but by early spring 1978, Frank finally relented.

Frank called and arranged to meet Sam at his office; from there, they went out to lunch. After about an hour of pleasantries and reminiscences that went nowhere, Sam finally asked in an exasperated tone, "Would you please show me what you've got?"

Frank laughed and pulled his resume from side pocket. "So Inga already called you?" Sam nodded.

121

Much to Frank's surprise, Sam did have something to offer. The Ward was involved in a nasty dispute between two companies over the patent rights for advanced aircraft transponders that had been developed by the military for application in World War II, Korea, and Vietnam, but for which there were lucrative civilian and military markets worldwide. Sam's firm represented a relatively new entrant to the field. They were arguing that formerly classified technology had been developed as a public asset and their adversary's earlier involvement as a military contractor in transponder development did not give them a right to cut off new technological advances through overreaching claims regarding patent rights. To make its case, the firm needed someone who could gain access to military records, help attain affidavits, and build support within the air force for a permissive policy toward commercial transponder and avionics development. Sam had already talked to his director after Inga's call and a position was there for the taking if Frank wanted it. Sam expected this particular battle to carry on at least through the next election, when Jimmy Carter's reelection or defeat would probably lead to a resolution between the parties.

The whole proposition annoyed Frank: Inga calling Sam behind his back, Sam setting up a job offer before talking to him, the crass commercial interests involved, and the political corruption he expected to encounter. On the other hand, dealing with such unpleasantries was certainly something that Southeast Asia had well prepared him for, and he definitely needed a job. He accepted. Within two hours, Sam had introduced him to the director and to Ted, Beth, Rafi, and Ben.

Inga was overjoyed when Frank told her he was offered a job with Sam's firm and had accepted it at a decent salary; she was oblivious to his resentments, particularly toward her. Frank's new employment status would allow her to save face and shed the embarrassment she felt when any reference to her husband arose in conversation, particularly at Langley.

There was no indication that Frank's former status had posed a problem to Inga's career. She had risen quickly to the position of case officer, enjoying the increasing demand for officers fluent in Chinese dialects that came with the normalization of US-Sino rela-

122

tions and the growing recognition that China was absorbing Western technology with little respect for intellectual property rights. Nonetheless, Frank's employment relieved her of an unwanted distraction. As she was being given increasingly heavy responsibilities for protecting Western technologies from Chinese industrial espionage, Inga had started to travel a lot, both to Europe and to the Asian and African countries where she had prior experience. The last thing she needed was Frank moping about, complaining of underemployment.

Inga also was happy that Frank would be working with Sam; she had been pleased with the depth of Sam's reporting in Africa, his sensitivity to what was important and unimportant, his low profile and discretion, and his naiveté toward his colleagues' motivations and mode of operation. Temperamentally, Sam was an ideal cut-out asset, willing to work diligently and to report objectively simply for the sake of objectivity, unlikely be branded as a spy, but, if detected, not be able to reveal much about principle agents or other assets, simply because he would have focused solely on the task at hand and not inquired deeply into those providing assistance along the way. So he was both valuable and expendable, an ideal cut-out, and he was even familiar with some of the high tech areas of deepest concern. The only problem was that he was working almost entirely in the U.S.

Perhaps Frank, with a proper infusion of new clients funneled through him from the Company, could influence a change in focus in that office that would provide an excuse for Sam to travel to places where she might best take advantage of his natural talents. Perhaps Langley could drop its opposition to declassifying certain aviation technology of interest to Barrington clients. If that failed, Inga had a back-up plan: Francesca, Frank's old acquaintance. Inga could induce her office for international exchanges over at the Smithsonian to arrange travel to key locations. Langley was as adept at setting up conferences and special events as it was in using corporate transactions as a front. It hadn't taken Inga long to realize that Smithsonian activities at home and abroad were incredibly eclectic, involving artists, collectors, spouses, friends, lovers, kooks, and assorted followers of art and culture. They took cultural exchange seriously. Sam would not stand out in that crowd. It could be a perfect setup to draw Sam into key locations with lots of time on his hands for contacts while Fran engaged in her own business at those awful, unavoidable wine and cheese parties that clung to museum events like sponges to a perfectly good reef.

Having known Sam for nearly ten years and Francesca now for almost three, she thought they would be a great match. Of course, Francesca was not exactly a honeypot. She had children, which sucked, but they were older and would soon be out of the nest. Maybe if Frank worked on Sam and she had a talk with Francesca, they could bring the two of them together. It might work. Sam would go along with the idea initially because he likes to play undercover asset. Anyway, he needs help meeting women. Francesca, she felt confidently, would not object to being set up. Travel for work and recreation, it had potential.

She had lunch with Francesca at the Castle the following week and came away feeling even more satisfied with her matchmaking plans. The woman was obviously completely done with her ex-husband and open to new companionship. In June 1979, Frank and Inga hosted a party as an excuse to introduce her to Sam. The two hit it off, took disco lessons together, and soon became "an item."

Basking in her success, Inga immersed herself in her work. Frank's new employment relieved her of a burden and he seemed to accept it more after bringing in an avionics client that brought appreciation from his new co-workers and their director. She only gradually began to realize that she valued little else in the marriage other than that preoccupation and the knowledge that Frank would be there for the children, no matter what. She even got to a point where she didn't care whether Frank had relationships outside the marriage. Eventually, she would accuse him of adultery and he would admit to it, but she never knew whether the accusations came before the act or not. There would be bitter words spoken, but the overreaching importance of her work always provided refuge. She was Madam Inga, indispensable to her new country, and whatever Rick said in *Casablanca* about personal troubles not amounting to a hill of beans seemed more true to her then than ever before.

CHAPTER 11:

Connecticut & K, 1979

The buses were jammed as Sam rode into work from across the Potomac along with tens of thousands of new commuters attempting to avoid long lines at the gas stations in that summer of crises and short tempers. He yearned for the delayed extension of the Orange Line to come about, but doubted at that point that it would make much difference. He got off at the Connecticut Avenue stop, across the street from where the Ward's offices were located, and spotted Ted loitering over at Bobby's paraphernalia stand.

A local curiosity, the stand had popped up at the corner of Connecticut and K after Carter eased up on the Nixon Administration's so-called war on drugs, favoring the decriminalization of marijuana possession in the belief that penalties for possession were more damaging than use of the drug itself. While laws against the sale of pot were enforced, police action against discrete users was minimal and paraphernalia was not targeted. The stand was laden with all manner of necessaries: bongs, cigarette papers, pipes, tweezers, syringes, snorting tubes, roach clips, mirrors, razors, small spoons, and more. Catering to tourists and K Street lobbyists trying to be cool, as well as proper drug users, the place thrived until the Reagan administration strong-armed the D.C. government into outlawing the trade, then cemented the ban with new federal drug laws. But at the time, with Carter's reelection appearing likely, it seemed to be a permanent fixture, one that fascinated Ted.

A young man calling himself Bobby McGee operated the stand, taking his name from the song, no doubt the Joplin version.

His patter was audible a block away in all directions: "We've got all you need except the weed"; "Our prices are lower so you can get higher"; and "Don't get caught without a razor or a spoon on a lazy afternoon." You couldn't buy drugs at the stand, Bobby was scrupulous about that, but it was an obvious rendezvous point for potential transactions of that sort. Regulars became aware that an empty display pipe meant no known pot dealers nearby, one full of fake weed indicated the presence of known sellers, and an upside down pipe warned of police in the area. It was a public service.

Ted rarely smoked anything other than the Marlboros he still was trying to quit, and then only free grass offered at a party, but he liked the singsong and the chatter around each transaction and would often peruse the displays for amusement. That November day he was staring at Bobby's collection of Florence flasks and other chemical lab equipment, trying to figure out what an addict would do with them, when Sam caught up with him. Sam was just beginning to explain crack processing from a purely academic knowledge of the subject when a woman's voice from behind broke his concentration. "Sam, I'll be damned. I never thought your interest in chemistry would take a turn in this direction. I might have to turn you in." Sam spun around, and was stunned to see Lillian standing there. It had been almost twenty years.

She had been attractive in her rumpled way as a teenager, but was now transformed into a beautiful, elegant, fully mature woman immaculately dressed in business attire, a deep red power suit, one of the small number of shades then current for professional women and Toyotas, complemented by a casually draped black trench coat. It was difficult to believe. She had seemed headed on a downward slide into a life as an abused housewife, living in poverty with a bevy of children. He was transfixed, and so was Ted.

The men stood there like statues until she finally raised a bag smelling of hot bagels and cream cheese in her left hand, asked Sam if he'd had breakfast, and offered to share a bagel in Farragut Square to catch up with each other. Sam quickly introduced her to Ted, asked him to cover for him for the meeting he was about to miss, and excused himself to cross the street with Lillian to the

126

square, where they talked for an hour, oblivious to the pigeons, bike messengers, and lawyers flocking around them.

Her story fascinated him: three failed marriages, two kids, a graduate equivalency degree, junior college certifications in computer science, and a career in the labor department. She had risen from a lowly clerical job completing layout sheets required for key-punching, the most menial job in the automated data-processing unit apart from emptying trashcans, to a mid-level public servant position. Sam was greatly impressed by her achievement, as only one with inordinately low expectations could be by a Federal bureaucrat.

Keeping to the Washington code of talking only business at introductory meetings, Lillian did not reveal much personal information beyond the names of her former spouses and children. She did mention that she was separated, hinting that she might be free to have dinner sometime if he was unencumbered. He was, but hesitated to accept, still having bad memories of their high school catastrophe and Frank and Inga having just introduced him to a woman over at the Smithsonian whom he would see again that evening. Still, he agreed to come to her agency's upcoming Christmas reception and take her to dinner later, a Greek restaurant, for old time's sake.

When the reception and dinner came a week later, the Greek restaurant proved to be a bad idea, as Sam could not get Ari's old advice to discuss Lillian's teenage troubles explicitly out of his head all evening. Nothing explicit said, Sam still could not help but conclude that Lillian, despite her put-together exterior, remained more of a minefield than even Ari or that she had been in her teenage years. He could not bring himself to probe any deeper that evening. He was having enough trouble in the office dealing with Nurse Ratched, as Frank had taken to calling Beth, and her perpetual guilt trips. He just couldn't take the thought of dealing with another complicated woman.

After he dropped Lillian at her home that evening, Sam vowed he would not see her again, but every couple of days she would call. Finally, he decided that Ari's advice years before was right; he needed to listen to her and uncover what was troubling her. He had a second chance to do the right thing. With trepidation, he called her at work and they arranged to meet in Lafayette Park for lunch.

It was a warm day for winter, but cold enough that there was no competition for a seat on a park bench. Thinking it might draw her out about what had happened all those years ago, he started talking about Vienna, noting that his parents had moved to Florida after his father sold his small hardware store; he had been unable to compete with the Hechinger mega-store that had opened there. He couldn't recognize much in Vienna anymore anyway, with Tyson's Corner Mall now open, so he didn't drive out that way often. She replied that she never did, that her mother had died three years after her first wedding, but her father was still alive and living there. She hadn't seen him since 1965 and wouldn't take the chance of encountering him at the mall. So, she had never seen Tyson's Corners, never would see it.

She tightened her coat about her and stared at her knees silently for a long while. "Sam," she finally said, softly.

He put his arm around her shoulder, comforting her and bracing himself for what surely must be a confession of what had happened with her family when she was in high school. He was prepared for anything. "Sam? Sam? I...I...I killed a man in New Haven."

Well, almost anything.

It all poured out, like a burst dam, her drug use, promiscuity, the concert, riot, rape and escape, the weeks of terror afterwards, the months of depression, after that the enduring cycles of depression and loneliness, interspersed with slippage into her old habits, chemical and sexual, more cautiously to be sure, but nonetheless her old dysfunctional self. Sometimes she wanted to go to the police, but to what end? She had been terrified that the rapist would break back into the apartment before she got on the elevator; she didn't intend to kill him, just get away, and it all happened a dozen years ago. What would they do to her? Put her in St. Elizabeth's mental hospital?

He comforted her, told her not to do anything, that he would be her friend, that she could call him any time, that he would be there for her as needed. Eventually, she walked back to her office, he to his. Lillian felt much better, and much less alone.

Sam did not, and cursed himself, Ari, and Lillian in no particular order. How did he end up being the tourniquet to staunch the bleeding of these wounded women? He was about as tightly wound as a tourniquet. On the short walk back to his office he mentally enunciated every curse word appropriate to having hit your thumb with a hammer, dropped an anvil on your big toe, or got your penis stuck in a zipper, and several that were excessive even in those circumstances. Passersby glanced at him warily as he emitted a long drawn-out "aarrrgh" in a tone pirates would adopt only if they were already at the end of the plank. Why him? Why did Inga tell him of her troubles with Frank, Beth of how she was hurt by Rafi's claim that she had betrayed him, Rebecca of how Ted's insensitivity wounded her?

Women, get a life. Don't lay it on me just because I look sympathetic. Oh, fuck, I am sympathetic. Ari, a prisoner of her own ethics; Lillian, suffering from her sensuality; Beth never quite properly acknowledged for her talents; Inga too dedicated to her profession; Rebecca with her ill health and second thoughts. Dammit Ari, how could you do this to me?

He closed the door to his office and brooded. He would be Lillian's friend, but only that. At one time, if she hadn't gotten pregnant, he could have fallen in love with her. But not now, he couldn't dive into that depth. He could not accompany her back in time to New Haven or Vienna or whatever other blackness lay back there... Maybe he could introduce her to someone new, someone that women hadn't dragged through their emotional coals once too often; someone with greater frivolity or less sensitivity. Maybe that's what he'd do. There was a knock on the door. "Sam, I've got a serious problem. Can you help me with it?"

"Get lost, Beth."

By April, Ted's marriage had fallen apart and Rebecca had taken their two kids to live with her parents, while Sam's relationship with Francesca had just begun to blossom. Theirs was a straightforward relationship, based on mutual understanding and steadily increasing affection, unbounded by the feminine emotional swamplands of his earlier encounters. So, when Lillian called in early spring to arrange a lunch in Farragut Square, he decided to ask Ted to join them. He did, and as Sam hoped, Ted was smitten.

Periodic lunches in the square, sometimes the threesome, sometimes just Ted and Lillian continued into the fall. In late November, the three met to hash over the election results, all agreeing that Reagan would be a disaster. Bobby McGee's days were surely numbered. As they were breaking up, Lillian turned to Ted and asked if he'd maybe like to come over to watch Monday Night Football in a couple of weeks. Ted had mentioned that he had often watched the Patriots play in Harvard Stadium and they would be playing in Miami on that Monday night. He eagerly accepted.

Lillian almost immediately regretted the invitation. Ted was fun to talk with, but he was not her type. Men like Ted were a game to her, a game she recently had tired of, and she could tell immediately that he would be interested in more than friendship but less than the real commitment she longed for.

Still, she needed companionship. She had hoped to build on her renewed friendship with Sam, but she could tell by his actions that he was not particularly receptive to the idea and it was good he backed off. Sam had proven to be frustrating in some ways. She admired his intelligence and appreciated his efforts to be understanding, but he was not especially forceful or ambitious. She had always thought he'd become some big-time lawyer or politician, but here he was working for some K Street lobbyist using a quarter of his brainpower. Perhaps he had his reasons, but his indecisiveness and lack of focus just didn't mesh with her own need for structure.

Lillian was only a mid-level civil servant herself, but thought her accomplishments didn't compare too badly to Sam's, despite his intellectual and educational advantages. She was proud of her office's contribution to fair labor practices and her role in it. She kept her shabby private life out of the office and out of her house as well. The girls suffered from her absences, but she did not endanger her children and she was proud of them in her way. Even Dom gave her some credit for that. Sam didn't even have children. No, she wasn't a great mother, but how could you be, when your primary objective was to ensure that your girls would not be the slightest bit like you?

These thoughts crossed Lillian's mind as she sat on a bench for a half hour after Sam and Ted excused themselves to dash to the office for some urgent appointment. She finally stood up and headed to Bobby's stand, where she purchased a mirror, razor, and spoon, admiring her image for a second before placing the mirror in her jacket pocket. She recalled how she had first met Ted there and immediately had been able to tell that he was a cocaine virgin just imagining a walk on the wild side. Perhaps exposure to some actual stardust would scare him away. Oh, hell, she didn't know what she wanted. Not with Sam, not with Ted, not with anyone.

Two weeks later, Ted drove out to Lillian's house in the suburbs. Her daughters were with an ex-husband that night, so they would be alone. The evening started out awkwardly, with Ted bringing a jug of Carlo Rossi Paisano he picked up at the drugstore, only to find a fine Bordeaux sitting on the table. It was the highlight of the meal, as Lillian was a terrible cook; she had learned from experience that the way to a man's heart is in no way through his stomach.

When they finished the lasagna, Lillian put on the television and directed Ted to the sofa. Still tempted by the thought of frightening him away without the unpleasantries of rejection, she sat down beside him, taking the mirror purchased from Bobby from the side table and placing it directly in front of Ted, where a line of white powder quickly appeared under the deft stroke of a double-edged razor. It looked to Ted like nothing so much as a Benihana performance. He kept the thought to himself.

"Join me?" she asked, straw in hand. To her chagrin, he did.

As the evening progressed, he appeared relaxed, his mild apprehension alleviated by the effect of the powder, dealers naturally providing a gentle blend, specially cut for a gentile civil servant class with more cash than voracious addictions.

The game served mainly as background for their conversation. It finally reached the fourth quarter and remained surprisingly close, keeping Ted on the sofa beyond the time he had planned to leave. Finally, with seconds left in the game, and the score tied at thirteen, the Patriots' field goal kicker started onto the field. But just as Ted rose to leave in anticipation of the game's end, Howard Cosell suddenly announced that someone shot and killed John Lennon outside of his apartment building on the West Side of New York City. The kick was blocked along with Ted's exit.

After listening to the news broadcasts, Lillian brought out Lennon's *Double Fantasy* album and the *White Album*, their mutual favorite among the old Beatles LPs. Bordeaux gave way to Paisano, new lines crossed the mirror, the sofa yielded to pillows on the floor, and the conversation led to embraces. The music moved to the bedroom, where the misfit couple sought solace throughout the night and much of the next day, making love repeatedly.

Both of them regretted the interlude. Lillian had moderated her risky sexual behavior after that near-fatal incident a decade ago in New Haven, but remained less than monogamous. A short-term liaison with someone she'd meet through normal social situations was not out of character for her in 1980, even if bar pick-ups had been abandoned. She was between marriages, after all. Still, something bothered her. In part, she thought, it was that Ted was Sam's friend and there was something unresolved with Sam, even after twenty years. Beyond that, she found herself liking Ted much too much. Sexual encounters had, for her, always been comprised of the seduction followed by a temporary descent into oblivion. With Ted it was more of a tender sharing in which she was an active partner. That scared the wits out of her. It was a fluke; it wouldn't happen again.

Ted wanted Rebecca back, and hoped she would regret leaving. He longed for his boys and yearned to fill the vacated rooms in his empty mansion. Even though Rebecca had given him ample cause to wander, he felt terrible about that evening. He took his vows seriously and even if he was right about Rebecca having left for a far more serious affair with an old lover, she had been ill, had been despondent, and was the mother of his children. He had responsibilities and should live up to them.

Ted decided to talk to Sam; Sam had been aware of the date, and equally aware that he hadn't shown up for work the next day.

Ted confessed to Sam that he had spent the night with Lillian, but had decided to back off. Sam was instructed to say that he was out of the office if Lillian called.

Back from lunch early, Beth sat in the next office in a foul mood with the door closed, overhearing everything. She did not wish to consider herself a busybody, but was appalled by Ted's confession of infidelity and offended by the assumption that if Ted just postured that nothing ever happened, everything would be fine. That wasn't fair to Rebecca or even that Lillian person. After Ted went back to his own office and Sam to a meeting, she placed a call to Boston and then went for coffee, pleased to have done the right thing for her gender and as called for by the scriptures, allowing Rebecca to make her decisions with the full knowledge of her husband's transgressions. Then, setting that aside, she and Ted completed a clever lobbying strategy for a chemical manufacturer resisting certain safety regulations. It was a little over the top, as Ted's initiatives usually were, but she had grounded the project with her computations of the disastrous financial impact of the proposed regulations. It was a successful team effort.

Ted had said after that long Tuesday in Lillian's bed that he would call her again soon, but never did. Months passed, Iran released the Embassy hostages, Hinkley shot Reagan and doctors finally diagnosed AIDS as the cause of the gay plague. Still, Ted never called. Lillian, telling herself she was content with that result, nonetheless felt offended and called Sam with a request to relay her message that Ted was an asshole. He apologized for Ted, adding that he was going through a rough time, was confused about whether he should reconcile with his wife, and was seeking a joint custody situation for his kids. He had a lot on his mind. "Just tell him he's an asshole." She hung up.

CHAPTER 12:

The Ward, 1980

It was another office lunch at the Mandarin Delights. The six seated there that day were about a block away from Barrington Associates, their K-Street lobbying firm. Everyone by then had picked up on Ted's rebranding of J. Ward Barrington's fiefdom as "Ward 22," even Barrington. Sharing a floor with a somewhat disreputable law firm, the Ward indeed had the atmosphere of an institutional facility both physically and in the ambiguity of its mission, supporting some clients benefitting from the Reagan administration's deregulation policy, and others that sought government intervention on their behalf. Working with diverse clients, it was a marriage of convenience with multiple partners, an open marriage in which some were gratified and others mostly just got screwed.

The Ward's senior staffers were pre-boomers, too young for the big war or Korea for the most part. In their early to mid-thirties when first hired and now hovering around forty, they found themselves in the lobbying profession almost exclusively for want of a better job. Still treated by their imperious director as interns, they remained to enjoy titles and progressively higher wages made possible by congressional openness to persuasion. Smart, avowedly liberal except for Frank, discontent, and disillusioned by the Vietnam War and the assassinations of the '60s, they shared little else in common than that they were having Chinese food together this day at the Mandarin Delights and still acting like interns despite crossing over to the western slope of the continental divide of life. When an uncontrollable pace of change makes everyone a novice, how is it possible to act otherwise?

Ted was pontificating about the boomers again, elaborating on his theory that they stole everything creative from his contemporaries, this time taking on the movies, expressing his annoyance in particular with *The Graduate*, released more than a decade earlier. Everyone knew about his marital problems, so they let him distract himself, condemning the film's portrayal, in his view, of pathetic boomer disillusionment with a world handed to them on a platter. It was especially annoying to Ted that the movie relied on his generation for anything creative, the screenwriters, the sound track, and actors. Dustin Hoffman, born in the '30s, especially offended him for betraying his generation to play a twenty-year-old graduating from college in 1967.

Sam was having none of it, pointing out Ted's inconsistency in accusing Hoffman of pandering to the boomers, but then claiming boomers exploited Paul Simon somehow for doing the same thing. Besides, some of Simon's lyrics were crap. "'Hear my words that I might teach you?' What an ego! Ted, what exactly have you learned from Professor Simon?" In Sam's view, every person was responsible for his or her welfare, so no whining about the generations, no moaning about the disruptions of war or great depressions on one's childhood, no bitching that fewer babies were born back in your day. He figured that X percent of people were into self-pity Y percent of the time in any generation, irrespective of the difficulties of the times; people related to their peers and contemporaries, and didn't weigh themselves against earlier generations. Boomer self-pity looked stupid because the times were so good compared to the times of their predecessors, but it was human nature. "Don't let it drive you crazy," Sam said, trying to be fair as always, but seeming a bit more willing to attack Ted than usual. He may have been a little more annoyed over Ted spending the night with Lillian than he would admit.

"Asshole," argued Ted, in response to Sam's logic.

"Sometime you sound like a boomer yourself."

"Oh, Sam, give Ted a break." Beth stopped playing with her chopsticks for a second and gave Sam a piercing glare. He figured she was trying to deflect the blame for ratting Ted out to his wife, as Ted had informed everyone in the office. Beth continued. "OK,

Sam, I don't think *The Graduate* was the best or the worst movie in the last twenty years, but it makes a pretty good case about how an affair can mess up your love life. It is pretty accusatory about the pre-boomer generations being a bunch of insensitive materialists, but none of us here went into plastics like the older generation condemned in the movie, so I guess we're as anti-materialist as the boomers, for better or worse. What's the point?"

"The point," Ted interjected, "is that the boomers are totally materialists when it comes to enjoying things; they're only anti-materialist when it comes to *producing* them."

"Like we're so into labor."

"At least we know what it is."

When Sam brought Beth into the firm with him, she and Ted became close for a time. Ted was attracted to her as a snake charmer is to a cobra, respecting her bite and thinking it commercially valuable. As Ted's marriage soured, however, Beth's sympathies turned toward Rebecca and she concluded that Ted was a complete idiot. He could have dealt with that—he was used to being underestimated—but her telephone call to Rebecca crossed the line and put an end to their office rapport. Her defense of him now had no authenticity and Ted cut it off by silence, returning Beth's gaze, recalling his favorite Saturday Night Live skits of a few years back. *Jane, you ignorant slut.* He would have loved to insert "Beth" and spit it out; even though he knew the phrase was a spoof on a man's inability to come up with a logical reply, it would have felt good. He had really liked Lillian, and not just for the sex, but he had not followed his heart with her because of Rebecca and the kids. Then Beth had stuck her nose in and made matters worse. Rebecca hadn't let the boys visit in weeks. Ted felt relief when Sam, Frank, and Rafi started exchanging experiences from Southeast Asia that captured all the men's attention, leaving Beth to her private thoughts.

Beth sat there, again feeling cursed in her business and personal relationships, her alliances with men faltering due to her efforts to compensate for male ineptitude, immaturity, and incompetence, and her disillusionment and frustration over chauvinism, disrespect, and latent racism. She gave these men multiple chances, but they never met her expectations, so she always was the one who had to kill or minimize the relationship. What's a woman to do anyway? It wasn't fair to her that they were so unperceptive and egotistical that they couldn't acknowledge her merits, but such was American culture, and she dealt with it in the best way she knew. For the most part she was nice about it. That, for the men, was the worst part.

Gazing silently at the guys across the table, Nurse Ratched saw little to change her clinical evaluation. Ted hated her now after she had done the honest thing and informed her friend Rebecca of his philandering. In the end, she rationalized, his being unable to see his kids could straighten him out and save his marriage. But did he appreciate that? Of course not. She had no expectations of that outcome.

Ben was so indisputably pedestrian, it was pathetic, but he was Barrington's gatekeeper on matters that were not of the highest immediate priority. He'd killed many of her best ideas and would kill more, but she had to put up with him for the time being. You had to work within the power structure, up to a certain point.

Rafi remained as full of ideological bullshit as he had been back in college. She was shocked to see him when she followed Sam to Barrington, since lobbying seemed completely foreign to his Trotskyite sensibilities. But the army, which had gotten him into electronics, changed him into a clone of the *MASH* Radar character. His new dogma was that personal computing and communications would save the world, now that revolution and flower power had failed to do so. He was wasting incredible amounts of time listening to the Village People on his Walkman while typing notes and calculations on his Apple II, especially since he had purchased that cheesy VisiCalc software back in December. The office had a perfectly good timeshare arrangement that she could never get him to use, employed a competent bookkeeper, and had purchased a thirty-five-thousand-dollar word-processing system with daisy wheel printers, but he would rather tinker around with his gadgets than do serious work.

Frank, the new guy, an unenlightened military sort, was simply out of his element, unsophisticated in social, financial, and spiritual matters, all of the pillars of civilization except maybe engineering, his never-used field of education. He had developed some kind of rapport with Rafi working for the avionics clients, mostly because of Vietnam, she suspected, but perhaps his technical training as well. Beth would not be judgmental about that. Frank was direct and might break down some doors in the short term, but in the end he would lack the imagination to be successful.

She had mixed feelings about Sam. He had brought her to the Ward and treated her more like a peer than the others, but the one time she needed his advice, he had come back from lunch in a terrible mood, locked himself in his office, and told her to go away. That was the day Ward Barrington had invited her to his house when her husband was out of town, with the clear implication that her acceptance would be reflected in the annual bonus. She had stormed out of the office expecting to be fired and had needed to talk to someone, but Sam wasn't there for her and she couldn't quite forgive him for that. As it turned out, the horny old widower didn't fire her and, in fact, gave her a nice bonus two weeks later, in return for her silence, she supposed. Sam should have been there, but he wasn't that day and he never followed up with her either. She hated her silence that she now felt powerless to break. Sam should have answered his door, dammit. She would have done so.

Ted had one thing right about the office; the Ward was just a way station, nothing more.

The Southeast Asia diversion having passed over quickly, Ben and Rafi leaned back in their chairs, awaiting Sam's next attack on Ted's generational paranoia, while Frank, being new, thought it best to just observe. Unexpectedly, Sam turned instead to Ben. "You fell for all that fake profundity in *The Graduate*, too, Ben. You know it, you just won't admit it. Hell, you probably identify with the Hoffman character, the good Jewish boy tempted by an older woman. The moral dilemma! Anguish. Hello darkness, my old friend."

Ben glanced around the room as if impatient for the waiter to start delivering the dishes. Then he fixed on Sam. "What makes you think the character was supposed to be Jewish, you bigot?"

Sam waved his hand, as if brushing away a fly. "C'mon, named Ben? Hoffman? Mike Nichols? Simon and Garfunkel? Lock the church door with a cross? Talk about your sounds of silence! Anyway, get this at least: the words of the prophets are not, absolutely not, not ever written on the subway walls. Anyone in his right mind knows that the words of the prophets are written in the men's room. That's the place for deep thoughts."

Ben raised his eyebrows. "Sam, you must just hold it all day. Have you ever been down the hall to the men's room we share with the lawyers? Are you really thinking that all the coke dealers, wife beaters, and rapists that are in and out of there can write anything profound? I sure haven't seen it."

"Yeah, yeah," said Rafi, "you're right as always. 'Here I sit in stinking vapor, someone stole the toilet paper.' Now *that's* poetry! Sure, sure."

Sam lifted a chopstick like an orchestra director about to cue in his own response, but was cut off by Ted. "'Alas, I can no longer linger, guess I'll have to use my...'"

"Ted! *No!* Guys, cut it out. We're about to have lunch." The men all looked at Beth a little sheepishly and Sam turned to a new topic.

"I was thinking after Ben's remark the other day," said Sam, "of how we all just drifted here, despite all of our education and high ambitions, and I've come to agree with Ted's theory that most decisions are fundamentally irrational and just triggered by the trivial notions that came into our heads as children, or maybe later on by catch phrases by Simon and Garfunkel or some actor. Rafi, for example, gets it into his head that he's going to be the next Che Guevara or Stokely Carmichael or something because of remembering older boys shouting 'Viva Fidel' as a kid. Who knows how many lives have been changed by some chance phrase, whether they're the words of a prophet or not?"

"Oh, please do enlighten us with some more examples."

"Don't be condescending, Beth. We know that you are the exception—the only one working for Barrington who was a practical adult from age six. Let me demonstrate. Ted, what was the second line of 'Here Comes the Bride' as you remember it from elementary school?"

"Uh, 'big, fat and wide'?"

"Exactly. You see, Beth, Ted will never take marriage and romance as seriously as you would want, because every time he thinks of marriage, that phrase pops into his head. At least half the men in the country answer the same way, something you should be aware of the next time you're tempted to waste your time trying to get us back on the straight and narrow. Now, if you want to know why Ted wants to use Catherine Deneuve in promotions to seek approval for the analog mobile phone system in the U.S., it's simple really... Ted, listen up: 'There's a place in France...'"

"'...where the women wear no pants!'"

"Precisely. It's not because they're already getting mobile phones in Europe. It's just because Ted will always be attracted to French women because he heard that ditty during puberty."

Ted feigned shock. "Well, yeah, but I'm more serious than that. I want a European woman as a spokesperson because American women of our age, like Beth or my wife, are much too conflicted, psycho, or both to make a technology pitch that's convincing to the average guy, and no one with any common sense would respect the opinion of a boomer girl making a critical recommendation on mobile phone technology."

"Jesus."

"C'mon, Beth. Have you seen the divorce rate? Guard your little daughter, Frank. Guys from their screwed-up boomer generation will be seeking out post-boomer girls before they hit fifteen. Now, when I want to sell the idea that you're *entitled* to something, like Rafi's precious Walkman, *then* I'll use boomer girls. They're all about entitlement."

Beth leaned back in her chair, "Guys, guys, how do you put up with this bullshit?"

Sam seemed not to hear, but Ben smiled and replied in a false whisper, "We're not as frustrated by your critical nature as Ted."

"Speak for yourself, Ben." Rafi stared at his empty plate to avoid Beth's eyes.

The conversation, which had stopped temporarily when the food arrived, resumed as soon as the waiter retreated from the table. "Remember that saying about how people in glass houses shouldn't throw stones?" Ted said between bites to no one in particular. "Well, I remember the story about the African chief who bought a new throne for his grass hut, so he stowed the old one in his attic. It fell through and killed him. People who live in grass houses shouldn't stow thrones. Pretty funny, huh?"

Sam looked quizzically at Beth, who, in turn, lifted her eyes to the ceiling and smiled weakly at Rafi before sliding the plate of mu shu pork toward Ben. He quietly placed a couple of large spoonfuls onto his plate, as Beth told Ted that maybe he should write fortune cookies.

"People would love them, too." Beth patted Ted on the shoulder in mock praise. The others lifted their glasses to Ted.

"Thanks a lot, Beth." Ted removed her hand from his shoulder as if brushing away dandruff. "I have something to tell you guys. I think I may get an offer from Burnham & Brown up in New York to do some contract work on the side. It wouldn't be until three or four months from now, but you remember they worked with us on the Dow campaign and liked my work. They handle advertising for a number of the Chemical Manufacturers Association members, so it's a great opportunity. It might eventually lead to full time. I've cleared it with Barrington."

"Well, I'll be damned," said Sam. "Congratulations Ted. I hope it works out. I guess with all of the chemical spills, toxic waste dumps, and plant explosions, the chemical folks may need you for more than our little efforts. 'And the people bowed and prayed to the neon God they made...' Now, Beth, don't you see it? Ted likes that song, so now he's going to go work for the neon Gods themselves."

"Sam, get a life. That's great Ted, but I hope you make it permanent someday soon, if it's what you want. We all do, I'm sure." Beth could be annoying, they were all sure of that.

After lunch, the group walked slowly back to the corner of Connecticut and K, past the optical store that once sold glasses to Abe Lincoln according to the affidavit in the window, glancing at the ATM famous for being shot a month ago by a drug-addicted holdup man enraged that it failed to hand over cash on demand, past the metrobus stop where another robber was arrested while eating a banana that, wrapped in black electrical tape, he had just used as a mock gun to threaten a teller, pausing to listen to Bobby at the paraphernalia stand sing out his sales pitch. "All you need…" It was autumn in the Nation's Capital and the times, slightly psychotropic, were changing.

They entered the lobby of their building, passed the carryout recently cited for thirty-nine violations of the city's "truth in menu" ordinance and later closed for something described as "domestic activity in kitchen," then up the elevator to the seventh floor, which was shared by the law firm and Barrington. Beth went directly to her office and the men headed, quite naturally, for the men's room. And there it was.

There, written above the center of three urinals, were four simple words: "The Duke Don't Dance." It was plain, stark, unpretentious, but elegant. A manifesto in four words. Block letters, upper and lower case caps, three and two inches respectively, hand printed in dark blue, not a stencil, but hand printed with no mistakes, clean, slightly arched over that central facility. They were transfixed, that is until Rafi bolted out the door calling for Beth to come see something.

Finally Sam spoke. "What did I tell you? Words of the prophets!!" For the next half hour, the dreary business of Barrington was sacrificed to a debate in the men's room, interrupted only when two of DCs finest escorted a rather unpleasant young man into the toilet, ordering everyone out. In that time, however, they discussed and provisionally dismissed many theories. Who was the Duke?

Rafi argued it must be Duke Snyder, the Brooklyn Dodger centerfielder who was one of the famed Boys of Summer. Rafi had secured an autograph from the Duke of Flatbush when he made an appearance at the Dodger's spring training camp in Havana in his rookie year and had taken a proprietary interest in his career ever since. That Duke was well retired in 1980, however, and not likely to be of much interest to the law firm's young ghetto clientele or the sleezeball lawyers, who were not much older.

Frank's choice was naturally John Wayne, a white guy's guess that didn't match the likely artist's profile, but certainly plausible as a candidate unlikely to dance well and maybe just tough enough to appeal to the local clientele, regardless of his ethnicity.

The front-runner, however, was Ted's Duke of Earl, Gene Chandler, founder of the Du-Kays, a rhythm and blues group with a strong rock-and-roll sound, with the number one R&B hit of the Duke's name. That hit was twenty years before, but Chandler made a living off that song forever. He was ethnically correct, but he could dance. Beth, when called in for the inspection, suggested Duke Ellington, but he also undoubtedly could dance, at least until he died six years earlier; perhaps that was the meaning behind the statement that he "don't dance" now.

Why the illiteracy? Yes, a lot of ghetto dwellers with less than proper English entered that facility, but the careful drafting of the statement seemed to imply that the writer deliberately selected the tense. Just as "I don't take no shit" is a declaration of bold defiance, but "I don't take a shit" is simply too much information expressed badly, a statement that the Duke doesn't dance would have been dully informational. The pronouncement that the *Duke don't dance* was forceful, proactive. No matter what you might want, you must accept the hard fact: he *don't* dance, and don't you forget it.

It was obviously a slow day and Barrington was out of town, so the discussion moved into the Ward and a forum convened, mostly out of boredom, but somehow also as a form of therapy for the tensions and failed communications over the lunch. They didn't call it the Ward without reason.

The first tentative decision was that the Duke of Earl was out of consideration, if only because Ted thought of it. Ben's late suggestion of Patty Duke was written off as the product of a youthful crush. More persuasive was another late entrant, Duke Zeibert, the proprietor of a legendary restaurant a few blocks away, popular with pols, lobbyists, and Washington sports figures. They had all dined clients there, and none could recall having seen Zeibert dance. Since the message was not that this Duke can't dance, but rather "don't dance," maybe that fit with the riddle. Sam favored that choice.

Driven to a second choice and influenced by Sam's reaction, Ted believed he had the answer, his two years of classical education at St. Johns coming to the fore. As Sam had suggested, the phrase must be the words of the prophets—or at least a prophet—proclaiming the non-existence of God or the unresponsiveness of any divine being to the supplications of mortals. No matter what you ask or pray for, the Duke *will not dance.* The line clearly refers to the ancient use of Duke as lord and leader, as in Jesus Christ, Duke of our battle, Satan, Duke of the deep. Or "the great Duke, that in dreadful awe upon Mount Horeb learn'd eternal law." *Dux a non ducendo,* "the Duke doesn't lead." That's it—"to lead" is a dance term. What could be clearer? It is the calling up of the Duke of the great reformer, John Wycliffe, defending the secular world from the dictatorial claims of religious zealots, calling on the common man in the common vernacular to deal with earthly affairs based on his own understanding and not the commands of religious authorities. "We concern ourselves with the verities that are, and leave aside the errors which arise from speculation on matters which are not," and so *Dux a non ducendo,* the Duke don't dance. Words to live by.

"But you're Jewish," Beth objected.

"Just another reason why the Duke don't dance," Ted replied.

This fine reasoning led the group to the inexorable conclusion, given such elaborate bullshit, that Ted must have written the graffiti. The interpretation was consistent with Ted's crisis of faith in his marriage and torment over his recent affair. This reasoning, however, confronted two obstacles: the writing wasn't there earlier when Ted and Ben left the men's room together, just in time to catch up with Sam and Frank, about to descend the elevator on the way to lunch. An even more daunting obstacle, Ted was clearly incapable of such flawless calligraphy.

Remaining suspect of Ted's guilt, but unable to circumvent the objections, they eventually agreed to accept his mystical interpretation as a working hypothesis. Each of them, after all, had reason to believe that fate, the Duke, or whoever was not dancing, and would not appear to them to conjure up any personal salvation. The phrase also paired nicely with a shrug of the shoulders or a final drink at last call. So the phrase became the Ward's quasi-official motto. They left at the end of the day with a renewed sense of something passing for companionship.

CHAPTER 13:

Capitol Mall, 1981

As the crowd gathered for the Fourth of July celebration, Lillian stood on the side of the reflecting pool, admiring her image and mentally critiquing that of daughter, Dominetta, now nineteen years old, still looking about twenty pounds overweight despite her recent diet, casually dressed in the most unflattering manner, and as judgmental as most daughters are toward their mothers. But at least her expression appeared less hostile reflected in the water than it had ten seconds before, viewed directly through the afternoon humidity. And so, Lillian chose to address the creature in the water rather than the one at her side.

"You may look older than me, but I'm still your mother. And Carl wasn't even your father…so where do you come off telling me I should go back to him?" A gentle move of her foot sent Dominetta's image into a ripple of colors for a few seconds. "It's none of your business," she said quickly. "None of your business. And, anyway, this isn't the time or the place."

Lillian was not in a good mood. It had been nearly seven months since that long Monday night with Ted, and the encounter still bothered her greatly in contradictory ways. She couldn't fathom how her emotions had managed to get so out of control, given that she hadn't much liked Lennon after breaking up the Beatles and didn't care for the album issued just before the shooting. She hated that her emotions had broken down her inhibitions with Ted and that she had reveled in the experience and then regretted his backing away, though the outcome was exactly what she had wanted at that moment in time.

The musicians on the Lincoln Memorial stage hadn't even started warming up, but it was getting crowded and noisy around the pool. A park policeman was headed toward them, surely to send them back into the crowds.

"Carl's been nicer to me than my real father."

"Then you marry the son of a bitch, Domino." Lillian finally looked up as the policeman approached. Looking past her daughter, lifting her short skirt unnecessarily to shake the water off her wet feet, she blew a kiss at the approaching officer.

"You're an impossible flirt." Despite being named for a Bond girl, Dominetta shared none of her namesake's emotive characteristics, cautious in romance, detesting her mother's promiscuity, abhorring her name itself for its implications of sexual aggressiveness, almost equally despising "Domino," the odd foreshortening applied to the character, again too masculine, too risk-taking to her ears. At least her mother could have named her Jennifer, the choice of about half the mothers in that era.

"I'm just exiting gracefully. I try to leave the law with good feelings, they're not paid that well."

"Such charity. You try to give the police a little joy and who else? Oh yes, anything else in pants." It was not really fair, she knew. Domino secretly admitted that to herself. As she came of age, she had begun to realize that her mother possessed a kind of sensitivity to men that she could only imagine in herself, a kind of radar that enabled her to find lovers that were thoroughly heterosexual, monogamous, and often long withdrawn from the company of women due to some unfortunate experience that still painfully lingered. Lillian had learned by hard experience to be much more selective than she was in her youth. She was hardly abstinent, but she was not indiscriminant and her daughter's words tore at her in both their truth and their falsity.

She wanted to be a good mother, but her own unspeakable childhood left her unable to do so. She kept her girls safe, never inflicted her affairs on them beyond not concealing their existence and was no more lax in their upbringing than any single working mother, but she was not a whole person and so could not

148

be a whole mother. And she would not pretend that she was, so accepted Dominetta's rebuke silently.

By age eleven, Dominetta was aware and appalled that her mother rationalized her seductions as somehow rescuing these inhibited men from the shackles of fidelity or post-traumatic symptoms of failed romances. That was bullshit, she thought, it was like throwing a drowning man a lifesaver with no rope attached, the man's joy in his good fortune soon dissolved as her mother sailed off in another direction with nothing in tow, and he left to drift aimlessly before surrendering to the sea. But that was a bad analogy. Lillian never pretended to be a rescue vessel, but was herself at best merely the unattached flotation device, barely able to keep herself above the waves and not capable of offering more than temporary respite for the men who reached out to her. She was adrift herself, and only Dominetta's own uncrushed spirit prevented her from seeing the fatal flaw in her comparison. That was Lillian's pride. She couldn't give her daughters direction, but she could preserve their will, whatever they might think of her.

A couple of hours earlier, Dominetta had driven her mother downtown to find parking within walking distance of the mall, thinking that the Fourth of July celebrations might be a fun afternoon, an opportunity to smooth over the mutual recriminations of past weeks. Her younger sister had opted out in favor of a picnic with high school friends and Dominetta was beginning to see the wisdom of that choice. Once again, her mother could not resist the impulse to compete with her like a sister, not at all like a parent. The park policeman was no older than twenty-five and her mother didn't look much older, with her restrained vitality clearly arousing his interest, drawing out the male's rescue instincts. How could a liberated woman compete with a struggling Fay Wray chained to the stockade? Dominetta was more amused than upset, but the day was already a lost cause for mother-daughter rapport, so she pleaded sick and asked her mother if she wouldn't mind taking the metro home. "Of course not," Lillian said, "I'll be fine."

Dominetta hiked to the car and drove off in search of Tikki and her friends. If the day was to degenerate to sibling rivalry, Dominetta would rather it be with her younger sister, where she held the advantage. As soon as her daughter was out of sight, Lillian walked over to the area where ground had been broken for the Vietnam Memorial and began to cry. As expected, passers-by took her for a widow and left her alone with her tears. After a half hour, she wandered back into the thick of the crowd, searching for something, anything, to fill the void.

———

Over at the base of the Washington Monument, Ted was distressed. Before his encounter with Lillian six months earlier, he, Rebecca, and their two boys had moved from their modest house in Silver Spring, Maryland to a very expensive one in Potomac, and things were not going smoothly. Mortgage rates were moving to an all-time high of over 20 percent and he had only been able to negotiate a fixed rate in the mid-teens. Nonetheless, he had been compelled to take the loan as a means of relieving Rebecca's almost continuous state of depression, not to mention to avoid constant reminders of her father's magnificent home in Boston. Within days of taking on the burden of the new home under those terms, however, Rebecca had walked out, taking the boys with her to her parent's house, telling him that she "needed space." She said it was only a trial separation, a gesture to reassure Ted that she loved him, and it was her not him and all that, saying all the comforting things that provide no comfort whatsoever. It was the opposite of comfort, like Reagan saying nice things about Carter in his victory speech, condescending, insincere or both. She may have needed space, but she gave Ted an excessive amount of it, bumping around alone in a five-bedroom house except for the twice-monthly visits from his boys.

Ted was hurt, insulted, and suspicious, as well as financially wounded. He came to the assumption that it must have really been about Rebecca's old boyfriend, a man who was Orthodox like Rebecca's mother, a man whose pacifism and flight to Canada led to their breakup, but whose adherence to principles was a topic of many dinner table conversations. That had to be the real cause of the separation, he was sure of it. He knew the man was back in the

Boston area, no doubt trying to rekindle the flame with Rebecca; maybe he was already sleeping with her. It ate at Ted, believing that he was second best to her, yet knowing that Rebecca had been his own second choice following Ari's disappearance. But that was different. As shallow as some thought him, as childish as his actions might sometime seem, as immature as he might really be, he was aware enough to know from the outset that Ari was a mirage to him, the timing terrible, her personality an unsolvable mystery. If Ari was unattainable, was Rebecca really a second choice? He didn't think so, not the way he was her second choice, anyway.

The Ward had taken sides on this family crisis along predictable lines. The pro-Ted faction included Ted's oldest friend Sam, the male chauvinist Frank, and the radical Rafi. Beth, of course, supported Rebecca, agreeing without hesitation to all of Rebecca's many variations on what was wrong with the marriage, no matter how contradictory. After Ben and Rachel had befriended Ted and Rebecca and had come to the awkward realization that Ted was almost entirely secular, Rebecca became the vehicle for their reform efforts, so of course they supported her. As cracks formed in his marital foundation, Ted came to feel that Ben and Rachel would not be averse to a breakup and to Rebecca taking a proper Jewish husband. It made for some awkward office lunches. To hell with them all; he would enjoy the concert with his boys.

On the rise near the Washington Monument a group of potheads raised a green marijuana flag. It quickly attracted a gaggle of decidedly mellow Woodstock refugees, men mostly in their thirties and women no longer quite flower children, many with small children in tow, awaiting the fireworks. It was all quite relaxed, no selling or at least very discrete transactions, but much sharing, particularly after the Beach Boys kicked of the concert with "California Girls" and the park police opted to enjoy the music rather than hassle the stoners. The territory around the flag became, in fact, an island of tranquility in a vast sea of overheated revelers, where tempers stoked by smuggled libations in hipflasks and thermoses fostered riptides of confrontation among the waves of humanity. Slowly, the emerald cannabis banner began to attract couples and families around the fringes, drawn not by the weed, but by the need.

At the bottom of the slope rested a row of Port-a-Potties and long lines of celebrants, drawn to each toilet like so many ants to a trail of breadcrumbs. The flag was one of very few certain landmarks, other than the obelisk itself. It was visible over a half million heads and became the point of reunion after one parent endured the long toilet wait with the kids or couples separated for their own benefit. By the time "Surfin' Safari" came along some folks were leaving their children with the flower ladies for a run at the johns and pot island began to take on the look of a day care center.

An older man named Bob with salt and pepper hair tied in a ponytail began inflating long balloons with exhaled reefer air, twisting them into somewhat psychedelic animals to the delight of the youngsters, while another mellow ex-hippie tried with modest success to recreate the magic tricks that he had learned as a child. Despite the drugs and tattoos, the relaxed good nature of the male smokers, the mother-hen fussiness of their women, and the sharp watchfulness of the ambivalent and disapproving on the borders gave an aura of confidence that everything would be all right. It was, too. In addition to babysitting, the ad hoc commune supplied more than a few exhausted celebrants with shade and water, almost certainly preventing cases of heatstroke. Bob actually gave one overweight gentleman CPR while a companion fetched an EMT from a fire truck over on Constitution Avenue. Peace and love, baby. Peace and love.

About the time "Surfer Girl" started, Ted was trudging up the hill from the johns with his two boys. It was his time with the boys and Rebecca, in town to visit Ben and Rachel and pick up the kids, had agreed to let him take them to the mall. As he walked the boys toward the pot-filled balloons, he told himself that his continued estrangement from Rebecca was all for the best. He plopped himself on the grass, slipped a flask from his pocket, and watched the boys attempt to make something from one of Bob's balloons.

"Hello, stranger." Ted looked up in astonishment to see a giddy, unsteady Lillian above him. She was obviously stoned.

"Well, hi. It's been too long." He sat there, awaiting recriminations for his boorish behavior but none were forthcoming, as Lillian struggled to maintain her balance and allowed his familiarity to overwhelm her conflicted emotions over their parting. He represented safety and comfort as he had that night of Lennon's murder.

She put a hand on his shoulder to steady herself, but involuntarily slipped to her knees beside him. "I…I made some friends here." Placing a finger to her lips, she brought her hand and face to his ear and whispered, "They gave me something."

"I can see that," he said. "Is it OK here? My boys are over there with the balloon guy."

"Oh, that's Bob. He's the sweetest man ever. Your kids will be all right with him. In fact, have a cookie, he's actually the one who gave me these." She opened a paper bag with some broken oatmeal goodies and he took a small piece. "Don't worry, he has real candy he offers the youngsters." She giggled and stretched her long legs across his feet as innocently as a child, as seductive as Salome's dance.

"You never called," she said hesitantly, as if uncertain of that recollection.

"I'm really very, very sorry. We had a wonderful time together and I was tempted, but, I guess Sam told you, I was still trying to save my marriage." Ted then called his boys over defensively to meet the nice lady, who was not feeling well. The eldest gave her one of his candies and they said hello nicely. But they wanted to get back to Bob as quickly as possible. Lillian had propped herself up by her elbows and watched their retreat, amused by their lack of interest.

"You've lost your body guard," she observed. "And?"

"And what?"

"Did you save your marriage?"

"Evidently not." He explained the situation as best he could and said a few words about Sam and his new friend. She rested her head in his lap, recovering from the cannabis. Ted sat still for perhaps fifteen minutes, looking north over the Capitol dome, watching his boys play with the balloons. The next song began while they remained silent. Finally, he stroked her hair and confessed. "It's no excuse. I'll never forget that Monday night and I was a complete ass afterwards. I can't get over it. When the spring came and the weather got warmer, I would go out into my backyard after dinner, and sit and watch the fireflies go on and off for hours, thinking of you."

"I had no idea you were that smitten. I thought you hated me."

"Yeah, you knew. You're just so used to all men being smitten that you forgot. But I hated your lasagna, if that helps."

Lillian laughed, but then suddenly looked away, exclaiming, "New potties! Ted, I'll meet you back here!" And with that she was halfway down the hill, running headlong to the end of the existing row of conveniences, where a flatbed with a large sign reading "Don's Johns" had just pulled onto the grass from Constitution and a forklift was approaching to off-load a half dozen or so fresh Port-a- Potties.

"Wait!" Ted shouted. He told his boys to stay with Bob and slipped him a twenty, which the balloon twister accepted with a wink. By the time Ted reached the bottom of the hill, he saw that Lillian had cajoled her way to the very front of the line to one of the new facilities. "That's my wife," he explained repeatedly, elbowing his way forward. "She's pregnant. She'll need my help if she's too sick from the heat." Reaching Lillian at last, Ted took her face in his hands. "Honey, if it gets too bad in there, open the door for me and I'll make sure you're all right. These good folks understand what it's like in the fourth month." He released her lips.

"Pregnant? Really?" With that, she quickly slipped into the toilet, quickly closing the door behind her.

About a minute later, the door opened a crack. "Ted, Ted, you have to come in." Laden with two water bottles, a bag of ice, and a clean tee shirt passed to him by crowd. Ted slipped into the john and locked the door. "Pregnant, well aren't you the inventive one?" Ted dropped the water bottles and brought her near, while she unbuckled his belt and unzipped the fly, letting his chinos and briefs fall to the floor. "Damn, I'm going to be sick," she shouted loudly, at the same time, her hands caressing his exposed manhood. And within a minute he was into her, her moans confirming to those outside that this was truly an emergency.

It was over soon. Passion slackening, Ted whispered, "Don't worry baby."

"Having sex in a box in the middle of a half-million people, are you kidding me? I swore once that I'd never have impulsive sex again unless there were people within earshot if I had to scream for help, but this is ridiculous."

"No, no. It's the song "Don't Worry Baby." We've done a better rendition in here than they're doing out there, though."

"Yeah, yeah. Let's get it together and get out of here."

Quickly dumping the water and ice in the toilet and throwing the wet tee shirt in the corner, they exited the toilet. "Are you quite all right?" the woman next in line asked.

"Perfect, after he helped me out," said Lillian. With Lillian leaning on Ted unnecessarily, they slowly ascended the hill, accepting applause and occasional high fives from the line as they homed in on the marijuana leaf and made their way toward Ted's boys, still playing with balloons. They sat next to the children and Bob, and Ted passed him an extra twenty.

"You all right?" Ted whispered in her ear, then turned slightly red as she wistfully stroked an inflated but untwisted balloon.

"Well, maybe the song should have been 'Good Vibrations.'"

"That's always saved for the encore."

It was, too, both on the mall and later at his house.

When the concert wound down they walked with the boys to Ted's car in the small company parking lot off K Street used by the Ward employees, Ted instructing his sons along the way to not upset mommy by mentioning the nice lady. He then drove to Ben's neighborhood, parked down the street, and walked the boys to the house to be picked up, as Rebecca had arranged.

Unfortunately, Nurse Ratched had been on the case. Ted had failed to observe earlier that Beth had also left her car in the company lot. On her return she spotted him kissing Lillian as he held the door for her to sit in the passenger seat. It was against her better judgment, but Beth reluctantly called Rebecca, who had asked her only that morning whether Ted's affair had ended. She hated being a snitch, but it was a direct question and the only righteous thing to do.

Fortunately, the irate Rebecca, having responded to Beth's call, had arrived at Ben's house two minutes after Ted left, departing with Lillian to spend the night in his own empty home. Rebecca thought of driving there and confronting him, but she had the boys with her now and wouldn't subject them to what would no doubt be a tawdry scene with the pick-up from the Mall

Without interruption from an angry wife, the evening went much as expected for Ted and Lillian. A nice wine, no cocaine, just a conventional, gentle romance with none of the adventure of earlier in the day. There was delicate, domestic warmth about it.

In the kitchen the following morning, Lillian breakfasted on orange juice, decaf, and muesli that Ted's wife had left behind in the pantry; he on Diet Coke, bacon, eggs, and Count Chocula. This appalled Lillian, who was as much a devotee of proper nutrition to maintain her youthful figure as she was a contrarian on conventional romance. Their incompatibility became even clearer when Ted noted that he had sent General Mills a proposed advertising campaign dedicated to convincing preschool-age kids that Count Chocula was a real person who would strongly object to other choices, except maybe Frankenberry. He thought they could draw on some music from the *Rocky Horror Picture Show* and add sly references to appeal to adolescent males, as well. Lillian was horrified. For all her faults, Lillian was serious about some family values.

After Ted dropped her at home, Lillian avoided an early confrontation with Dominetta by retiring to her room with the morning paper. Thinking over the previous day and evening, she began to feel an emptiness quite unlike the blend of exhilaration, guilt, triumph, and righteous self-punishment she normally experienced after such encounters. Ted was different. Yes, he was a man normally devoted to one woman, and yes, he was traumatized by his recent breakup. Still, she had not seduced him, not rescued him from his troubles. He had no false illusions that she could save him from anything and it was quite likely that he would not call her, just like the first time, and that she would never see him again. She really liked the man, he was a kind and considerate lover, but she was just a target of opportunity, a random sex object, despite the nonsense about the fireflies. That was the weird part of it, to be hurt by thinking she was just a sex object, when being a sex object was a carefully crafted skill that she had perfected, a state deserving of admiration, most triumphant when imposed on the unwilling.

And then it became clear: he was a lot like her. He, too, was self-medicating with the momentary relief that sex provides from pain, harboring no expectations of anything permanent, willing to take risks for the relief offered, accepting of any consequences from his actions. *Shit, he's such a jerk and he's just like me.* "Damn it," she yelled.

Dominetta, who was making coffee in the kitchen, jumped at the anguished cry. "Is something wrong?"

"You think? Christ, I just got screwed by Count Chocula in a fucking Port-a-Potty!"

Dominetta rolled her eyes, looking skyward, clinching the coffee pot in a death grip. *I've got to get out of this place.*

———

Ted, on the way home, contemplated whether yesterday's occurrence on the mall might perhaps have been a bit too impulsive, not fully reflecting his serious nature or the depth of his feelings, at least his prospective feelings, for Lillian. She was a nut case to be sure, but aside from the sex, he was beginning to think he really cared for her, maybe even loved her. The sex itself was not the main thing. In fact, it was arguably better in the anticipation than the performance, soothing and more wistful than ardent. Before their marriage he thought he had really loved Rebecca, at least believing he loved her; every nerve sated from her wanton passion to satisfy him in every way, but he wasn't sure that he had ever liked her all that much. He never could empathize all that much with her parental conflicts, and hated her many signals that his religion, or lack thereof, was a liability that he was obligated to constantly overcome, an obligation fulfilled partly by

157

succumbing to her succuban love-making. He despised being tolerated, detested being drained of life emotionally and physically. Lillian probably thought he was an idiot and maybe he was, but he was sure that she would see his good and bad qualities as separate things, and if she saw the good side as more attractive than the bad was repelling, she'd let it go at that. She wouldn't demand some continual compensation for his deficiencies. Lillian hurt inside, he could see that, but she wouldn't fill him with guilt as a cure for her own infirmities. There could be a real life with her.

He arrived home to find Rebecca and the children waiting for him, thinking at first that she had come to tell him that it was over, girding himself for an argument over custody, feeling almost relieved, knowing he was sure to obtain joint custody, anticipating a new, more adult pursuit of Lillian. It was not to be. Rebecca had almost left him for good the first time Beth had called and she had been prepared to let him go until Beth called again and told her not to be a fool, that her religious tenants and her marital vows meant something and she should hold her man to them, not let Ted just make it up as he went along. Rebecca had finally received a diagnosis for her anemia, a rare form of lymphocytic leukemia that was debilitating, but might persist for years before finally resulting in death. It was terrible, that diagnosis, and she could not be all to Ted that he wanted her to be and perhaps, even, she had made a mistake in marrying him, and would have been better with her first love. But Ted, like Beth's Tom, had made the commitment and he must be held to it. The doctors had made the diagnosis, but Beth prescribed the treatment: Ted must support her. Emboldened by this kindred spirit, Rebecca had decided to return to Ted with the children.

Ted's first instinct was to send her away, but he could not bring himself to do it and welcomed her home with all of the warmth he could muster. He composed a letter to Ari asking her advice and Ari's response convinced him that he had taken the right course and that he could take refuge in raising his boys. Ari, unlike Beth or Rebecca, did not rely on religious precepts to dictate her course, but lived with the implications of her own choices. For Ted, that inward assessment brought him to the same place as Beth's religious dictates. Eventually Ted had dinner with Lillian, despite an extorted promise to Rebecca never to do so, and explained the situation and his second disappearance. Lillian was moved by his dilemma, and found herself more attracted to Ted than before. Only the finality of the evening dampened the sense of resolution that it brought to both of them.

As they walked from the restaurant, he took her face in his hands, kissed her, and recited Bogart's farewell speech from Casablanca. Of course, "We'll always have Don's John" doesn't quite have the charm of "We'll always have Paris," but it would persist in their memories equally well. At last he said, "Here's looking at you, kid," and watched her as she walked off into the fog. Then he went home and watched videos with his teenage sons on the new MTV channel.

CHAPTER 14:

Paris & Montego Bay, 1982

Ari had made a decision. It happened in Paris after a dreary day in the classroom and was as irrevocable as the one she had made twenty years earlier.

The passing years had reaffirmed the irreversibility of her fate to live without marriage and a conventional loving relationship, a course foreordained decisively by the act of abandoning her one true love. Continuing to teach in schools across America and Europe, she had had a number of affairs since that loss. The boys at the university nearly twenty years before had wished for what she could not give then, so she gave nothing, but she had not forsaken sex forever. In the two decades following, having the normal hormonal drives of a woman in the prime of life, being continually in the presence of willing partners, as attractive females inevitably are, and possessing the natural allure of loneliness, she passed through a number of short-term relationships. Her irrevocable rejection of long-term commitment, however, remained unchallenged, and her intelligence and uncompromising standards ultimately intimidated partners. The IQ tests she once used for defense were not needed to cool the male libido, as the mere presence of a superior intellect had the same result. The ebb and flow of life continued, accompanied by a multitude of pleasant personal interludes and professional accomplishments.

But if fulfillment could be obtained through being an inspiration to thousands of students and hundreds of peers, maintaining the highest standards in one's profession, assisting many people in resolving their personal crises, experiencing sweet romances that ended in enduring friendship, and being admired by lovers,

161

friends, colleagues, superiors, underlings, and even critics, why was Ari unfulfilled?

Ari experienced no inner reward from academia or leisure, an emptiness requiring, and yet intensified, by introspection. True to her heritage, Ari held the view that an unexamined life is not worth living, but Socrates' advice serves better as a retort to one's accusers than guidance for a fulfilling life, certainly for Ari in her contemporary world. Exploring every dark corner of one's soul, questioning every motivation, insisting that one's actions be entirely honest, committing to logic over the vast array of manipulative devices always at one's disposal, all this demanded more courage than the philosopher acknowledged and more tolerance of pain than might break a tortured prisoner. And so Ari took no pleasure from her teaching skills, remaining to her mere performances, charades that tricked her students into learning, successes that only sufficed to meet her obligation as a custodian of the cultural heritage she transmitted to her classes.

Friends who knew Ari's aging mother often thought that the old woman's harsh dismissal of Ari's achievements was the source of her persistent discontent. Her mother had made her brutal critiques quite transparent to all, deliberately and hostilely. But Ari had thoroughly explored that musty corner only to find a tunnel behind the cobwebs that led deeper into her mother's own past miseries, beyond the failed marriage, beyond any fascist collaborations, and into old misfortunes and rejections—failures that, with the early symptoms of Alzheimer's, were progressively being lost to memory, leaving the old lady's disappointment in her daughter a pure malevolence, free from fetters of personal regret or responsibility. Her mother's state saddened Ari, not so much out of sympathy, but more from the conclusion that she hated the woman, hated her with passion, hated her with just cause for transferring her own blighted hopes into automatic and highly predictable denials of her daughter's achievements, hated her cowardliness, no longer challengeable, sheltered by mental incapacity. It was ugly, not the way things should be, pathetic in many ways, but Ari was strong and a mother's rejection did not mold her into her current state.

Her mother was right to an extent, Ari being acutely aware that her potential lay well beyond her achievements and almost certainly would remain so. As she vowed years before, Ari did not intend to change that situation, as the price of ambition was too high, requiring too many compromises, would take her too far from the isle of her self-imposed internal exile. Any extraordinary achievement would have to come by fate, by an accidental circumstance, an accident not likely to occur, just as impossible to imagine as a repetition of her one great love. So, *Primum non nocere* became her watchwords. "First do no harm." That gave her some solace as a prisoner of her own convictions.

Yet despite those convictions and the internal torment they created, Ari's introspectiveness was rarely detected, she remaining a social animal, genuinely curious about others' thoughts, eager to experience new things, open to different cultures, ready to hear any argument and debate it in generous spirit. Prior to abandoning her eternal love, this outgoing nature and adventurist spirit were natural expressions of youthful exuberance. In a sense, they remained so, but increasingly in a compartmentalized manner, a part of her life disconnected from the pretense of career goals that either posed no challenge or that she would not abandon her principles to pursue. She did not view her social pursuits as trivial, her support for friends as meaningless; she was never condescending. But it was all transitory; perhaps sincere, sometimes delightful in the moment, sometimes of passing great importance, but transitory nonetheless.

Then, on that damp summer evening in Paris, she wandered into a showing of *La Guerre du Feu,* a film about a primitive people's struggle for fire and a young woman who was rescued by cavemen. The woman enlightened a dense Neanderthal about how fire could be made, rather than captured from an accidental blaze, and about how the sex act could become a gentle, sustained pleasure, rather than the rapid extinguishing of pure instinct. Although the plot was not entirely convincing and the instruction in the missionary position laughable, she found herself warmed by the scenes where the lithe woman, Ika, transformed the man into a proper lover. And then, during the final scene, when the man,

Naoh, discovers that Ika is pregnant with their child and caresses her while they both gaze at the brightly lit moon, Ari made her decision: she would have a child.

A child was what she lacked; parenthood was a responsibility that was more than a passing entertainment or a brief contribution to solving someone else's riddles. She thought it over, testing her resolve, and attempting to sort out rational thought, emotions, and pure instinct, and finally concluded that she must bow to the demands of natural selection to reproduce herself, striving for a more perfected form than she had reached or would ever reach. Perhaps this was a sound conclusion or maybe just simple curiosity. Curiosity she concluded was ultimately the font of her successes and her failures, the driving force, the reason she had rejected conventionality for forbidden love, the reason she explored all the dark corners, the reason why she was often miserable, but never afraid. She needed to know what it would be like to have a child, to raise a child. She needed to know if she could be a better parent than her mother or her father. She needed to test whether she could be as competent in reality as she was in the artificial world of teaching.

For years, Ari had asked the question of whether there was a God, ultimately deciding she didn't care. Or maybe, she thought, the question was irrelevant unless she could positively resolve a different question: was there an Ari? She must satisfy herself that she was not just a random combination of biological and environmental forces that determined her actions, emotions, and so-called rational thought, little more than a cinema projector that could not itself claim responsibility for what appeared on the screen. She needed to feel that she was real or accept her derivative pseudo-existence. Perhaps having a child might lead her to a conclusion. If she loved the child as she hoped she might, loved the child despite the rejection that could be forthcoming, then maybe she could believe herself a real person.

She must have a child. But with whom? She didn't want a husband or a lover, just a child. She pondered her options, unwilling to leave something this important to a one-night stand, and knowing that having passed forty she would need to act soon. She felt that her prior lovers were unlikely partners, either now platonic friends with new romantic entanglements or, in a few cases, resenting Ari for their breakup. She was attracted by a sperm bank's combination of donor screening and non-involvement, all pressing her toward the technological, but sterile, solution. But in the end, she came back to her holistic, naturopathic belief that normal reproduction guided by instincts of natural selection would lead to the best outcome. She must have sex, but not with just anyone; it had to be someone who knew and sympathized with her, someone who would stay the course until conception was assured, someone who would then consent to go away and not bother her, someone who would be there in some fashion if her child wanted to know the father.

That narrowed the choice greatly. She thought about Ted, whom she knew would eagerly assent, but in her latest letter she had just convinced him to stay with his chronically ill wife and his children and couldn't be so hypocritical as to put herself in the same adulterous bed that she just helped drive him away from. And after her great lost love, she had vowed never to have another affair with a married man. Despite what others said of him, she knew Ted to be bright; after all, she had subjected him to an IQ test, so he would provide good genes, but no... Ted would be impossible.

Then there was Sam. He was still single and, as far as she knew from Ted's letters, still had the illusion of her being the perfect woman. He loved her in a kind of ethereal way that was neither platonic nor sexual, that asked for nothing, that demanded no reciprocity, that was without conditions. She knew now that all those years ago, she had made the mistake of drawing him into her labyrinth of doubts, fears and incessant quest for answers to the unanswerable that compounded his own futile search for some fate, some calling, some star, as Shakespeare wrote, to guide his wandering bark. And after all these years, during which she had followed him only through her correspondence with Ted, he remained in that labyrinth. A reunion might go well, but the proposition she had in mind would not, not with that terrible bond of his knowing her wounds too well, the abandonment of

165

her father, her hatred for her mother, the sacrifice of her lost love, her potentials and why they would never be fully achieved, and yet her inability to set these things aside would be seen in his eyes only as her courage to forge deeper into the darkness to confront the monsters within. She knew Sam was steadfast; he could be counted upon not to abandon her, to stay aside as she wished, to be a good father if needed, to transmit his own intelligence to the child. This is exactly why she could never ask him. She could not condemn him to the labyrinth.

Then, she thought of Frank, whom she had met briefly on an airline stopover in DC a year or so before. Traveling between teaching appointments, she had hoped to see Ted and Sam then, but Sam was out of town. Ted had spoken well of Frank when they met at Ted's office, and related the story of Sam recruiting him for their firm, feeling his military discipline might reinforce Rafi's resolve on technology matters and even give some backbone in defending himself with Barrington. Ted respected Frank's innate abilities and commitment to his children, the mark of a real man in Ted's eyes, and forgave his right wing, down-on-the-farm posturing and his decidedly non-monogamous sexual proclivities.

Ted invited Frank to join them for lunch and the three went out to dinner a day later, where they talked mostly about Sam and his new girlfriend and Frank's marital problems. Frank was amusing in a bantering, overly macho fashion that he obviously employed to conceal his troubles. She liked him from a sort of anthropological perspective. He was bright, intolerant of stupidity and pretense and his amorality, she felt certain, would be fully offset by her over-endowment of ethical concerns, a genetic flaw if there ever was one. In his last letter, Ted had mentioned that Frank was divorced, he and his oriental wife having at last given up on their marriage after difficult years of attempting to reconcile their separate careers. He would be perfect, as he lived far away from where she taught in California and Europe, and was unlikely to refuse such an invitation. Plus, there was no way in hell that she could ever be romantically attracted to the man.

He could be her dense Neanderthal. But Sam, how would he take it? Not well, certainly, if she sought out this hunter-gatherer directly. But according to Ted, Sam both admired and disrespected Frank's primal disconnection of the physical and emotional; Sam would know there was no chance that Frank could compete for the emotional bond Sam sealed with her twenty years ago. What, then, if she spent a couple of weeks in Washington and renewed acquaintances with Sam, gradually expressing her feelings, and then asked for his advice, confessing her plan and all the emotions behind it, and indicating that she was considering Ted and this Frank, among others. She would make it quite clear that all she wanted from the man was a sperm donation. Would that work? Sam would certainly reject her consideration of Ted as her donor and would even take a great deal of pleasure in confirming her doubts on that score. He would not himself ever consent to fathering a child that he couldn't care for, and he would respect her decision to be an unhampered single mother. Hopefully he was as enamored with his new friend as Ted thought. It all came together as an epiphany. With proper preparation, Sam would accept her judgment that the child could provide the escape from her despair, see the validity of her plan and that would be the string in the tunnel, for him at least, if not for her.

Two weeks later, Ari arrived in Washington on the excuse of an educational conference and arranged to have lunch with Sam. The call practically paralyzed Sam, anticipating that some trauma lay behind the meeting and fearing where it might lead. When the day came and they sat down together, the conversation unfolded just as Ari had planned: a serious but restrained discussion of their careers, the problems of the world, their satisfactions and dissatisfactions, his new lady friend and her impressive job, Frank and his wife and their breakup. Sam introduced Ari to Francesca one evening and they attended a concert at the Kennedy Center together. There followed additional lunches, with and without Ted or Frank, pleasant conversations that seemed to reflect some level of tacit understanding of the logic of their coming together at that point in time. Finally, at a seafood restaurant alongside the Potomac, she confessed her revelation. Her plan initially staggered him, of course, but he eventually saw the logic of it and the plausibility that it might possibly give her a modicum of happiness. Ted, of

167

course, was out of the question. He himself could not possibly volunteer, as he and Francesca had just moved in together.

A liaison with Frank made some sense. Yet Sam also realized that Ari was manipulating him; she had known exactly how he would react and had already made up her mind about this planned liaison. He told her so and, as lunch turned into a long afternoon strolling along M Street with stops in bars along the way, he extracted her confession. Her proposition was more painful to him than she imagined, but he confirmed to Ari's relief that his relationship with Francesca was serious. That eased her concern substantially. In the end, Sam agreed with her on every point, not begrudgingly, but because he was convinced that this was a path she needed to take.

They joked about her charade over Ted's candidacy and he related tales of Frank in NKP. He talked a little about Francesca, about how her marriage had ended badly, but how she seemed to be coping well, even caring for four children. He and Francesca didn't talk much about her problems and, unlike his compliance with Ari's advice regarding Lillian, he admitted to Ari that he felt no need to probe Francesca about her past. Was that wrong? "No," she responded, "not all women are problems to be solved, some are solutions to be accepted." She was pleased that he had finally found someone who was good for him.

Ari left Sam with a sense of inner peace, convinced regardless of the right and wrong of it, that he had accepted her plan with genuine equanimity, to her the most important of immeasurable virtues and the most absent in her own soul. She approached Frank with her plan the next week. He accepted, a decision requiring no amplification. They departed to the Caribbean a week later.

The two weeks Frank spent with Ari were possibly the worst in his life, certainly the worst spent with someone he actually liked; there was no spontaneity whatsoever and no common interests to discuss except their mutual friendship with Sam, which only made him feel guilty. Curiously, the stud farm aspect of things didn't bother him all that much. While there was pressure to "perform" and neither of them wanted any chance of repeating the evolving debacle after the first couple of days, he had managed to distance his emotions from the physical act of sex. Ari was still attractive at forty and they had not been intimate before, but she had a weariness about her that destroyed any newness or sense of adventure.

The resort itself didn't help. Ari had made the arrangements at the newly opened Sandals in Montego Bay. It had introduced the all-inclusive concept, offering its guests water sports, classy rooms with upscale furnishings and service, Jacuzzis, multi-channel televisions, fine dining, free drinks, and swim-up bars. Ari had paid for the whole thing, so he was immersed in decadence and unable to pay for anything, both deeply offensive to his male sensibilities. He had always been in control, or thought he was, whether with lovers or prostitutes, but he wasn't in control here and it bothered him greatly, especially in the aftermath of his failed marriage.

On the last day of Frank's term of confinement, Ari consented to let him pay for a lavish dinner at the best restaurant outside of the resort and he felt much better. She was sure their "project" had been successful. If it had, she would let him know and then would honor her promise not to see him again and protect his anonymity. If her child eventually asked about him, she would contact him then and allow him to make the decision about seeing the child, as long as he would not see her or dispute her custody. They had gone over all this many times before and even had a notarized agreement, but it was reassuring.

After returning to the hotel, they agreed not to make love again, but had room service deliver piña coladas to drink on the balcony overlooking the ocean before retiring. Ari apologized for the awkwardness of the stay and they had a pleasant conversation, not exactly as friends, but more like fellow passengers stranded together in a strange place after their flight had been cancelled. She revealed little of her inner life that she had shared so completely with Sam, but confessed that she had a habit of trying to control her relationships with men and apologized for having made him suffer the same way. He lied that he was OK, that they had had a nice time together.

They went to bed, and while she slept peacefully, he mulled over the conversation. He always had had to be in control of his relationships with women and he didn't know why, always presuming that was the natural order of things. It hadn't been that way with Inga, but he had assumed that was because she turned out to be such a ballbuster. But hell, he thought, maybe he did try to control the marriage too much. After all, it was his fault that they had had kids earlier than she wanted, that he had resented having to be the more active parent, and that he had felt driven to make more money than she did, to take more of her time than the damned Company, to be reminded of how much he had done for her by making her an American. Well, that was water over the dam. There was nothing he could do about it now.

Looking at his sleeping companion dimly visible in the moonlight, he couldn't fully understand why Ted and Sam idolized the woman so much. Her hang-ups about men were of her own making; it was pathetic, really. But what did that make him? He was doing the exact same thing—his way or the highway. Maybe he could change; he could try to be a little more flexible. He fell asleep sometime around three.

In the morning, they flew first class back to Washington and upon their arrival, he kissed Ari goodbye on both cheeks, and took a taxi to pick up his kids from Inga. From there, he went on to the rental house in the suburbs he'd occupied since the divorce, arriving in time to watch the Redskins come from behind to beat Miami in Super Bowl XVII on Riggins' famous run. Ari took the evening flight to Paris. The in-flight movies included a censored version of *Quest for Fire*. It was better in the original.

A couple of months later Frank received a letter from Ari with no return address stating that she was pregnant. Several months after that a similar letter arrived, stating that she had had a healthy baby girl she named Triana. Sam and Ted each received birth announcements. Frank said nothing of his fatherhood to either Ted or Sam…or to Ari, since he did not have her address. She had his address if she wanted to reach him.

In any case, Frank's attention had turned elsewhere. Shortly after Montego Bay, Sam had invited Frank to join him for a lunch he was having with an old friend. It was an incredibly timely coincidence, to meet a woman who was actually a Doors fan, a multiple divorcée who would have no basis for condemning his numerous

170

adventures, a woman whose children were adults who she thought hated her and, in any case, would not interfere in their relationship, a woman who was a bit on the wild side, who could no doubt stay with him drink for drink or joint for joint, who shared his working-middle-class background, who was clearly smart despite her marginal education, and who was at least as sexy as Nancy Kwan.

Lillian cleared his mind of Ari immediately. When he received word from Ari about the birth of their daughter, he was happy for her and promised himself that he would provide financial support to the girl if it were ever required. But he did not dwell on the event. Not for more than a day, at best.

CHAPTER 15:

London/the Vatican, 1983

Sam was pleased to receive the assignment when Inga approached him in August, surprised that their connection had outlasted her marriage. "As John Cougar sings," she said, "'life goes on, long after the thrill of livin' is gone.' We've got things to do." It was the first side job Inga had offered since he accompanied Francesca to Ireland a year earlier, before the big split. That one hadn't amounted to much.

In the meantime, Sam and Fran had settled into stable domestic routine, she now allowing him the privilege of the familiar name, though never Frannie. When Inga called, Fran was preparing to undertake preparatory work for exhibition exchanges in Rome and London, a potential "Hidden Treasures of the Vatican" tour of small sculptures and paintings not normally accessible to the general public and a Cecil Beaton photographic exhibit that might be shown at the Victoria and Albert. Inga wanted Sam to undertake an investigation in both locations and his spousal accompaniment of Francesca would be a perfect cover.

The previous year, London police had found the body of one Roberto Calvi, chairman of Banco Ambrosiano, known as the God's banker due to Vatican holdings in the bank, hanging under Blackfriars Bridge in the financial district. The death was termed a suicide but widely thought to be a murder, probably because of some obscure Mafia vendetta. Inga's employer didn't give a damn about who killed Calvi, but was concerned that an investigation might lead in an undesirable direction. Calvi had been a member of a Masonic lodge—illegal in Italy—called Propaganda Due or P2. Members of P2 referred to themselves as *frati neri* or "black friars," and the connection with Blackfriars Bridge seemed too direct to be coincidental.

P2 was, in turn, suspected of complicity with the Company in Argentina's Dirty War and—this where Inga became involved—with the so-called Berne Club, an informal association of European intelligence agencies formed in the '70s to counter Soviet clandestine operations in Europe and Soviet domination of liberation movements in Africa and elsewhere. Critically, some said without proof, the Berne Club received clandestine cooperation from the PRC Embassy in Berne on matters where Chinese and Soviet interests diverged. "For obvious reasons," Inga emphasized, "this is highly sensitive and nothing in the Calvi negotiation should lead the police back to Berne. We need to be aware of any police inquiries or press reporting that could send the investigation in that direction."

The assignment excited Sam, and Inga's next revelation overjoyed him. "We have thoroughly vetted Francesca since we last talked. She's clear and likely to be willing to help you out, especially since she's disillusioned with the Catholic Church and since her ex-husband may have been involved with P2 in some way and has now disappeared. While there's no love lost there, I suspect she'd want to know what happened to him after he returned to Italy a few years ago, especially if it involves Vatican intrigue. Something could turn up when we investigate the P2 connection. It could be an inducement. You have my authorization to reveal our arrangement to Francesca and, if she agrees, to use her as a translator and interpreter since she is fluent in Italian. Your kids—that is, her kids—are now all out of high school and beginning their own lives; she might be able to travel longer than before if we need to extend the investigation. When you have her agreement, I'll brief you and Francesca on the details and you can then make arrangements to accompany her on the Smithsonian mission." Feeling guilty about his secret agendas on earlier trips, this was exactly what Sam wanted to hear.

He surprised Fran with his disclosure that evening and she took the revelation surprisingly calmly, indicating that she had known that he was up to something on the Irish trip since he had skipped most of the spousal events and seemed to be more preoccupied than his claim of private tours would justify. She wasn't sure, she said, of how she felt about his working for the CIA, even in such a limited, academic way, but it was a relief to know what he was doing and that it didn't extend to any true cloak-and-dagger stuff. Sam was vaguely disappointed that she wasn't more impressed.

Fran hemmed and hawed about helping him out with translations, saying she had mixed feelings about the CIA as far back as college and she needed to take care of her paying job first. On the other hand, her oldest girls remembered their father and would want to know what happened to him. By bedtime Sam had convinced her to be complicit in his secret world, though all she would agree to do was the translating. Tell that to Inga, she insisted.

"This could be the beginning of a beautiful relationship," he said as he turned down the lights.

"Shut up and go to sleep, Sam," she replied.

"Call me Zulu, Foxtrot."

"Oh, grow up."

The flight to London was uneventful, as was the week in the city before they proceeded to Rome. Fran tended to her negotiations at Victoria and Albert and Sam was on his own. Inga, through a series of secure phone calls from Langley, arranged briefings at the American Embassy on the Calvi episode based on connections with Scotland Yard and SIS, the secret intelligence service famed in Bond films as MI6. Those meetings and a follow-up at SIS headquarters near Waterloo railway station yielded little beyond speculation—rumors about rogue Masonic factions, the Mafia, Opus Dei, secret Nazi cells, and the like. There was some discussion of Banco Ambrosiano's clandestine funding of anticommunist operations in Latin America through a Luxembourg bank, but that was fairly common knowledge in the intelligence community and was not linked in any way to Calvi's death, so it was not a concern to Inga and her superiors. If Scotland Yard or SIS knew anything about a Berne or PRC connection, they weren't telling the Americans. A series of meetings with reporters from the tabloid press did not uncover anything troubling either. Although some suspect dealings between Calvi and Swiss Banks came to light, no connections with either the Berne Club or the PRC embassy surfaced. Sam was instructed that one can often serve intelligence best by confirming that events remain undetected, rather than detecting leaks and their perpetrators. His initial findings would please Inga.

Complications arose when Sam arrived with Fran in Rome. The Vatican exhibit was far more important than the small photography show that the Smithsonian wanted to place at the Victoria and Albert, and Fran was involved in intense discussions at the Vatican, taking up most of the day, every day. While Fran disappeared for those purposes, he pursued the leads provided by Inga with Italian security, police, and newspapers, gathering articles, investigative reports, and other documentation. In the evenings, often late evenings, as Fran's negotiations dragged into the night, they would go over the materials, with Fran scanning everything for any Swiss connections and translating key passages.

Except for the late-hour translations, it was a lot like London and yielded similar results, but it felt more like Johannesburg a decade earlier. Inga had provided him a contact in the Servizio per le Informazioni e la Sicurezza Democratica, called SISDE, a recently established state domestic intelligence agency separated from foreign intelligence after a scandal. Sam imagined it was like creating a new FBI as a spinoff from a CIA in the wake of a corruption investigation, with all of the divided loyalties complicated by a legacy of corruption, organized crime, radical politics, and, of course, obscure machinations of the Holy See. Sam's driver, assigned from SISDE, was as adept in botching appointments as the one in South Africa, and Sam knew he was tailed whenever he took taxis. *Per aspera ad veritatem,* "through difficulties to the truth," the SISDE motto, seemed an unlikely outcome to Sam's mission.

Compounding the tension concerning who, if anyone, could be trusted regarding the Calvi matter, was the ongoing "Mattanza," the so-called Second Mafia War between the Corleonesi based in rural Sicily and the urban crime bosses throughout Italy. It was a power struggle to be avoided at all costs, but elements of the Mafia were almost certainly involved with the Blackfriars Bridge incident. Further, many of the rumors circulating among the police and the press came from *pentiti*, Mafioso collaborating with the authorities for retribution or protection. It was getting to be, to use the technical term, hairy.

For that reason, Sam was not altogether surprised when he returned to his hotel one late evening to find Madam Inga sitting at a table across from Fran, a compact handgun on the table in front of her. It looked smaller than the gun she had carried in South Africa, he said, in the absence of any other coherent thought. "Newer technology," Inga replied tersely, motioning for him to sit down at the table. She had arrived, she explained, to emphasize the seriousness of the situation; neither of them should attempt to meet anyone not specifically approved by the contacts within SISDE, not even other individuals in that organization. It now seemed that any internecine conflict between CID and KGB related to the Blackfriars mess would not see the light of day, so Sam could probably wrap up his report after a lunch meeting with SISDE the next day and they could return home whenever they would like after the weekend, when Fran's Hidden Treasures talks wrapped up. No more poking around with the press or the police.

There was, however, one more thing to be done. The next day, when Fran visited the Vatican, she would have to serve as a courier to dispose of Inga's gun. She would meet a member of the Swiss Guard who would identify her by her last name, and she should pass him the gun; that would be all. Fran tried to object, but Inga insisted it was critical, and she relented.

Inga then showed the gun to Sam, gratuitously adding that it was a SIG-Sauer P225, citing its advantages over her old Walther for its size, reliability, and widespread use in police and security agencies throughout Europe. Even the Swiss Guards carried a variant of this model. Never, she advised Sam to no discernible purpose, carry a weapon that is not in common use in the area you are operating, preferably by the police. That requires attention these days because there is such a growing diversity in the small arms market. If you need to dispose of the gun, it is best not to be carrying anything exotic or associated with James Bond movies, but rather something that may give authorities pause to pursue the matter aggressively, thinking that the gun might be a link to one of their own. That was especially a worthwhile precaution in Italy, given the high nine-millimeter casualty rate in recent months.

Sam asked incredulously, "You expect me to carry a gun sometime?" He definitely wasn't up for that.

"No, but such things are good to know. Francesca needn't worry about tomorrow, for example. It's not the best option by far, but if the Swiss Guard doesn't appear as arranged, Francesca can safely toss the weapon. There's no great risk. If it is turned in, it wouldn't be the first P225 picked up by police this month."

When Inga left the hotel room, Fran gingerly picked up the handgun in a silk handkerchief, inspecting it quickly to see if the magazine was full. Seeing that it was, she shuddered, and tenderly placed the weapon in her purse. "God, that woman scares the hell out of me! A fine thing to be toting into St. Peters."

"You can unload it if you want."

"There's no way I'm going to touch the thing until I hand it over. What have you gotten us into, anyway?"

The next morning, Sam stayed in the hotel room to finish work on his report on his new Compaq suitcase computer. He was delighted when Fran returned for lunch to report that the transfer of the weapon had gone smoothly. With just a soft "Signorina Ghiardelli" at the appointed corner, she had opened her purse for the young guard to lift the gun, still wrapped in silk, and slip it into his pocket. He politely returned the scarf. She was free for the afternoon, but had to return that evening to the Vatican to see if she could close on the exhibit. It was not looking promising, but she was going to give it her best shot. In the meantime, they could be tourists for the afternoon.

They headed first for the Trevi Fountain, crowded with countless tourists as always but still delightful for both the Baroque fountain and people watching and a good spot to grab a gelato. Fran was pinched on the behind once, and whispered to Sam that it was too bad she was no longer packing. After a brief ten-minute walk from the Trevi Fountain to the Pantheon and an hour spent inspecting the splendid edifice, they found a pleasant restaurant to have wine and a light snack and watched the sun slowly set. Fran was resigned to an unsuccessful outcome of the hidden treasures negotiation that evening, but Rome can be a treasure just in the enjoyment of it. They toasted Inga for at least allowing them the pleasure of the afternoon.

The next day at noon, Sam sat in a small restaurant located in an alley near the coliseum, awaiting the arrival of his SISDE handler for the debriefing, sampling a seafood appetizer fresh from the Mediterranean with an exceptional glass of Tocai Friulano. The agent finally arrived full of apologies, pleading a very busy morning, and Sam passed over the floppy disc containing his report, a quid pro quo Inga had arranged to secure the unit's support. It contained nothing new to SISDE, but the contact welcomed that news as much as Inga did. The agent feared that the Calvi affair would never be resolved.

The reason he arrived late was that a clue had come in regarding the disappearance of a teenage girl, Emanuela Orlandi, a resident of Vatican City who, Sam might remember, had disappeared in June and some suspected, among other theories, that she had been kidnapped as a warning to stay away from the Calvi affair. An informant connected to the criminal gang, Banda della Magliana, claimed the girl knew a gang leader through a church where she studied music. He had promised SISDE further information, but earlier in the day the police found his bullet riddled body dumped in the river. That was a fairly common end to matters involving Vatican corruption, he sighed. Sam could not help but think that Inga might have had something to do with it, with that weapon she had had Fran pass to the Swiss Guard. But no, that was absurd and bringing it up would only disturb Fran. He put it out of his mind. Over the next few days, he and Fran toured, drinking and eating their way through Rome and taking a delightful side trip to Capri before flying home.

CHAPTER 16:

La Paz & Elsewhere, 1984

W hen 1984 came, it did not much resemble the Orwellian
world of perpetual war, pervasive government surveillance, and incessant public mind control. Reagan's feel-
good persona may have blanketed his administration's share of
political manipulations but the concepts of big brother, double-
think, thought crime, etc. seemed further from people's consciousness than they had been in some years, particularly with the cold
war slowly dissolving. American politics these days were centered
on debates about an old lady's hamburger ads complaining about
not enough beef. The era of supersizing meals and downsizing
political expectations was beginning.

Frank had decided to leave the lobbying firm in late '83, concluding that it just wasn't his thing. He had made a contribution,
he knew, but his heart wasn't in it and it was exhausting to be the
firm contrarian. Beyond that, Lillian's prior entanglements with
his Ward colleagues were more than a little disconcerting. And his
voluntary service to Ariadne was more than embarrassing while
working alongside two guys who idolized the woman and actually
meant something to her. He felt like a gigolo in their company and
worse, a man of easy virtue. And on top of that, Sam and Francesca
were working with his ex-wife. The main reason why old friend-
ships fall apart, he reasoned, was too much familiarity, too much
information. And there was far too much information circulating
in that office.

Besides, he had a better opportunity, one that finally made
some real use of his experience in Southeast Asia as an independent contractor. Frank was decisive. He walked into Sam's office,

explained his situation, secured Sam's support, and then marched into the director's office to tender his resignation. That evening he asked Lillian to marry him and, on her assent, found a Virginia judge to perform the civil service, departing with her to New Orleans a week later, where he would establish a new base of operations.

Lillian was not especially shocked to receive Frank's proposal. She had lived with him for over a year, which was almost as long as her earlier marriages had lasted. Both of her girls were now over twenty-one and had moved out of the house, with Dom pursuing a career in psychiatric nursing and Tikki pursuing men. Both had let her know in unmistakable terms that she had been a terrible mother, from the moment she gave them such ridiculous names until they became adults, and, although Dominetta at least had forgiven her, neither wanted her intruding in her present life. It was difficult to argue with that. Even apart from the natural tendency of daughters hating their mothers or being embarrassed by them for the better part of their lives, she had done a truly horrible job of raising them. That, in fact, made her more inclined to marry Frank, whose children were not yet teenagers. The boy thought she was a goddess who would be the perfect mother and the girl despised her slightly less than she detested her natural mother, whom she regarded as a control freak. Both offered Lillian a second chance at raising children under more favorable conditions.

The prospects of a new and different life contributed to her decision to say yes, Lillian never living outside of the DC area or traveling outside of the mid-Atlantic region. At the same time, she had no family ties to bind her to the area and her other associations with the region were more negative than positive. There was nothing to inhibit her acceptance of Frank's proposal, except perhaps that the alliance would be more rational than romantic, more practical than passionate.

That objection of insufficient ardor was not only insufficient, she concluded, but misguided. She and Frank were both deeply flawed people. She had issues that stemmed from childhood and he had lost his way and his confidence after the swashbuckling days of Isan. He could have been seen as a war hero if the war had

182

turned out differently. In fact, he was still seen as such by some whom Frank didn't particularly respect, those who saw the mere risk of death confronting a uniformed soldier as conferring hero status, no matter how involuntarily he arrived at that position or what self-serving or ignorant motivation brought him there. Lillian could see that Frank, who was now over forty, placed no greater value on his past than on hers. They were both survivors. That was what was important and made their alliance the proper choice. And, besides, Ted and Sam were off the table unless she seduced one or the other out of pure meanness. She couldn't do that; they had been too good to her, and it was enough to know that she could if she wanted to.

Lillian transferred her house to the girls to re-sell on the booming Washington area market at a nice profit, took her vows, accepted congratulations at the Barrington Associates farewell party, and departed with Frank. She did think that she would miss Sam a little and Ted more so, now understanding his reasons for deserting her, but the stars had not come into alignment with them, so she would be content just to remember them both fondly.

Frank's new opportunity had come with the expansion of the Drug Enforcement Agency, an initiative sparked by the Reagan Administration's anti-drug stance and the rising tide of crack, turning cocaine from a relatively upscale recreational trifle to a serious hard drug with all of its collateral concerns. It was becoming evident that domestic action could not address the problem without a more concerted attack on foreign supply than cocaine -producing countries were willing or able to mount. In response, DEA began to develop aggressive interventions in Latin America directly and through contractors, involving air assets for both crop eradication and combat support against the cartels' guerilla forces. Combating violent, mostly leftist drug cartels seemed to Frank a socially responsible occupation, more so than the Reaganites' broader avocation of overthrowing elected leftist governments. When contacted, he could not resist the opportunity to exploit his FAC experience and his covert operations familiarity, especially as a contractor to DEA. The offer appealed to his inner cowboy and he was happy to work for an organization that was independent of the CIA. At least no one could claim that his ex-wife helped him to get the assignment.

After reaching a contract with DEA, Frank and two similarly oriented entrepreneurs founded a company named Snow Angels, LLC, a name chosen because such angels are illusive, disappearing in sunlight as would all traces of their operation. The name might dovetail nicely with Operation Snowcap, DEA's cocaine eradication war in the late '80s. The company would have an office in New Orleans but be registered in Dominica, and its main assets were two Cessna A-37 Dragonflies, one T-41A aircraft financed through classified government sources, and partial ownership of a couple of old Hueys. They were not mercenaries, merely service providers—a distinction Orwell himself might well have appreciated.

The first assignment was in Bolivia, where they initially would work for Umopar, the Bolivian anti-drug police, taking on eradication and interdiction activities that were not politically acceptable for formal U.S. Army assistance programs or that conflicted with the complex double-game operations the CIA was playing with parallel suppression, sting operations, and shady arms deals, thanks to Oliver North. "A fine mess, you've gotten us into now, Ollie," was pretty much the Snow Angel motto. They would fly chancy missions in their small aircraft, easily mistaken by ill-coordinated friendlies for those used by the cartel, or in their old Hueys in dubious mechanical condition, or, worse still, choppers leased from Umopar. "Let's go someplace like Bolivia; let's *go* someplace like Bolivia." Damn, Frank loved that old movie, but he never could figure out whether he wanted to be more like Butch or Sundance. It didn't matter, really. If he were to put his life on the line again, Bolivia would be perfect. It was too late to grow up to be a real hero, so he might as well follow his fantasies.

Frank brought Lillian with him to La Paz for a year, then Medellín and Tingo María. She had a wonderful time in the colorful, chaotic cities. The tall, striking señorita with paler skin and shinier black hair than the native girls was a celebrity in every market, nightclub, and social gathering. As Don Henley might have sung, all she wanted to do was dance… and fake romance. She had largely lost her appetite for seduction now, eliciting interest was

184

sufficient. Still, Henley's music set a theme for the first three years of the marriage, insulation from the heat coming off the streets of La Paz, Dominica, New Orleans, the diverse lounges, air strips, and markets, the last gasp of the life beyond the pale before the boundaries of age pulled them back to civilization.

Passing fifty by the end of the decade, they eventually would settle in New Orleans and vacation in Dominica or Martinique, Frank for the most part beginning to allow young bucks to spray the crops and attack jungle camp sites, content to manage the operation, and to passably contribute to the maturation of his children, who gradually came to spend more time with them than with Inga. They left home shortly after turning eighteen, Frank's son to pursue a musician's life and his daughter to endure the sexism of the U.S. Air Force Academy, following in her father's footsteps without either his encouragement or disincentive.

Lillian was not as loved by either as much as she had hoped, their loyalties and time divided between her and Inga, but at least they didn't reject her with the decisiveness of her own daughters. That was more than enough. A full life involves both adventure and responsibility. She and Frank gave them adventure; Inga reserved that for herself, so she could handle the responsibility.

———

Although Frank was arguably the least essential of the Ward's senior staff, his departure had triggered a rapid disintegration of the lobbying firm. By early '84, Beth had followed him to become the chief financial officer of Frank's fledgling company, tendering her resignation to Barrington with enthusiasm. She had wanted to return to her native city for some time and her husband Tom had taken an investment banking position in New York. It was more convenient to split time between New York and New Orleans than New York and D.C., given that Frank would be in Bolivia or elsewhere more than half the time and she could perform much of her work in Manhattan. That was an irresistible combination, quite apart from her contempt for Barrington after his sexual overture.

She blew off a client campaign with Sam and preparation of Congressional testimony for Barrington and left on short notice.

Beth's departure greatly annoyed Barrington, who felt that her compensation fully excused any indiscretion on his part and was relying on her to supply the numbers underlying his testimony before Congressional committees and regulators. But Beth had no regrets. The unspoken grievance aside, she knew that Barrington would never give her any credit for the success of his testimony, no matter how thorough and convincing her calculations might be. Besides, when push came to shove, Ted would simply pull numbers out of his ass and Barrington would fly with them. It wouldn't be as convincing without her assistance, but Barrington wouldn't recognize any falling off and, if he failed to achieve his client's objectives, would blame some idiot in the client's legal department or outside counsel, not any weakness in his own presentation. Sam, stuck with a heavy workload, was stoic and said nothing.

Beth proved a competent financial officer, as Frank knew she would be, and she had ample time to pursue independent financial consulting opportunities and investments allocated from a nice nest egg accumulated over the years from her prior employment and severance packages. Frank had encouraged this, satisfied with perhaps 25 percent of her time being devoted to his company. Beth had burned her bridges with most of the men at the Ward, which Frank saw as a positive. Lillian and Beth held each other in mutual disdain so there was little social contact. In fact, the degree of interaction between Frank and Beth was remarkably limited for officers of the same company. That continued satisfactorily for some years.

By 1985, Ted had finally left for New York to pursue his dream to make it big in advertising with Burnham & Brown. Rebecca's father had died and her mother had moved to New York to live with a widowed sister, so it made a lot of sense to Ted. Rebecca could complain about him to her mother rather than Ben and Rachel, so he would continue to have a buffer, but wouldn't have to hear about his faults secondhand at work. Apart from that, the advertising firm still worked with some of Barrington's clients and Ted would keep in touch with his colleagues. Unlike Sam, Ted did not burn bridges or allow them to collapse through lack of maintenance. He would occasionally even have lunch with Beth.

By 1986, Sam had resigned, resuming his interrupted international career through a small group of privatization consultants contracted to USAID and international development banks. Inga had recommended him based on his confidential work for the Company when traveling with Fran. The new venture would come with a quid pro quo for continued reports "on the side," he knew. However, he'd grown to like the relationship, having shaken off the paranoia of Africa and Rome. He thought it was fun to play clandestine operative without the guns or cyanide pills, and he wondered how Inga could get away with paying him for his reports.

His contacts abroad, who were not explicitly told that he was an asset by Madam Inga, seemed to suspect that he was employed by the CIA or some sort of intelligence agency, so he knew that his sources were passing on public information or misleading insider data, motivated by personal or institutional disputes, all taking up real agency resources to verify. Still, they were willing to pay him. He loved the experience of working in many different cultures and political settings and much enjoyed his new life away from the Ward, whether it be mundane project work, his reporting to Inga as an adjunct to those projects or his continuing spousal travels with Fran.

Ben and Rafi remained with the old firm until 1989, uneasy as the prospects of merger or dissolution grew, leaving only when Barringer announced his plans to retire on his considerable savings accumulated over the last two decades. Ben obtained an appointment as vice president at another lobbying firm and Rafi pursued his interest in the new computing technology, co-founding a software development firm creating specialized applications layered over the new spreadsheet technology.

CHAPTER 17:

The Hermitage, 1987

I t was a cold interlude in the midst of a great thaw. Perestroika was underway, the beginning of market reforms in the Soviet Union, reforms that eventually would fail to meet the goal of making socialism work more efficiently, leading instead to regional political competition and the rapid disintegration of the union. Through summer and fall, however, the new policy of openness and transparency introduced by Mikhail Gorbachev appeared to bear fruit. Reagan had challenged the Soviet Union to take down the Berlin Wall without great protest on the Soviet side, leading to its destruction two years later. The two sides signed a missile reduction treaty at mid-year, followed by a half dozen more arms control agreements over the next decade. The Smithsonian, eager to take advantage of the new spirit of détente, negotiated exchange exhibits of each country's paintings from 1850 through World War I, symbols of a new spirit of understanding between the Soviets and the Americans and a Soviet concession that art and culture had existed before the ten days that shook the world in October 1917. In November, seventy years after that event, Chairman Gorbachev's wife, Raisa, opened the American half of the exchange in Moscow's Tretyakov Museum.

A few days after the opening in Moscow, Sam and Fran were sitting in a coffeehouse in Leningrad, taking refuge from the freezing cold and blowing snow and thinking that the invitation to a private tour of the Hermitage, part of the cultural exchanges associated with the exhibits, was not as great a dividend as they had imagined earlier. The Celsius and Fahrenheit scales converge at minus forty degrees and Sam was arguing that they might reach

189

convergence that very evening. It had been warm enough inside the museum, but the trek to the coffee shop, an impromptu stop on the way to their hotel, was miserable.

The cultural exchange had exceeded expectations thus far, at least for the Smithsonian contingency. A tour of the Kremlin and Lenin's tomb, nights at the Bolshoi and Kirov, visits to various palaces, orthodox churches and, of course, museums, all given an air of excitement that any trip behind the iron curtain conveyed in those days, customs officials searching pockets for any stray kopeks, severe-appearing guards everywhere, and manifestations of most of the spy movie clichés of Soviet paranoia, prejudices that you rejected at the outset of the journey, but were confirmed by your experience. It was a successful tour from which the Smithsonian would extract large donations from the liberal elite contributing to the exhibit. There were, however, other business aspects to the visit, as well.

Sam had another small assignment from Inga. While a good year in Soviet relations with the West, 1987 still was problematical in terms of USSR relations with the PRC. Although Chinese leaders publicly professed not to be concerned, China's Ministry of State Security, MSS, successor to the old CID, was not happy with the Soviet base established at Cam Ranh Bay in Vietnam, the Soviet Union's improved relations with North Korea, the presence of Soviet troops in Afghanistan and Mongolia, and large troop deployments in the Far East, along with nearly two hundred SS-20 intermediate-range ballistic missiles and one hundred nuclear-capable long-range bombers.

The Soviet Union enjoyed tactical and strategic nuclear superiority and exceeded China in terms of mobility, firepower, air power, and antiaircraft capability. While MSS reportedly did not consider a Soviet attack to be imminent or even remotely likely, military superiority created political leverage and relations were tense. As Inga explained to Sam, it was not in the interest of her superiors that glasnost alleviate these concerns; their continuation would place economic pressures on both countries and adulterate their political and military strength vis-à-vis the West. Sam was to make selective inquiries into ways to forestall Sino-Soviet détente. Most of his contacts would be in Moscow, and two in Leningrad.

One possibility for stirring the pot lay in rumors of Soviet Ministry of Defense and KGB interest in biological-pathogenic warfare, missile warheads, or clandestinely delivered devices laden with anthrax, weaponized smallpox, Marburg virus and microbial weapons with new properties of high virulence, improved stability, and new clinical syndromes. Of considerable concern to the West, these threats were even more troubling to China, with its vast exposed hinterland. Sam needn't take risks to uncover anything definitive. All he needed was just enough suggestive information to undermine Gorbachev's initiatives to moderate tensions with China.

Fran had no Russian language skills and need not be involved. In the meantime, she had her obligations for special projects. The exhibit exchange itself was under control, but there was more to be done. The less rigid ideology represented by glasnost and the financial stress on the Soviet economy provided opportunities for compromise and better prospects to appeal to individual egos to close deals that were not possible earlier under rigid state controls.

The preceding day and that morning had been a distraction for Sam, but not for Fran, as they had been given a thorough tour of the Hermitage holdings. The materials on exhibit were far outnumbered by those gathering dust in attics, underground facilities that had served as bunkers in the Great Patriotic War and special climate-controlled storage scattered across the vast building. Fran and Sam were guided through the museum by an elderly museum official who had served as an assistant to Joseph Orbeli, the famed director who had accomplished the evacuation of the museum treasures to Sverdlovsk in the Urals in 1941, just before the Nazis closed the ring around the city. Fran had explained to Sam that she was interested in an exchange that might tell the story of that heroic event, which required the labor of all levels of museum employees and volunteers from all walks of life in the city. He accompanied her to help provide historical perspective; an exhibit, if one proved feasible, might include items perhaps stored in attics since their return to the Hermitage, selected as much for the particular story of their rescue as for their intrinsic value.

Fran had not been aware of the extent that the general population had participated in the evacuation. After sorting out initial confusion over their guide's repeated reference to "Peter," which turned out to be a nickname for the old St. Petersburg and current shorthand for Leningrad, Fran grew even more excited with the story of the city's great collective triumph in the Hermitage evacuation. She arranged multiple meetings with people who had lived through those days or their descendants.

Sam found her idea interesting, but was also happy that she would be fully occupied while he pursued Inga's instructions. In addition, her inquiry, sanctioned by the authorities, would provide a convenient cover for him to poke around on his own at some of the spots that she visited. They would join prearranged tours of the Winter Palace and other cultural landmarks together, but would otherwise have ample time to pursue their separate objectives. Shortly after noon they had finished the Hermitage tour and trudged in the snow down Nevsky Prospect to find shelter from the cold and blustery winds.

Sitting in the café, warming up after the walk from the museum, Sam was having mixed feelings about the last two days. Although the tour was interesting, he would rather have been having conversations with leads at Leningrad State University, since Inga assumed that any clandestine bioweapons development in the region would likely have some affiliation with one of the university's faculties, perhaps chemistry, biology and soil studies, or medicine. He was eager to narrow the search. One of the Amazonian guards present in every exhibit room of the Hermitage had given him an envelope as Inga had promised, and perhaps that would be useful when he looked at it later.

In the meantime, the discussions of the evacuation of the Hermitage collections might uncover something useful. Sam was free to talk to Fran about his mission in generalities, so offered his opinion that glasnost surely would especially appeal to university faculty members and academics, like the museum types who offered their hospitality throughout the trip. He thought that violations of chemical and biological weapons treaties would especially trouble such people and they might well leak information on such activities if they existed.

Fran replied that Inga must have had him reading too many spy novels. Couldn't he see the national pride in the stories they had just been told? If anything, the educated elite in the university and museum worlds were more patriotic than the average Russian. They'd probably be less susceptible to cash inducements and bright enough to avoid scandals. Men are never bright enough to avoid scandals, he replied.

At about that time, the waitress came over to ask him if they wanted something besides coffee and he responded that a late lunch would be fine if they were still serving. "*Natürlich,*" she replied, "*Was möchten Sie essen?*" Sam realized she was speaking German. Although he was mostly from German stock – and looked it—his college German did not take him to the necessary next step. He took a deep breath. "*Meine Frau spricht...uh...fließend Italienisch und Französisch. Sprechen Sie...uh...nicht?*" A flurry of incomprehensible Italian ensued, followed by the best meal they had had in Russia. The standards weren't that high frankly, but it was very, very cold outside and the meal was hot. Actually, it was a nice fettuccine with puttanesca sauce. Who would have thought it?

Sam patted his stomach and began buttoning his coat to venture outside for their walk to the hotel. "What would I do without you?" he said to Fran.

"I have no idea," she replied.

The next day they found themselves in different faculties of Leningrad State University, he in Petergof, pursuing the names slipped to him by the museum guard, and she in the university's principal buildings on Vasilyevsky Island, the city's historic center situated just across the river from the Winter Palace.

It was at Faculty of Biology and Soil Studies' research center in Sergievka that he picked up his first rumor of potential value. Yersiniapestis, a strain of the plague virus, was said to be under study in a secure facility, supposedly a civilian facility requiring heavy security simply because of the nature of the subject matter, not because of military applications. His source claimed the laboratory was affiliated with an enterprise known as Biopreparat. The academic, perhaps lulled into talking freely by Sam's praise of the Hermitage tour and the great wartime evacuation, noted that yersiniapestis was used as a biological weapon in World War II, when a Japanese airplane flying over Chekiang Province, China released rice and wheat laden with rat fleas carrying the plague, killing well over a hundred—and perhaps a few thousand—people. With modern delivery systems, that number could be multiplied by more than a thousand. Of course, the Soviet Union would never engage in such terrorist exercise, the academic assured him. This, Sam thought, would be perfect for Inga's purpose. Given the prior use on their population, nothing would incense the Chinese more than the prospect of a plague outbreak, perhaps delivered in a fashion not detectable as deliberate.

The next day, Sam followed up with a Russian scientist referred to him by the prior day's source. That man noted that the mysterious Biopreparat had discovered that one could readily modify yersiniapestis genetically by inserting a plasmid containing the gene for myelin toxin. The design was simple and would be deeply disturbing to the Chinese. If doctors treated a patient diagnosed with pneumonic plague in normal fashion, the antibiotics would attack the plague cells, thereby releasing the plasmid coding for myelin toxin, which would cause paralysis, high blood pressure, irregular heartbeat, and death, a deadly one-two punch. Of course, the informant said, the research was only for defensive purposes, but for Madam Inga's needs it didn't matter, even if there was a remote chance this were true or if the whole story was completely wrong. Inga wanted to poison Sino-Soviet relations, not the human organism.

Sam discussed his findings with Fran during another walk in the cold, assuming that there was every prospect that their hotel room had been bugged. She was interested and supportive of his work as always, but more nervous about his involvement with the nasty world of biological warfare than she had been with the Vatican-Mafia nexus in Rome. She pleaded with him to contact Inga and see if he had done enough on this assignment before proceeding further. He agreed. His next steps would be in Moscow

194

anyway, so he could reach her through the embassy and confirm that it was absolutely necessary before he did anything more.

On Sam's return to Moscow, a visit to the American Embassy made possible a secure transmission of his findings. They again pleased Inga, who quickly assured him that he had done enough. It was almost as though she anticipated the transmission. Sometimes, he thought, he was only a citation to Inga's fully formed opinions, a superfluous footnote. This was one of those times.

In her Langley offices, Herminia J. C. Ng pored over Sam's reports, which were concise, objective, and well written, as always. The latter didn't mean much as far as intelligence value was concerned, but so many assets were functionally illiterate that Sam's reports were always a pleasure to read and of great help in getting the attention of her superiors. If only Frank had been able to write decently, he might still be affiliated with the Company and they might still be married. Ah, well... water over the dam.

MS. HJC NG. NCS HUMINT, as the nameplate on her desk read, was already well aware of the existence of the Soviet Ministry of Defense Biopreparat program and its Institute of Ultra-Pure Biochemical Preparations; there was nothing new in Sam's report, really. However, Sam had found some new sources for information already known and that was of some significance. It meant that she could route information to China's Ministry of State Security through her contacts in Macao without giving up the identities of more important CIA assets. It was better that the Chinese be panicked by rumor mongers on the fringes of bio-weapons development, who might themselves have exaggerated fears of capabilities and potential uses, than give up the identities of current or potential assets within the program who were truly knowledgeable. She certainly would not want the Chinese competing with the Company's own operatives for the attentions of potential defectors or double agents like Pasechnik or Alibekov. Sometimes low grade information is better than high grade information. On the secure line with Sam, Madam Inga could hardly contain her excitement over the large pile of horse manure she could now drop on MSS, thanks to Sam's inquiries. She practically purred with pleasure.

CHAPTER 18:

New York, 1990

Liberated from commitments to particular products or agendas, Ted rapidly made his mark on the advertising business.
He advanced from the bottom rung at Burnham & Brown
to senior levels in less than five years, rising through what most
of his colleagues and comparisons considered lucky breaks, yet
reflecting a powerful psychic connection to the inner logic of
American enterprise. Producing fewer and fewer tangible products in facilities located anywhere near company headquarters
where marketing decisions were made, most large companies
instead controlled intellectual property claims on diverse goods
and services produced in remote locations, largely abroad. Ted
sensed that, aside from the geek elite in Silicon Valley and a few
other boutique enterprises, mainstream corporate management's
pride in their products and services was increasingly disconnected
from any understanding of how they functioned or were produced. This freed the advertising executive to be more creative,
unfettered by the pedestrian outlook of old-school managers who
walked the shop floor and took pride in particular specifications
and quality standards that customers could care less about, or at
least those customers whose buying decisions could be influenced
by a thirty second TV spot. Put another way, both buyer and seller
were searching to find the merit of the product, making the advertisement at least the equal of the product in terms of value added.
The advertisement had become, in a sense, a part of the product
itself.

Ted's epiphany came in observing an IBM ad campaign based
around wide shots of quiet woodland scenes evoking Thoreau-like

contemplation and the slogan, "Not just data. Reality." At the time, IBM was struggling against innovative competitors that were taking advantage of its lack of market responsiveness. The company was embracing a campaign that did not refute its stodgy image through any defense of its products and services, but rather asserted that, in some indefinable ethereal way, IBM might make you, your perception or the world more "real." IBM was marketing reality, and Ted got it. If IBM could pour millions of dollars into Zen-based advertising, there must be thousands of companies that had lost touch with what they were doing and could be convinced that they needed to appeal to the customers' spiritual awakening, to a realization that the purchasing decision would be a self-actualization of their inner needs. A positive response to the advertisement would be a fulfillment of the impulse to convert oneself into what one is capable of being; it would help restore the consumer to the natural order of things.

It sounded like bullshit, Ted admitted, but IBM did buy off on that Zen-like message and maybe its customers also did to some indefinable extent, even though there was less content to the campaign than the first line of your average haiku. In the end, Ted concluded, the appeal of Zen and dharma is to allow the adherent to achieve a state of comfort and self-satisfaction and that state is not attainable through the complications of analysis, but through the simplicity of synthesis. The simplicity of synthesis. He would develop his campaigns around this realization and the knowledge that comfort and self-realization stem from three sources: sexual satisfaction, the confidence of familiarity, and a return to the verities of childhood, before you began to realize that the world is so exasperatingly complicated. His campaigns would employ physically attractive, semi-clothed models, familiar images and sounds, mostly music from a previous decade, and childhood references that bypassed the sophomoric for what impressed you in kindergarten. At first blush, the combination of sex, rock and roll, and potty-mouth humor might not sound particularly spiritual, but that's merely a confusion of the spiritual and the profound. Spirituality is not progression to a higher state, but regression to elemental perception.

Guys understand that. Take that, you New Age morons.

Some people laughed at Ted and disparaged his approach, but he sold the ads anyway and the ads may have helped to sell the product. Ted never forgot that the purpose of advertising is not entertainment for its own sake but to entice people and leave them feeling unfulfilled; to create a state of temptation that only can only be satiated by purchase of the product. That's how Ted and others like him took a small population suffering from clinical impotency and created a nation of fifty million chronically limp dicks yearning to soak in one of the twin bathtubs alongside some hot, nude chick.

All things considered, 1990 was a good year. The Soviet Union had fallen apart, Germany reunited, and Nelson Mandela was freed. These occurrences unfettered Ted's liberal sensibilities and created potential commercial opportunities for his clients. The Rolling Stones seemed to be on tour everywhere, contributing to a nice wave of nostalgia, Ted's stock in trade. On the other hand, Milli Vanilli was caught lip-syncing, Céline Dion started singing in English, and "We Didn't Start the Fire" overtook "Sounds of Silence" as the apex of boomer self-denial of responsibility for anything.

Ted was now approaching fifty and his beloved sons were twenty-five and nineteen, so he spent a lot of time at home with Rebecca, who had become increasingly frail since her mother died and more demanding of him in terms of physical and psychological assistance. She was also decreasingly critical of his disabilities as a human being. He was never sure whether she had just given up on his potential for reform, had concluded that he was a better person than he had been in the '70s, or had just become more tolerant. He went through the motions of being more attentive to her religious convictions, attending synagogue with her and honoring the holidays, but at the same time buffered his boys from her demands in that area and they grew up decidedly secular. Ted still believed that the Duke didn't dance and he certainly wasn't going to confuse his children on that fundamental truth.

People accused Ted of being a cynic, but you are not a cynic if those around you are in fact ill-motivated, untrustworthy, and unvirtuous, and you just happen to be a good observer. Ted was not scornful of the behavior he observed in the present, and he was, in appropriate measure, optimistic about the future. That a person can't be trusted doesn't mean that they're incapable of good things. On that basis, Ted still kept in touch with the Ward alumni; with Sam despite his perpetual state of distraction, with Ben and Rachel for his wife's sake, with Rafi, with Frank, somewhat resentfully, even with Beth. Of course, an optimistic outlook does not account for everything. In Beth's case, it didn't hurt that her husband Tom had risen to a moderately important position with Shearson Lehman Hutton, where Ted's eldest son sought employment. Shortly before Shearson Lehman shed the Hutton name in 1990, Ted Jr. was hired and Ted invited Tom and Beth to dinner at the newly opened Tribeca Grill as a thank you. Beth had spent over half of her time in the city since leaving the Ward in the mid-'80s, anyway, so he wasn't surprised that she was able to join Tom and him for dinner, but the revelation that she had abandoned Frank's firm in New Orleans took him aback. He had spoken with Frank by phone the week before and he had said only that the firm was doing well and that he and Lillian were enjoying the New Orleans life style and cutting back some on touring the drug capitals of Latin America. After asking Frank to say hello to Lillian, he'd inquired about Beth, but Frank was in the middle of some Bolivian war story and never replied before he begged off to take another call.

According to Beth, Frank's firm Snow Angels was undergoing a DEA-required audit when she had uncovered certain irregularities with the Dominica-based corporation improperly sheltering income. Beth was not going to get involved in any money-laundering scheme, so she had reported the problem to both the drug and tax agencies. That resulted in the suspension of Frank's firm for six months while undergoing the IRS investigation. DEA eventually reinstated Snow Angels with IRS imposing no additional tax obligations for the shareholders, but the firm lost over three million in contracts while under the suspension. Under those circumstances,

Beth was obliged to resign and abandoned New Orleans for New York, leaving behind many friends from her church choir and the several charities in which she was active. She blamed Frank for the dubious bookkeeping that compelled her departure, flaws which she suspected that DEA later covered up in an equally dubious manner. In benevolent moments, she would forgive Frank for simply being caught up in a corrupt system operating outside of acceptable rules. If he understood that error in judgment, they would not have a problem.

Frank didn't give a damn what Beth thought. He blamed her for the loss of business. In his profession, narcs were not respected, and he wrote her off as he would any snitch that had outlasted his or her value. Remembering Beth's phone calls after Monday Night Football and the Fourth on the mall, Ted felt a twinge of sympathy for Frank. Beth was a piece of work.

Wherever the blame lay, Beth moved on, expecting never to see Frank again, satisfied that she had done the right thing and even more convinced that men—with the exception of Tom—would all inevitably prove dishonest or incompetent. She joined the Boston Company, a Shearson investment management subsidiary catering to pension plans, endowments, intermediaries, and mutual fund shareholders. Her role was to help the business recover from a massive income-underreporting scandal and help prepare the unit for spin-off or sale. Beth had again landed on her feet, and was now independently wealthy, having bailed out of the market a week before Black Monday on rumors of Congress taking away tax advantages for leveraged buyouts, then jumping back in at the bottom of the crash. Virtue is its own reward and timing the greatest of virtues.

Ted was mildly annoyed by Beth's success, but amused by the fact that she had gotten so wealthy simply by knowing when to fold, when to cut and run. Hit the road, Jack; she could've done backup for Ray any day. Still, Beth's expertise at timing markets and relationships didn't seem to require nearly as much talent as did his own profession. She would never have been able to appreciate that images of bikini mud wrestling would actually improve the perceived taste of light beer.

Shortly after their meeting, Ben and Rachel arrived in town to visit relatives and Rebecca. They had not changed much over the last decade; they were still good citizens, regulars at synagogue, comfortable but not wealthy, as proud as Ted of their now-adult children, nominally liberal in the fashion of suburbanites who had paid off their mortgages and were obliged to hire tax attorneys to shelter income.

Ward Barrington had died of a heart attack weeks earlier and only they and Rafi had attended the services. Ted, who could not leave Rebecca that week due to her ill health, had sent white lilies, and Beth had sent a weird arrangement of basil, coriander, and orange lilies that looked like something in a Haitian voodoo shop. Ben was mystified and had hidden it behind the vase of roses he and Rachel had purchased. Frank and Sam were apparently both in some godforsaken places around the world and did not attend or, as far as he knew, send anything. It was a sparse turnout, but Barrington was a private man whose children were grown and whose wife had died even before the lobbying firm was established. As far as Ben knew, he was the only member of the firm Barrington had ever invited to his house, probably because he had known the family before the wife died. Ben recalled that one evening each year, before bonuses were awarded, they would have cognac in his library and discuss each employee's performance; then Barrington would reminisce about his time with Patton in Europe.

"Barrington was in the army with Patton?" Ted's younger son, David, had joined the army in an act of rebellion and was now with the First Cavalry Division awaiting deployment to Kuwait. Ted was hoping Iraq would withdraw before that happened, but now had an even greater interest in military affairs than he had had in the '60s, when he was wondering whether his deferment would hold up.

"Hard to imagine, isn't it? Yes, he was a grunt, like Rafi in Vietnam. I think that probably had something to do with Rafi's hire in the first place. Rafi was always a little different from the rest of us, the MAC among all us PCs." Well, if Rafi could survive Vietnam, David should be able to survive Kuwait or Iraq or whatever came about. Ted nodded appreciatively, still coming to terms with his son buying off on "be all you can be," even though it had a distinct resemblance to "not just data, reality" – "not just war, self-esteem;" simplicity in synthesis or whatever.

Thinking it best to back off war talk, Ben switched topics, telling Ted that Rafi's roommate had died. They had shared an apartment, which they described as a bachelor pad, in Alexandria back in the '70s and '80s and periodically had joked about entertaining ladies, but there was little evidence to support that. When Rafi went to seek his high-tech fortune in California, the friend had gone with him. After his friend's death, Rafi sold their house and moved into a condo in Cupertino, but planned to retire in Virginia, where he had relatives and old friends. He had more money than he knew what to do with, especially since he was not in great health; Ben and Rachel had had to look after him quite a bit at Barrington's funeral.

Ben didn't know what the roommate had died of, but Ted could guess. And that was as far as the discussion went, or ever had gone. Everyone always avoided discussing Rafi's private life, just as he desired. Even Beth left Rafi's personal life alone. He may not have been black enough to be in the civil rights movement, but she never questioned his masculinity. Of course, being masculine was not exactly one of the virtues in Beth's eyes, so she was happy to leave him in the company of heterosexuals or whatever. It made no difference to her, the gender's fatal flaws being in the mind, not other organs.

Ben and Rachel managed to revive Rebecca for several hours, so Ted had welcomed their visit. They were boring and predictable, but that's not always a bad thing. They said the right things about Ted Jr.'s bright prospects and their faith that David would get through the mess in the Gulf in one piece; they would prove to be right in both cases.

CHAPTER 19:

Riverside, 1997

Ari had returned from Europe to teach in the classical studies program at the University of California Riverside, part of the ten-campus University of California system. Triana, who had just turned fourteen, was in full rebellion mode. Even with four years of high school ahead of her, she already was arguing with her mother about colleges. Triana was campaigning to attend UCLA or USC with a drama focus, as she desired a career in the movies, television, or theater, which Ari detested as artifice. Ari argued that Triana should be a traditional literature major, preferably somewhere on the East Coast. Triana had demonstrated exceptional writing ability as early as the fourth grade. Writing books, plays, or scripts was something Ari could understand and honor, but not acting, not being a puppet for someone else's intellect.

The arguments over Triana's college and career choices, however, were not solely about those subjects. Much like inserting the point of a knife under a jar lid probing a little here and a little there, so that with maybe a tap on top or emersion in hot water, a tightly compressed seal would move just a little and eventually open, Triana had adopted the dispute as a mechanism to force her mother to treat her as an adult. After all, a concession won about college might then compel her mother to reveal more about her heritage, about her grandparents and how they came to America, about Ari herself, and, especially, about Triana's father.

Aside from her mother, the only relative Triana had ever met was her grandmother, who was now confined to a nursing home and unaware of her surroundings, reeking of urine and excrement despite the best efforts of the nursing home to keep her clean. Lingering in the final stages of dementia, priorities had shifted from any hope of patient improvement to palliative care for the relief of pain, symptoms, and emotional stress, requiring twenty-four-hour care seven days a week. Despite Ari's lack of love for the shell of a woman, she had attempted to provide that care herself with only a part-time nurse until 1995, when the burden became unbearable. She was compelled at that point to enter her mother into the nursing home. By that time the old woman was almost always drowsy and unaware of her surroundings, knew no one, was wholly uninterested in eating, and had little bladder or bowel control. She never spoke except for obscenities uttered occasionally through the summer of that year, when she stopped speaking altogether. The angry glare in her eyes, which may have signaled something that remained inside her, faded a few months later.

Ari, herself now over sixty, visited regularly, paid not only the facility's base fees but also any supplemental care that might provide comfort, inquired regularly about options, and did all of the things a loving daughter would do, as if she were such a daughter. She was not, but once she had decided that providing the best care for the woman was the proper, ethical course, her determination was unshakable. It didn't matter that her salary was modest, that less expensive institutions were available, that her efforts were despised somewhere within her mother's mental cocoon, if they were detected at all. There was a right and wrong of it, and that was all that mattered.

In 1997, the fetid fishwife comprising the remains of Ari's mother finally expired, well beyond the date than any benign supreme being would have mandated. Her death provided long-overdue relief to Ari, but left Triana bereft of the last trace of her heritage. Ari did not want to talk about herself, her feelings about her mother, or her terror that she would die in the same fashion. Faced with this silence, Triana eventually concluded that she did not wish to know any of the details of her mother's life and would not ask. The silence could only mean terrible secrets, scandals, moral failures, veniality, transgressions, personal and family curses, perhaps passing through generations. She was having enough trouble with her mother in the here and now, without looking back into some sordid past.

And yet the point of the knife remained under the edge of the jar lid, whether the purpose of removing the lid had been lost or not. They argued daily, and the confrontations never went anywhere; it was difficult to ascertain what the harsh words were all about, if for no other reason than it being unclear to those who uttered them. Ari meticulously declined to express any emotional distress over her daughter's academic missteps or other adolescent mistakes; she would not become her mother. Triana did not appreciate that self-control and could not know its causes. To her, Ari seemed cold. It was like coming home from school only to have another teacher at home, going through the paces of some curriculum that had nothing to do with her. Ari wasn't a harsh teacher or unfair in her evaluations, but was objective and unemotional to a fault. She was supposed to be a *mother* for Christ's sake. The difference between home and school, of course, was that Triana could shout at her mother, roll her eyes to the sky, say "I hate you," and walk out of the house. It was, in other words, a shadow dance, a perfectly normal mother-daughter relationship, only more so.

Ari's difficulties in coping with her daughter were compounded by her promises to herself and to Frank. She wanted to reveal his name and let him see her daughter if he so chose, but when she tracked him down and approached him on the subject, he had not wanted to do so, he said, until his children had come of age. But then, nearly three years ago, his twins had turned twenty-one and Frank asked for more time. That was annoying; she tried to contact Sam and, failing to reach him, contacted Ted instead. Ari had made them co-godfathers after Triana was born and they had responded with small birthday gifts each year. Now the time had come that they could do something more.

On taking Ari's call, Ted made two decisions: first, he would approach Sam to see if he could persuade Frank to allow Ari to reveal his name to her daughter, and second, he would arrange for Ari and her daughter to get access to the Internet, so that he needn't be an intermediary on such awkward matters. By then, e-mail had become simple enough for anyone to use. Ari was, he was sure, the opposite of a computer geek and he doubted that her daughter would be much more adept, but he believed the new AOL release would overcome any reluctance. Sam and Frank had embraced e-mail early on, so Ari and her daughter could reach them easily, if Frank assented. So, Ted concluded, his next birthday gift to Triana would be the latest model Dell Pentium II with AOL and the most current Microsoft operating system pre-installed.

Ted next composed an e-mail to Sam marked urgent, explaining the situation, asking if he would pitch in on the birthday gift to Triana as usual, appealing to him to find out what was up with Frank, and attaching an advertisement for the computer he had in mind and four pictures of his sons—Ted Jr. standing with a group of eight suits from some company ringing the opening bell on Wall Street, and David in his major's uniform earned in the years since Desert Storm.

A day later Ted received a polite reply, bearing the words "you stupid motherfucker" in the subject line. Apparently the download had taken seven hours on the dial-up line in Almaty, Kazakhstan, with a usage charge of $375. Sam was inexplicably unimpressed with pictures of a PC and Ted's bell-ringing, ribbon-laden sons whom he hadn't seen in over ten years. Aside from his typical male disinterest in other guys' kids, he had Fran's four children, who had occupied more than enough of Sam's time and patience, to the extent that he had lost any inclination to have children of his own, which was fine with Fran.

Sam made an exception, however, for the goddaughter he shared with Ted. Like Ted, he had never seen her in person, but he knew that she meant everything to Ari, despite the war of attrition between mother and daughter, or maybe even because of it. Raising a daughter hadn't been easy, but it certainly cut back on the time that Ari would have devoted to self-inspection. So, yes, Sam would go in on the birthday present with Ted; in fact, he suggested two computers because it was foolish to think Triana would share use of a single computer with her mother. They could make the second one a laptop, with a docking station, monitor, keyboard, and all the trimmings, and Triana could eventually take it to college.

He also agreed to e-mail Frank. He suspected that Frank's reluctance to acknowledge his daughter had nothing to do with his children or with his ex-wife and everything to do with Lillian. Frank was dedicated to making Lillian feel that he was dedicated to her only, to making her feel whole after her difficult life. Sam honored that, and so should Ted if he cared as much about Lillian as he said he did. But Frank needed to honor Ari and his daughter as well and Sam would make sure that he did. Ari, Sam knew, would never contact Lillian and he was sure the same would be true for Triana.

Ted was relieved. Calling on Frank's better nature to contact his daughter was the right thing to do, but he wanted nothing to do with it directly. Sam obviously understood why.

Sam agonized all day over his note to Frank, but he finally pushed the "send" button and dispatched the note, explaining that Triana's desire to know him had become a bone of contention with her mother and that it would be a major favor to everyone if he could let Ari know that it was all right to reveal his name and some personal history, even if not where he was now or how he could be contacted. Frank could send the e-mail through him so it would be untraceable. Sam had edited his document several times, replacing "Triana" with "your daughter" and laying on other guilt-inducing touches wherever possible.

It was almost a week before Frank replied. And when he did, his response was a little like a treaty of surrender. Yes, he would allow Ari to give Triana his name, but he didn't want his whereabouts revealed and he would forward his e-mails through Sam. He attached a general description of his life as he approached sixty and said that Sam could edit it if he wanted to do so.

The note was a disaster, poorly written with innumerable typos, describing events so incomprehensibly that Sam could barely recognize them, despite having lived through many of the incidents with Frank. It also contained much too much irrelevant vitriol concerning Inga and an especially lame fictional description of how he and Ari got together. It was obviously composed with the aid of a fifth of Jack, requiring a full week of rewriting before Sam was satisfied with the product and sent it to Ari. The end result read well, he thought, at least well enough to prevent Ari from being ashamed that she had slept with the man fifteen years ago and Triana from getting the first impression that her father was a total alcoholic and misogynist.

In the revised note, Frank came off as sort of a gallant hero of both Isan and the drug wars, a sensitive man whose affection for Triana's mother was only curtailed by commitments to his one true love. He was an honest man, a loving father who would do the right thing by the daughter he did not deserve, and by a twist of fate was doomed never to see.

One thing in Frank's original draft did touch Sam almost to the point of tears, and that was his description of how Ari's advice had helped him to accept Lillian for who she really was and how doing so had changed his and her life for the better. He felt that way himself about Ari's advice regarding Fran, and he'd heard Ted say much the same thing concerning Rebecca, despite his problems with her. It made him proud to call Frank a friend and even prouder to value Ari so highly. He didn't do much with that section of Frank's letter before he sent it off, a copy by regular mail with a note indicating that an e-mail attachment would follow when she set up an e-mail address on the computers they had sent her.

Ari took her some time to work up the courage to tell Triana. When she did a month later, Triana wrote to Sam under the AOL screen name "trianamiller," asking for the electronic version of the note. Sam replied with the attachments and once or twice a year thereafter would find something from that address in his in-box.

Ari was grateful for the communication from Frank, and within a couple of weeks had relayed her thanks to him through Sam with the screen name "Ariadnexxx." She was happy that Triana now knew his name and thanked him profusely, not mentioning that the revelation had added yet another dimension to the mother-daughter disputes based around innumerable "what-if" scenarios of what might have happened if Ari had done things differently over the last two decades.

Triana accused her mother of coming to a fork in the road and then wandering off aimlessly into the underbrush. Triana was proud of her sarcastic little homage to Robert Frost until her mother responded, "What the *fork?* There was no fork, it was all woods! No path, more traveled or less. What do you think you are, a guide dog? Going to show your mother the right path, are you? At least I brought you to where there are some paths. You'll show me the way to grandma's house, all right."

Triana marched off to her room and began searching on AltaVista to find Frank Miller. After several false leads, she finally located Snow Angels, LLC, based in Dominica and New Orleans. It fit with the information her father had sent a few weeks ago. She started typing an e-mail. "Hi Dad," she began.

CHAPTER 20:

NYC/Kampala/D.C., 2001

The turn of the century was not the best of times, it was not the worst of times; it, more or less, just sucked. On the positive side, computers kept working after 11:59 p.m. on December 31, 1999. That was good news for the faint of heart in the high-tech world, but the attention given to coding might well have been placed elsewhere. The so-called "dot-com bubble" broke in early 2000 with the NASDAQ collapse, precipitating Rafi's retirement from the software giant that had bought out his company back in the late '80s. Economic growth slid to nothing, driving Beth to restructure her portfolio and Ted to focus his marketing efforts on prescription drugs, which were always countercyclical.

The focus of anti-drug efforts shifted from cocaine production in Bolivia and Colombia to methamphetamine production in your neighbor's rec room, undermining Frank's modest enterprise. A political malaise equal to the last year of the Carter Administration accompanied the economic downturn. Too much information over Clinton's scandal and Gore's fear of its potential impact undermined the unity of the Democratic presidential campaign, leading to the Florida debacle and the ultimate appointment of Bush as president by five conservative members of the Supreme Court. That was Ted's interpretation, anyway. He didn't think dancing to the Macarena at the convention had helped much either.

Then al-Qaeda brought down the Twin Towers of the World Trade Center and things did get worse, much worse. Beth and Tom, as well as Ted and his sons, frequently did business at the Twin Towers. Ted especially liked to entertain clients at the Greatest Bar on Earth or Wild Blue on top of the North Tower. They all knew staff members who died and considered themselves fortunate not to have been there. They might not have been so lucky if the attack had come later in the day.

As with all great disasters, the events of September 11 triggered diverse reactions. Beth devoted more time to her church, grew more nostalgic about New Orleans and vowed to return there. Tom began to worry about his mortality, devoted less time to work, and sought unsuccessfully to engage Beth in simple leisure activities. Ted and his boys adopted the stiff upper lip of stalwart New Yorkers to the extent that Ted almost forgot that he was a Red Sox fan. Rebecca fell into a deep depression that Ted could not curtail.

Those from the Ward who lived outside of New York were affected as strongly. Ben and Rachel devoted themselves to Jewish charities for the victims. Sam and Frank each threw themselves into their work with renewed energy, which was their way of being patriotic. Fran began turning down international exchange assignments to devote more time to her several grandchildren. Lillian cut back on her visits to beauty parlors and spas, bought a puppy, and with canine assistance significantly reduced the size of her shoe collection. Ari and Triana declared a truce that lasted at least two weeks. Rafi had a stroke, and with the help of Ben and Rachel moved to an assisted-living facility in northern Virginia.

Sam was in Kampala in the November following the attacks, completing an assignment Inga had set up through the World Bank, while Fran was spending time back in the United States with her youngest daughter and her two children. Inga had asked Sam to investigate rumors of Chinese interest in building a railway line out of South Sudan to export oil and minerals via Mombasa or a new port in northern Kenya. The work had been going well, but an outbreak of Ebola in northern Uganda and an upsurge in the Lord's Resistance Army's insurgency against the Ugandan government disrupted the mission.

The Chinese threat, if one could call it that, was long term and Inga had no problem postponing the assignment, but Sam was stuck at the Sheraton for an additional three days due to a massive airline screw-up. The trip had been one long headache, and was made even more painful by the hotel dining area's insistence on hosting constant performances by the worst female lounge singer in existence. An entertainer from the Philippines, the girl knew about five songs, headed by a particularly grating "Smooth Operator," part of a mix that seemed to also include only "I Will Survive," "You Light Up My Life," "I Did it My Way," and (as she sang it) "The Boy from Ipanema." She was on her second or third cycle of these tunes as about forty guests waited in the lobby for a rumored airline pickup in the next hour.

After forty-five minutes or so, the hotel concierge announced that there would be no flight for at least another four hours, prompting a dispersal of the crowd to public areas of the hotel, the management having rebooked the rooms of the departing crowd. An attractive woman in her early thirties announced that she was off to see if the Swiss instructor in the exercise room would like to get laid (Generation X, bless her heart), a cluster of guys headed for the big screen TV in the bar to look for a football match, and a mixed group of businessmen and vacationing families settled in for a Jean Claude van Damme festival on the movie channel in the breakfast room.

Sam, with time to kill, decided at last to call Ted, who had sent him an e-mail that he wanted to discuss something important, but only over the phone. Cell phone service had arrived in Uganda and he was able to go off to a far corner of the patio, far away from the singer, to make the call. He reached Ted at breakfast. It was the first time they had talked since the Ari crisis four years before, though Ted had been meticulous in sending annual New Year letters, two-thirds of which detailed his sons' accomplishments. He feared the conversation would have something to do with one of Ted's sons. Perhaps it was an offer to get in on the ground floor of some exotic financial deal or maybe his help was being sought to work out an issue with the US Embassy in Lebanon. Ted's youngest son was trying to get a visa for a girlfriend he had met in Kuwait, now studying at the American University of Beirut. Ted always believed that Sam had infinitely more influence in such places than he actually had.

To Sam's surprise, the call was about Ari, or rather Ari's daughter, Triana. After their intervention in '97, Ted had exchanged e-mails with Ari, who planned to return soon to her native Greece to retire. Triana, however, was now eighteen and applied to the University of Southern California; she hoped to attend the School of Theater there. She was accepted, but Ari had managed her money badly, having had no interest in such mundane matters, and was afraid she could only afford junior college. She had consulted Ted to help her investigate what was possible for her to manage through student loans and it didn't look promising, not for a drama degree at Southern Cal. Ari would never accept assistance from him or Sam, but Ted had an idea.

Ted was willing to help and knew Sam would, too, but it would have to come through Frank. Ari was aware that Triana had reached out to Frank, and suspected that it was to a much greater extent that her daughter was willing to reveal to her. Naturally, Ari had mixed feelings about that, but as far as she could tell Frank had been careful not to undercut her parental authority and, in fact, seemed to consistently support her. She was grateful for that. If Frank would assume responsibility for the financing, she might accept it, reluctantly to be sure, but he had the leverage of being the father. If Frank would just agree to be the front man, they should collectively be able to cover the annual forty-thousand-dollar tuition. Perhaps Sam could give Frank a call and bring him around. "After all, we all know you're some kind of secret agent, so you should be able to pull this off easily."

Sam stood silently for a minute, with Ted twice asking if he was still there. Finally he replied, "I'll think about what I can do on the plane and you can mull it over with Rebecca if you want. I don't know where Frank is at the moment and he dropped his AOL account, but I can get in touch with him through his ex-wife. That'll get his attention"

"Rebecca is dead, Sam. That is the other reason why I called." Again, the line fell silent; the discordant strains of "you give me hope to carry on" filtered through the atmosphere and satellite relays. Ted winced and then had to laugh. "Are you being tortured?" Ted offered his condolences and accepted Sam's for Rebecca, outlining the funeral arrangements that would take place in Boston should Sam wish to attend after he returned from his trip. Sam said he'd be there; then the call was dropped.

Late in the afternoon, the airline bus finally arrived and took the passengers off to Entebbe. The flight home was difficult, with a long layover and painful new security procedures at Heathrow. Inga had him traveling coach and flying U.S. carriers due to recent budget cuts. The leg room was minimal, the plane old, the flight attendants older, the in-flight meal tasting older than that and the in-flight movies were *Meet the Parents* on the first leg and *Crocodile Dundee in Los Angeles* on the second. Surviving the flight on wine miniatures and peanut substitutes, or whatever they call those little bags of chemistry experiments with sesame toasted flour products, Sam was beginning to think that, having turned sixty, he was too old for all this.

Upon his return home, Sam called Inga, got Frank's "coordinates," the new term for contact information, and called his cell phone. He was somewhere in the Caribbean with Lillian, and even put her on the line for a minute. He sounded relaxed. Sam broached the subject of Triana's tuition at USC, anticipating immediate rejection. It appeared, however, that Frank had slowly developed a close relationship with Triana, through a frequency of e-mail conversations with her, that Ari could not have imagined. He was quite aware of the financial burden that threatened Triana's education. In fact, at about the same time that Ari was frantically relaying her dilemma to Ted, Frank already had told Triana that he would solve the problem. Ted and Sam could pitch in if they wanted, but it wasn't necessary. He eventually agreed that he would pay eighty percent of Triana's tuition and room and board, with Ted and Sam each covering ten percent and enabling Ari to cover the incidentals and offset the fees as she was able. He had arranged to see Triana with Ari and had already made his flight reservations to Los Angeles. He planned to drive to Riverside with his fatherly demands. It would be awkward, but he was sure Ari would assent to Triana's desires.

———

After Sam arrived in Boston with Fran, he relayed Frank's plans to Ted, brightening an otherwise somber day. Ted appeared totally grief-stricken, far beyond Sam's expectations. For all of the troubles they had experienced twenty-five years earlier, he and Rebecca had come to some sort of resolution somewhere along the way.

On returning home from the funeral, Fran asked Sam if he was finally ready to retire from his surreptitious work for Inga. It had been all right for him to do amateur spy work when he accompanied her on Smithsonian trips and she knew he was OK, but she was getting more and more nervous about him taking on potentially dangerous assignments under the cover of flimsy privatization projects that seldom seemed to have any results. Eventually someone would see through the pretext and he might find himself in trouble; besides, he was getting older. There's a reason why Hollywood doesn't make many spy movies about guys in their sixties bumming around places like Sudan. Well, there was Harrison Ford, but he had stand-ins; Sam didn't. She would be fine with him taking legitimate consulting jobs, but she really wanted him to stop being an asset for Langley.

Sam had enjoyed doing the occasional reports for Inga as well as the regular work he did with a small consulting group, but he was finally ready to stop. He agreed.

"Great," she replied, "Then I think it is time to have the house thoroughly cleaned."

Sam had no idea what she was talking about since they had a monthly maid service come by and Fran was always happy with the results, but she must have had something special in mind. She made an appointment for a week from the following Thursday and suggested that he make plans for that day. Sam agreed, but when the day arrived, he wasn't feeling well, having pulled a muscle doing yard work the preceding afternoon. She agreed that it would be all right if he stayed home, a bit reluctantly, he thought. At precisely ten o'clock Fran went to the window and announced that the cleaners had arrived and told Sam just to sit in his chair by the desk and stay out of the way.

A van appeared in the driveway; it was black with tinted windows and an odd antenna on the roof. Four large men in dark suits got out, with no cleaning supplies in sight. Fran greeted the men and a few minutes passed as they reviewed papers and IDs. Three men then came in while one remained at the door, talking on the wireless Bluetooth connection to his cell, his right hand gripping something in his coat pocket, his eyes scanning the road. The three who entered scattered without saying a single word, one carrying a device looking something like a metal detector that he ran across every surface of each room, one viewing each of the three computers in the house, copying the hard drives to a portable drive, inspecting certain flash drives identified by Fran, and then taking Fran's laptop and replacing it with one from his briefcase, and the third pulling something from one of Fran's closets, then disassembling the living room table from its pedestal base. From the base he pulled a large bundle of cash that he simply handed to Fran, along with a colorful stack of passports of various countries. Placing them on the far end of the desk from Sam, he picked each up in turn, holding the document so that he alone could see the personal information page and comparing that information to a checklist placed on the desk, mouthing a name for each that he recorded.

The last of the stack, Sam could see, was a Republic of Ireland passport, with *Éire* clearly visible on the reddish-brown cover. The man, obviously relieved that all was in order, whispered the name a little louder than the others. Sam caught a glimpse of the photo as the man placed it in the stack. He then placed all of the documents in his briefcase and passed it to the man at the door.

One of the men emerged from the bedroom carrying a handgun and asked if Fran wanted to keep it. She replied no, not with her grandchildren visiting; those days were over.

Sam sat in awe while the men inspected every corner of the dwelling, reassembling and connecting everything that they had taken apart. Finally, one said, "You're good." With that, they were gone.

Sam was dumbfounded. "What the hell was that with that gun?"

"Oh, it was a Glock 23, forty caliber. The police don't use the nine millimeter SIG-Sauer P225 over here, so it would be stupid to carry that. The tradeoff between the stopping power that cops prefer and accuracy isn't that significant. Not as far as I can tell, anyway."

Sam was confused. "I mean, why in hell did you have it?"

"Personal defense, dear."

"Why do you need a Glock for personal defense?"

"I don't. I just gave it up."

Frustrated, Sam persisted. "What was that with the passports? And why is there an Eileen Moran with your passport photo?"

"Covert ops, love," Fran explained softly. "Inga was my case officer and you were my cut. You remember the research she had you do at the archeological museum in Dublin to uncover whether an American agent helping the English might have been disposed of among their collection of bog bodies? Well, based on your report, we found the agent's body and I had to pass for an Irish G-2 agent in order to have the body transferred to a proper cemetery in Dublin. Inga had him disinterred later and got him to the U.S. from there. It gets complicated sometimes. No agent left behind, though, especially if he has a microchip embedded in his armpit. It was shortly after the Maze Prison escape and we weren't really sure if anyone from G-2 might have been involved, so we had to pass for G-2 ourselves. I picked up the passport in the snug of the pub we visited on that rainy afternoon in Dublin after the holy hour."

"And Rome, what was going on there? The SIG-Sauer P225, that was yours then?"

"Guilty. Inga brought it for me and you walked in on us. We had to make up the story about the Swiss Guard. I'm sorry."

"The guy who was killed, the one who knew something about the girl who disappeared, did you know something about that?

"He was a double-dealing little Mafioso who may have known something about my ex-husband's disappearance also, but he'll never talk about that, or the girl or Berne either. You know that's all I can say."

"And Leningrad?"

"Well, now that it's St. Petersburg again, I really wish the Smithsonian would do a show on the Hermitage evacuation. Wasn't the old man who showed us around delightful? But I suppose you're talking about the plague. You remember Dr. Vladimir Pasechnik, the Soviet biologist who defected in 1989? He was part of Biopreparat, a network of secret laboratories. Dr. Pasechnik was in charge of one known as the Institute of Ultra-Pure Biochemical Preparations in St. Petersburg. I was happy that he defected. He was a very nice man. The same with Dr. Alibekov. That's all I can say about that also."

"So you worked for the CIA, not the Smithsonian Institution?"

"I only worked for the Smithsonian for about six months back in '75, and I never said my office was part of the Smithsonian. I said it was *associated* with the Smithsonian. And I suppose it never occurred to you that the full name of my unit was Special Projects and International Exchange Service?"

"Special Projects... oh...uh... I don't think you ever said 'Service.'" Sam dwelled on that for a while, feeling miffed. "Wait a second. Your cut? Your cut? You mean I was expendable?"

"To Inga, dear, never to me. Never to me."

It took weeks for Sam to get over it.

. CHAPTER 21:

Big Easy, 2005

D espite fairly convincing evidence that George Bush had not accomplished his mission in Iraq, he narrowly defeated John Kerry, the latest of the silent generation to fail in a quest for the presidency. Admittedly, some of those who tried may not have been the best men for the job. Ted acknowledged as much when Beth met him for lunch before leaving New York. However, the Red Sox lifting the curse of the Bambino had dried any tears in Ted's eyes. Without such solace, a sense of disappointment in her generation and the election results dwelled in Beth's mind as she completed arrangements to move back to New Orleans. She arrived in January on the date of the Bush's inauguration to his second term, which was also her sixty-third birthday.

A decade before, Beth had purchased a large home for her parents on Audubon Place, a gated street next to Tulane University. It was terribly overpriced, but she felt compelled to do it, partly just because she was able to do so, partly out of spite to the university for the disappointments of her youth. She figured that the president of Tulane would be uncomfortable with his new black neighbors and it would serve him right, not thinking that her parents might be even more uncomfortable. Still, her parents had enjoyed the house, if not the neighbors, for some five years, up to the day Beth's father died. Her mother then became increasingly frail and isolated, with only the companionship of a nurse and servant. She had few visitors and was lonely. With that in mind, Beth decided to move to the five-million-dollar house herself and retire there.

The decision came with the collapse of Beth's personal Berlin Wall, an event as inconceivable as the destruction of the wall itself, as unforeseeable as the disintegration of the Soviet Union. Five years earlier, on the eve of the new millennium, Tom had announced that he wanted children. It was the worst shock of her life. They had agreed, no children, and then, when she was fifty-eight, the asshole wanted children, a ridiculous idea she would have rejected even if she were still of a suitable age to conceive a baby. They struggled privately with Tom's change of heart for two years and even their closest acquaintances had no idea that anything was amiss. However, he was determined and he found a partner, a woman at Goldman Sachs who had broken through the layers of big swinging dicks at that institution to reach a position equivalent to his at Lehmann, but who was still in her late thirties.

Jesus Christ, Ted was right all along, she should never have married a boomer. He had to have it all, a marriage without the burden of children and then, when he was rich and could afford it, he wanted children on the side with some sweet young thing. She'd have preferred him to have turned out to be gay.

It was a betrayal of the first order. It didn't matter that Tom claimed that his attraction to the girl came solely from his desire for a son or daughter and her willingness to have children, not from a love affair that led to the desire. It didn't matter that he made it plain that he would stay with Beth, if only she could tolerate his secret family on the side. She wasn't European enough for that, she concluded, or African enough, either. Beth cried and went to church every day for about a month. Then she got over it. It was just another confirmation of the fundamental unworthiness of men, a defect somewhere in their DNA back to some point in evolution when selfish inconsistency and obliviousness were valid survival techniques.

After the split became apparent by Tom renting an apartment and Beth scheduling many office visits with lawyers, Beth took her young assistant Jennifer into her confidence. Eventually, the two began sharing more than their unfortunate experiences with men. Beth didn't consider herself to be more than a recreational lesbian, and looked at Jennifer as a welcome distraction. It was likely to be a passing fling, but she had standards that were more flexible for women than men.

Beth was pleased when the settlement papers under her pre-nuptial agreement arrived at her office. She couldn't believe that Tom had actually signed the agreement over thirty years before, but she had the higher income then and he was young and naïve. After the settlement, maintaining luxury homes in both New York and New Orleans would be easy.

By Mardi Gras, Beth and Jennifer had settled into their luxury accommodations, taking in the krewes on parade days, partying in the Quarter, Jennifer even flashing her breasts in exchange for some finer strings of beads. Beth's mother simply accepted her daughter's new sisterhood as a symptom of the times, not knowing or wanting to know too much. The girl was infelicitously white and assertedly Unitarian, basically an atheist wearing religious lipstick, but being Tremes, her family held to its own faith and was tolerant of that sort of thing in the less well bred. In April, they all enjoyed Ellis Marsalis and Kermit Ruffins at Jazz Fest and Beth was again content.

In the months since she moved back, Beth had not contacted Frank, who still lived in New Orleans somewhere. She had no reason to consult him for business reasons and doubted that she would see him by chance. She had never had any interest in his soldier-of-fortune activities or his idiot companions. The last time she had talked to Frank and his partners, in order to get the final payment under her severance agreement, it was "Talk Like a Pirate Day" and she had to endure the idiots calling her a bilge rat in order to set sail with her booty. They would never grow up. No, she didn't run in the same circles as Frank and his disreputable wife.

Then, at the end of August, fears began to grow that Hurricane Katrina, having brushed by southern Florida, might deviate from its second projected landfall in the Florida panhandle. Beth and Jennifer were not too concerned within their secure gated community; Frank was a little more so in his residence above the Snow Angels' offices near the Saturn Bar on St Claude. Late on August 27, the mayor called for voluntary evacuations and Frank was able to get tickets for Lillian to fly to D.C. the next day, where she could stay with Dom. He would remain in New Orleans and take care of the property.

The outlook became steadily worse the day of Lillian's departure, but it was not until the next day that the mayor declared a mandatory evacuation. At that point, Beth and Frank had one thing in common: the compulsion to protect what was theirs. They ignored the order.

The residents of Audubon Place, for the most part, had heeded the hurricane warnings, stocking up on provisions necessary for a few days of inconvenience, trusting in their solidly built dwellings to weather the storm, and in some cases purchasing fuel for electrical power generators and having contractors or handymen provide some additional storm protection. The determination to ride it out changed quickly, however. After New Orleans officials confirmed the breach in the 17th Street Canal levee and reports of breaches at two other canals were broadcast, most of those Audubon Place residents who hadn't evacuated earlier did so. Actual hurricane damage on the private street was relatively minor, not seriously affected by flooding. The concern now was vandalism, home invasion, and robbery, so armed guards were employed to defend the abandoned properties. A prominent electronics millionaire on the street hired Israeli mercenaries to protect his home and those of his immediate neighbors. They quickly appeared, hanging around the arched front gate with AK-47s or similar formidable weapons on display.

Beth's home was not on the select list of properties to be protected, and with three defenseless women in the house, she wanted greater security. Having retained all the particulars on Snow Angels, she was able to reach Frank by cell and pleaded for him to contact the Blackwater types he sometimes worked with and arrange twenty-four-hour protection for the duration. Frank responded with a string of obscenities that blew past Beth with the speed of Katrina itself, but it was a small price for achieving her objective. For old times' sake, she just told him to belay it and hoist anchor on her proposition.

Money talks, especially to pirates, and Frank needed an immediate influx of cash to deal with his own situation. Beth knew Frank and his books well enough to be aware that most of his assets were sheltered offshore and he would have trouble getting to them under the present circumstances. In the end, Frank relented and he contacted a couple of hard cases whom he had trusted when they were DEA assets, just returned from Iraq after the place became too hot for contractors who could afford only small private security details. He arranged for them to come in via helicopter as part of the search-and-rescue operations.

Beth was surprised that the men Frank recruited were both African American. Being blissfully unaware that the mercenary business was well integrated, she had assumed that he was enough of a bigot to engage only stereotypically white Blackwater types and was insulted that he must have engaged these two just because she was black. Unfortunately the two would stand out in her neighborhood, Beth thought, but her mother liked them and the armored vests and automatic weapons would be sufficient to distinguish them from looters. After a few critical words to Frank, she deemed them acceptable.

The security team brought in ample supplies and serious communications gear and settled into a downstairs section of the house near her mother's master bedroom, while Beth and Jennifer watched DVDs and satellite TV in one of the upstairs bedrooms. One of the guards turned out to be an excellent cook, and struck up a rapport with Beth's mother. All in all, the five had quite a pleasant time over the eight weeks or so of the guards' presence. It wasn't exactly a vacation but it was an adventure, and Beth was disappointed when pressure from the authorities to eliminate the paramilitary presence in the city and disarm the population forced her to release her mercenaries in favor of a couple of racist rent-a-cops moonlighting from their police jobs in Metairie.

Things were not quite the same for Frank, who had hunkered down in his compound off St. Claude, surrounded by a brick wall topped with concertina wire, living on MREs, without heat and with only Lillian's pit bull, Daisy Mae, for companionship. The flooding was not so bad in his immediate corner of the ninth ward, just a few inches that lingered only a few days, not anything like the heavily flooded districts. The area, however, seemed to him to be like Mogadishu; certainly the Bush Administration seemed to see it that way, initially keeping the National Guard out of the city in fear of the dispossessed black population, whose trepidations were real but exaggerated. Trigger-happy police prowled the neighborhoods along with scavengers and looters until FEMA and company and more levelheaded military minds at last accepted that the city was part of America, not Somalia. For those days in the interim the symbol of the Super Dome seemed more like the Thunderdome, with a Mad Max or Master Blaster at every street corner.

During the day, Frank was able to use the helicopter that brought in Beth's Praetorian Guard to better purpose, performing a number of uplifting rescue and sobering recovery missions. At night he would batten the hatches, share an MRE with the dog, and sip Bushmills, occasionally entertaining volunteers working on the city's recovery. He didn't go out much; the Saturn Bar was closed and it wasn't prudent to wander over toward the French Quarter even if you were packing, as Frank always was.

After six months Frank decided to give up on the city, at least for the present; he had always preferred to do business out of Dominica anyway. He resolved to leave the office and dog in the charge of one of his helicopter buddies, and fly west to visit his son Rick in Los Angeles, taking an extra day to attend Triana's graduation from USC. He would then return to New Orleans to wrap things up before rejoining Lillian in Maryland. He was approaching seventy and it was time to move on.

A long weekend on the West Coast went smoothly. Rick had a couple of gigs at local clubs preparing for his alternative rock band's first national tour. They were entertaining for Frank, even with his country western bias, loud, but not more so than the dives in Naked Fanny or the R&R bars in Bangkok. Rick focused so intently on those sessions and the upcoming tour that he did not even question Frank's daylong absence for the graduation. The next night, Frank almost choked when he thought he saw Triana at the club where Rick was performing, but the place was packed and dark, and filled with college girls, so he must have been mistaken. Of course, she might have been there, since the group was popular with kids in their twenties. At least Rick was not into bubble-gum pop for the pre-teen set. He wondered when teenage boys stopped being turned on by mature women like Monroe and Jane

Russell, or Nancy Kwan for that matter, and started lusting for thirteen year olds like Miley Cyrus. He was happy his son had a more mature outlook and audience.

The flight back to New Orleans was uneventful, but the city had become an occupation zone. In the better part of a year, it transformed from Thunderdome to something more like he imagined Kandahar to be, except with slightly less violence and many more hookers by night. He secured his office-residence, determined to sell it at a later date, and drove miss Daisy Mae to Annapolis, leaving the shattered city in his rearview mirror.

Much to Frank's surprise, Lillian and Dom had actually gotten along passably in the latter's small house in Annapolis. Dom had never married and had long ceased to be competitive with her mother, unlike her younger sister, for whom Lillian's success with Frank was more annoying than her prior series of bad marriages. Dom had come to admire Frank for his protectiveness of her mother and his soft spot for his children, and even for her and Tikki. Her mother was still too self-centered in Dom's opinion, but it didn't interfere with her adult life and was amusing to watch now that it no longer enabled her to get everything she wanted. Vanity is not so annoying when it is less justified. The two women were now in alliance, in any case, both campaigning for Frank to agree to move to Annapolis.

Upon his arrival, Frank found himself more impressed with the town than he had anticipated. He had always mocked the naval academy, having been loyal to his biases as an air force academy cadet, but it did have a certain comfortable familiarity. His time in New Orleans and Dominica had at last undermined his Rocky Mountain discomfort with being at sea level. It might be a nice place to retire. He could now afford a respectable oceangoing boat and he and Lillian could spend six to eight months in Maryland and sail to Dominica or Martinique for the winter. So, it was final; the Big Easy was behind him.

Beth stayed. Despite Federal incompetence, local corruption and the glacial pace of recovery, New Orleans was home and she deepened her commitment through her church and philanthropies. Her young friend Jennifer loved the city as it was in the months before the storm and gradually would become again, the reviving nightlife offering an occasional balance to evenings with her aging mentor. As Tulane slowly returned to life, they both were able to take graduate classes. Offering Jennifer more freedom to enjoy the city, Beth accepted a part time instructorship, conducting occasional lectures on naked credit default swaps, certain related specialized derivatives and other exotic financial instruments. Being paid even symbolic amounts of money by Tulane seemed a measure of revenge for their denial of her aspirations years before. For those who followed her advice on derivatives in the ensuing years, but lacked Beth's skill at hedging, it turned out to be a potent revenge indeed.

CHAPTER 22:

Athens, 2008

A t around two in the morning Ari turned on the television in her Athens apartment to watch the American election returns. She had voted much earlier by absentee ballot, and was filled with anxiety as she awaiting the results. Ted and Sam had separately called in the afternoon after they had voted and Triana around midnight, phoning from Los Angeles in excitement over her first presidential election, having been a few days too young for the first Bush election and missing the second during her hectic senior year at USC. Everyone in that group, to no great surprise, had voted for Obama, and she took it as a good sign that Triana had made it to the polls. She was certainly into the arts much more than politics, and was much less versed in such matters than Ari had been at that age. Back then, the cold war was at its height, colonialism was crumbling, and the political world was torn between Camelot and Dante's *Inferno*, stirring the young to activism, not driving them to seek careers in information technology, business administration, and even theater, anything to insulate them from the political banality of the last twenty years. Triana actually voting perhaps said something about the enthusiasm of Obama's supporters and their desire for change. Ari hoped so.

The election returns came in slowly. Only a few polls had closed by three o'clock Athens time. Ari felt increasingly tense about the uncertain outcome, but felt warmly gratified by Triana's enthusiasm for the election. They had argued constantly over one trivial thing or another, and once Triana went away to school there had been months on end when they hadn't spoken. Still, not a year passed without hearing "I hate you" more than once, and there were days when that phrase seemed to mark the minutes more than the hours, but it was never about politics or race. Triana was a liberal—or, as she preferred, a humanist— like herself. She had friends of all races, including intimate male friends with whom romance had evolved naturally, not through some adolescent rebellion against family and society, not out of guilt over the prejudices of her mother or her father. Ari had purged those aversions from herself and shielded Triana from her Frank's prepossessions; he wasn't a bigot, really, but she was content with her accomplishments as a single mother and was grateful for his restraint. Triana voted for Obama because he was intelligent, open to the world, promised change and had kind eyes, much the same reasons that caused Ari to fall in love years ago, but it seemed so easy now and was so terribly hard then. The world was changing. Maybe it was about to change even more.

By four the results began to come in, favoring Obama. However, for Ari the promising returns seemed to transform the increased happiness of the last hour back to nervousness and fear. It was the approaching reality of the promise that frightened her, the prospect of a new shining city on the hill rejecting the prejudices of centuries. It seemed as close to fulfillment now as her great love had been forty-five years before. Therefore, it was a promise that could still be lost with the next declaration. Perhaps the Western states would crush the dream, not California to be sure, but those mountain and desert states, places that produced people like Cheney and elected cowboys like Bush. To relieve the tension, she finished the first bottle of wine and started on another.

Alone in her apartment, she wondered if her lost love was following the election returns. He had never contacted her since fleeing Boston decades ago. But he had returned to his country and followed his ambitions, rising to become a government minister and serving on regional commissions after that, which is exactly the life she had hoped for him. She didn't know about that for years, but with the advent of the Internet she had searched for him and was gratified by his accomplishments, satisfied that her sacrifice had not been made in vain. He must be following the elections now, that strong and honest man with the soft eyes and vulnerable heart. She found that comforting.

By five, the outcome seemed inevitable to almost all the world and by six the commentators were beginning to declare Obama the winner; yet Ari trembled with fear. Never strong in mathematics, the wine impaired her ability to sort out popular and electoral votes and she remembered the stolen Gore election. Perhaps Pennsylvania or Ohio or some other state would move from blue to red. Such things have happened. Her heart beating wildly, she thought again of Triana and how many arguments they would have had if she had admitted the truth about her great love. Triana would have thought her an idiot for her steadfast commitment to a man who had seduced her while married, had lied to her about that, and had abandoned her without ever betraying any regret for having done so. Triana had accused her of depriving her of a father, learning Frank's name only at twelve, meeting him for the first time only briefly at eighteen, never knowing how sordid and unromantic the transaction was. How much worse might it have been if she knew the truth of her one great love, knew that she sacrificed everything to preserve it? Would Triana have felt that not only had she sacrificed herself but deprived her daughter of a normal life?

At least now, half a world apart, she and those she cared about were all eagerly anticipating the same outcome: Ari, most of all, Suluhu, certainly, Ted, no doubt concealing his feelings in lame jokes at some election party, and Sam and his wife at home together, feeling vindicated in their political and social views. The only sore loser would be Frank, who almost certainly voted for the Vietnam War hero, but at least he, along with Ted and Sam, she had discovered later, had enabled Triana to follow her dreams. They had done it for Triana, but they had done it for her even more. She was grateful for them all, even loved them all, as best she could.

Shortly after seven in the morning, Obama began his victory speech and the Athens morning sun began to brighten the room through the shades. She was afraid, even then, that a sudden shot might come from somewhere in the massive crowd and end it all.

But the speech was moving and the Chicago crowd tumultuous. Ari began to feel very warm, as if she were being embraced by all those with whom she had shared the long and lonely evening. Crying, she finished her glass of wine and rose to open the window for fresh air. Raising the shade she faced the blinding golden sun of a new day. "It has finally come," she thought, just as the brightness exploded in her head and turned to black.

———

Triana called by nine, but no one answered. Repeated calls and e-mails followed with no response, and Triana began to receive concerned e-mails from Ted and Sam, who also had tried to reach her mother. She e-mailed a note to a young man in Athens who often helped Ari with computer issues, asking him to call on the apartment. An hour later, he relayed the sad news: Ari was dead. He had found Ari's lifeless body on the floor next to the television, the American election results blaring.

Two days later, Triana arrived in Athens to mourn and attend to the necessities following a sudden death. That would include confronting an enormous clutter of paper Ari had left behind in a disorganized fashion with which Triana was quite familiar, one of many bones of contention between the two over the years. Mother and daughter had moved frequently and the amount of household goods that they brought with them from place to place was quite limited; most of their residences were furnished apartments. Papers, however, were not subject to such constraints. Ari respected the written word to the extent that hardly anything covering five decades was thrown away—letters, student papers, magazines, articles, books, bills, contracts, anything typed or handwritten. Ari's mother had destroyed all of her papers when she left for college fifty years before and it would never happen again.

Consequently, boxes and suitcases filled with documents accumulated. Ari had a simple filing system: if you don't move it from where you left it you can always find it there. It was a thoroughly effective system, its sole flaw being that well-meaning visitors or her daughter would always seek to organize things, destroying the natural order. Ari had resented it, but was too polite to resist the intervention of self-appointed personal secretaries.

It took Triana a week to go through all of the papers and separate the essential records and indispensable remembrances from reams of recyclables. She formed separate piles of correspondence with Ted, smaller piles with Sam and Frank, and a few notes of her own; there was no trace of any communication with that accomplished African man her mother had mentioned on rare occasions. Triana was about to finish packing the small number of valuable files and a few mementos to bring with her to America when she finally came across her mother's will. It left Ari's modest estate to Triana and specified that she wanted to be cremated. Triana knew that and already had seen to it in the first days, but the will also outlined her wishes for the disposal of her ashes. They were to be released into the Charles River from the Weeks Memorial Bridge in homage to those she met, loved, and learned from many years before. It was mostly homage to Suluhu, but Triana could not know that and thought of Ted and Sam.

The will did not specify any memorial service, but Triana thought there should be one, so she contacted Uncle Ted, as she now called him in e-mails, and asked his advice on whom to invite. In the end, he suggested only Frank, in addition to Sam and himself. Ari's professors back in the '60s would all be gone by then and he never knew how she had felt about them. She had a good friend from Africa, but he'd learned from Sam that they had had a falling out and that he would not welcome an invitation, even if it were possible. Frank, he thought, would want to come even though he had not met Triana's mother until much later in life.

On a cold November morning the four of them gathered on the designated footbridge. It was a passably quiet spot near Dunster House, where Ted and Sam had lived as students, where on warm spring days young men would throw Frisbees to eager dogs, rowers would pass below the bridge, and lovers would recline in the grass. This was not the scene on that bleak wintry day, as they scattered Ari's ashes gently into the Charles. They had a warming lunch in Harvard Square afterward, sharing memories with Triana that her mother mostly had not. Then Ted suggested they go to the Harvard-Yale game about to start in the stadium. It was one of his flaky ideas but it would give them three hours to huddle together and talk. So they purchased cold-weather gear from the Harvard Coop and trekked to the stadium. Ted and Sam reminisced, enjoying their first-time face-to-face acquaintance with Triana and a ten-nothing Harvard win. She looked a lot more like Ari than her father, and Sam and Ted were enchanted. Frank, for his part, shivered in the bitter, gusty wind, cursed under his breath, and concluded that it was the worst college football game he had ever seen.

CHAPTER 23:

LA/Potomac, 2010

Frank wrestled fitfully with his retirement. While not exceptionally wealthy, he was nonetheless financially secure with accounts both in the US and in Martinique, the former simple IRAs, the latter accumulations transferred from the corporate holdings in Dominica when Snow Angels closed for good in 2005. He may not have exactly properly reported the Martinique assets under Beth's interpretation of IRS rules, but the Federal government was to blame for that. The Martinique nest egg was all "off the balance sheets," so to speak, and Frank took the position that it was his patriotic duty not to blunder into a security breach through indiscrete income tax reporting. It was important to do the right thing.

After Katrina, Frank moved his personal Cessna to an airfield in northern Delaware, from which he still took on the occasional contract job independently and flew for recreation. He settled on a property in Annapolis that he upgraded into a fine retirement home with his own physical labor, limited architectural talents, and extensive contractor remediation. Then he acquired a fifty-three-foot Super Sport ocean yacht for travel down the coast and into the Caribbean. That was all rewarding, but it was now done and he lost interest in the mundane tasks of maintaining the Annapolis property, the small house in Martinique where he and Lillian spent several weeks each winter, and the financial devil's triangle that the Super Sport represented. By 2007, he had transferred the Martinique house to his son Rick and daughter Nancy and split occupancy with them as a kind of family-based time share. He then had a small second house built on the Annapolis property for

Dom, from which she would manage both houses. Lillian insisted he keep the yacht. After years of feeling like the underdog, the reality crept up on him that he had been too successful and now had much too much leisure time.

It was late in coming, but after Ari's death, Frank had decided that he must see Triana for more than the passing hours they had spent together on three occasions. The first time in 1997 had been uncomfortable, the second at her college graduation too short and too filled with distractions, the third at her mother's frozen memorial too somber and much too Ivy League for his tastes. He wanted to spend a week or two with her now, getting to know her and letting her get to know him. It might be awkward and it wouldn't make up for not being in her life at all for two decades and then barely for another, but it was something he should do.

He had paid for most of her college education and Triana knew he had helped, but being an email father was not enough. He still felt the need to distinguish himself from Triana's godfathers by spending more time with her. That could be awkward, and he was reluctant to expose Lillian to this legacy of his past, but still he felt he should try to get to know his second daughter personally.

Coming to the end of the year, Frank was finally close to closing a deal on the property in the Ninth Ward. While the country as a whole remained in the doldrums, New Orleans was slowly coming back and the old place was in a decent location and had come through the disaster relatively unscathed. The right buyers appeared to have come along and Frank wanted to complete the transaction before Christmas. Perhaps he could visit Rick and Nancy in Los Angeles first, as his daughter was now stationed with the 61st Air Base Group in El Segundo. Then he could see if Triana would agree to a road trip to New Orleans. That would give them plenty of time to get acquainted. He'd bring his Willie Nelson and Outlaws CDs and they'd have a good time on the road, and they could celebrate an early Christmas in the Big Easy.

When Frank called, Triana accepted his proposition, but with some trepidation. He was her father and she had always suspected that he had a lot more to do with paying for her education than he let on. He seemed to be a nice guy and they had exchanged quite a lot of e-mails over the years, but he was a horrible writer, unable to express his emotions well at all, and she never felt that she truly knew him. He was her father, but not her parent; only Ari had played that role, and she missed her terribly. How he became involved with her mother was a total mystery. That was even more reason to get to know him better, she supposed, but the idea of four or five days of meandering through the Southwest with a seventy-year-old geezer listening to Willie Nelson, as he suggested on the phone, was not her idea of a good time. God, he'd probably listen to Rush Limbaugh, as well. It wasn't an attractive prospect, but there was one possible solution.

Ten days later, Frank flew into Los Angeles to be met by Rick and Nancy, Rick wearing what might be called alternative casual, Nancy looking more like an air force officer than Frank ever did. He was proud of them both. Frank planned to spend three days with them, and then, when dropped at the airport the next day, he would rent a car instead of taking a flight home. From there, he would pick up Triana and head off toward Vegas, then detour through Arizona and New Mexico, visiting the Grand Canyon along the way, before making the long drive to Austin and eventually Louisiana.

First, however, he would have a good time with the children he had known all their lives. They had a casual meal at Rick's house the first night, with Nancy filling in details of her high-tech military assignment and confessing to a budding romance with a young officer of equal rank, a man she thought a bit of a dolt when they were at the academy together, but had begun to see differently in recent months. Sitting across the table from her, Frank studied her face, admiring her; she had the oriental facial expressions of her mother, but they blended with his into those exotic features that you know to be foreign but can't quite place. She was five inches taller than Inga, more angular than either her or the actress from whom Frank had borrowed her name, and had steely black eyes, just like her mother. This guy had better treat her right, for his own sake. Frank would have warned the young man, but he was away from the base that week.

The first day in the city was spent mostly with a tour of El Segundo space and communications facilities, as well as Rick's recording studio. Despite their vastly different scales, both were technologically impressive, in large part for the substitution of human resources by electronics. At the air base, Frank remembered the old NASA television footage of hordes of white guys in white shirts and pocket protectors, each with their own keyboards and monitors, contrasted with the compressed, miniaturized facilities of El Segundo, controlling far more assets with far fewer people. Hell, even Ben Hoa and NKP were more labor intensive, as he remembered them.

Rick's studio was just a modest rented room with lots of expensive computer hardware. He and the other band members operated the whole thing themselves, producing CDs, DVDs, streaming videos, you name it. No wonder there's such unemployment, he thought. You can practically run the whole economy on a do-it-yourself basis. And stuff was so cheap that you only needed a part-time job, a few gigs like Rick, or a room in someone's basement in order to compete with the Rolling Stones or to hatch a plot with some dipstick in Pakistan. It was crazy; they say the middle class is disappearing and he supposed it was in many ways, but everyone today had cell phones, one or more computers, cable and satellite LCD TVs, and the like. Poverty is not what it used to be, Frank thought.

They capped off the day of touring with an adventure at a garlic-heavy restaurant called The Stinking Rose. Another busy day followed, with Rick and Nancy taking advantage of being tour guides to do the things they would have been embarrassed to do with their contemporaries. The day ended with reservations at the Wilshire. Frank would have preferred a steakhouse each night, but with his kids turning vegetarian, what could a father do, anyway?

They were reviewing the menu at their table when Triana walked in. Frank nearly melted into the floor. Rick stood up, walked over, and kissed her on both cheeks, giving her a big hug, as well. Frank was both cornered and appalled. Finally able to speak, he stammered, "Uh… uh…She's your half-sister."

"We know, Dad, we know."

It took considerable time over dinner and dessert and a long evening afterwards to work out what had transpired over the years, but it started with Nancy getting into Frank's AOL account sometime after 1997 and finding their father's old e-mails to Sam and his replies. Simple Internet searches put the three in touch and e-mail yielded to My Space, and then to Facebook and Twitter. Rick met Triana for the first time shortly after she entered USC and Nancy finally met her younger sibling after she transferred to El Segundo three years ago. They were both happy to have a little sister to look after. They had been spending a lot of time together and Triana had helped Rick with lyrics on his last CD. A couple of years ago they had resolved to tell Triana's mother of their friendship, a decision lost when Ari died suddenly on election night, but they were there to support Triana emotionally through those dark days. They had kept all of this a secret because Frank had wanted it that way and because they didn't want their real mother to know; she'd probably have everyone investigated. But their father was stupid not to tell Lillian. Lillian was a survivor. She could handle it.

After the restaurant, they all went to a quiet bar that Rick knew and Triana told her side of the story, how it felt good to have older siblings, how they helped her work out problems with her mother because they seemed like a real family even though they only became so as adults, how they had made life so much more bearable after her mother died. She had enjoyed working with Rick and was going to appear in his DVD. He even had found her an agent to help with her nascent acting career. Nancy, she said, was a good role model because she knew how to deal with aggressive males like Frank, just as important for a woman in the showbusiness world as in the military; in fact, more so, because showbusiness types are more deceiving. It sounded a bit like an insult, but Frank was flattered.

Then came the announcement. They would *all* take the road trip, using the Roadtrek camper van used for Rick's band, adding a few days to the adventure. There was one condition, however. Frank would have to tell Lillian. Rick and Nancy were pretty sure she knew something anyway, probably had for years, but their father had to man up and call her. The next day he did. Lillian

sounded surprised, as most women would after hearing such a revelation. Still, she knew he was a reckless son of a bitch when she
married him and her reaction was muted, perhaps just because of
that, perhaps because she knew more. He would find out over the
holidays. Enjoy the time with your children, she said; she looked
forward to meeting this new daughter someday. In the meantime,
she and Dom were off to Martinique. He could fly down from
New Orleans and they would spend Christmas and New Year's Day
there.

The road trip went well, although there were times when Frank
felt that he was competing with his own children, particularly Rick,
for Triana's attention. Rick and Triana were the creative ones in
the van and it was apparent that Triana was more in awe of Rick
than of Frank and his wartime exploits. She was a pacifist, a liberal,
and a Democrat, and it was clear that he had missed his opportunity to influence her in a fair and balanced direction. On the
other hand, together with Inga he had raised Nancy from day one
and even though Inga was a bigger neocon than he was, Nancy
turned out to be a liberal, a Democrat, and a near-pacifist, even as
she served in the air force. Then there was Rick, who was an anarchist, as far as Frank could tell.

He was outnumbered. They let him play a little Willie, a little
Outlaws, and quite a bit of the Doors, but no Hank Williams Junior
or George Jones, no soundtrack to *Apocalypse Now,* a tight limit on
Jimi Hendrix and Credence Clearwater, and a nix on the Animals'
"We Gotta Get Out of This Place." And of course, no Rush Limbaugh on the radio under *any* circumstances. Filling in for Frank's
rejected offerings were a lot of songs from Radiohead, Green Day,
Linkin Park, the Chili Peppers, and the Rentals and a host of tunes
unfamiliar and incomprehensible to Frank. Frank thought that
they enjoyed some of his music a lot more than he did theirs. It
wasn't that he hated it; it was just that it didn't have the edge to it
that his music did.

They discussed his reactions to current music and related matters at casinos, national parks, tourist traps, and Motel 6s all the
way to Louisiana. By the time they reached New Orleans, Frank
was feeling like a fossil, but he opened the door to his fortress off

St. Claude with some degree of new understanding. They aired the place out and sprawled out on the sofas with bottles of cheap wine and whiskey strewn across the tables, along with a paper bag full of muffalettas and fries they bought in the quarter. It would be an early evening after the long trip, but Frank had been brooding behind the steering wheel and wanted to get his thoughts off his chest.

"The music in the car over the last week made me think," he began. "Your music seems to be about such small stuff. We were more messed up than you are today back when we were young, but at least we felt that we had clear enemies. A lot of us considered ourselves to be young and 'fought the power' until we passed forty; some still do. Reagan was already seventy his first year in office for Christ's sake. There were always old farts in charge until Clinton; well, we tried youth with Kennedy and he got shot for his troubles in less than three years. Politicians seemed to be larger than life then, for good or evil, and at least they were taken seriously.

"It's different now, the enemies aren't so clear except for al-Qaeda, the adults are all over the map politically, still as messed up as when they were in their twenties. The kids in the military, like you, Nancy, are so small in numbers that you don't affect society at all, and civilians, like you, Rick, aren't at risk and don't have anything to protest against. I like your music, Rick, but it's got no bite, nobody's mad as hell anymore, just sad as hell. It's a lot harder to get worked up about incompetence and pandering than about good and evil. Our villains were all about good and evil; your villains are basically petty shoplifters with big appetites, and the good guys are like rent-a-cops taking money on the side and not doing their main jobs. Screw 'em all.

"Triana, you know I'm so sorry about your mother, but at least she left feeling something big and positive happened that election night and hasn't had to witness the nonsense of the last three years. I almost envy her for that. I place more of the blame on the president than all of you, but it's the pettiness all around that's so tiring. It's funny, we used to say don't trust anyone over thirty, but most of us didn't really believe it. You don't say it these days, but really ought to."

Nancy and Rick were not supportive, having heard Frank's rants before. Rick pulled out his guitar and they entertained him with selections from some of the lamest songs from Frank's day, including renditions from Brenda Lee, Johnny Horton, Del Shanon, and Theresa Brewer. They then hit him with a medley of *People*, *Feelings* and a couple of soft rock Manilow tunes. Frank threw up his hands and went to bed.

All in all, the road trip had gone well. They had another four days before Frank would fly to join Lillian and Dom in the islands, so the younger set toured the recovering region by day while Frank attempted to close the pending deal on the property. They would rendezvous each evening to enjoy the reviving nightclub scene. Frank's transaction went smoothly except for one minor glitch: the need for signatures from one of the new owners. Fortunately, he lived in Potomac, Maryland and Frank could easily drive to his home after returning to Annapolis after the holidays.

Martinique was delightful as always, and Frank's anticipated confrontation with Lillian about Triana never came about. He finally asked her if she had known about his second daughter, and she replied that of course she did. "How long?"

"Oh, since about 1984," she said. "But it was nice of you to protect me all these years."

But how did she find out? "Who would you think? Beth, of course."

That seemed to eliminate the need for any further discussion. Frank had come away from the journey judging that Triana was a lot like her mother, feeling that they had a good rapport but without the intimacy that came from raising Rick and Nancy, concluding that there was no way that it could ever be any different, and now realizing that there was no need to feel guilt over agreeing to impregnate Ari. Triana was 100 percent Ari's child; that's how Ari wanted it then and how Triana needed it now. The last thing that he told Triana in New Orleans was that her mother taught him everything that he ever needed to know about women and he treasured her memory for that. That was a good place to leave it.

Frank, Lillian, and Dom stayed in Martinique until early January, then returned to Annapolis. The lawyers had finished the paperwork on selling the New Orleans house and on January 26, they arranged to meet Frank at the buyer's home in Potomac for the final signatures and notarization. It was a miserable, blustery day from the outset and the early afternoon meeting stretched into the early evening, as the lawyers raised and resolved one minor question after another. It was dark and the road was icy when Frank departed for home, driving a little faster than prudent, eager to get away from the narrow road paralleling the river and onto the Interstate.

Then the sledders appeared in the headlights. Frank was still a pilot and didn't waste time having his life flash before his eyes, but instead recalled evasive maneuvers over the Plain of Jars or the Altaplano. Instantly he turned the steering wheel sharply to the right, sending the car into a spin, kicking up gravel on the shoulder, slowing the vehicle almost imperceptibly, missing the sledders by a foot or so at most, and hurtling the car over the embankment.

"Damn, I've still got it," he thought, as the car sank rapidly into the icy waters.

CHAPTER 24:

Arlington, 2011

"**N**o, it's not about you, you idiots. It's *fiction!*" Ted was explaining his new project to the small group gathered at the Hotel Palomar in Rosslyn for the reception following the services at nearby Arlington Cemetery. He decided last night, he said, to call it the end of a good run with the advertising agency, retire, and write a novel. The story would be about the Silent Generation—their generation—and would chronicle over fifty years, an epic in scope, but told with all the cultural sensitivity of, say, a Viagra commercial. And, yes, he would draw on incidents and conversations that came up at the Ward, and even some from the wake last evening, but he would scramble the plot in such a way that no one could recreate personal histories. He would merge some aspects of the real participants into the characters in his drama and deconstruct others into multiple characters, fooling with their romantic liaisons and shifting around offspring. Hell, he might even turn Beth white. In any case, he informed the assembled, they'd all come off better in the novel than they do in real life. Everyone would have at least some redeeming characteristic, as difficult a task as that would be for him to attempt. "As long as it makes you happy," Beth uttered to no one in particular.

Driving to Arlington in the early morning for the military ceremony, Lillian was grateful that Frank's relatives hadn't imposed their fundamentalist religious beliefs and right-wing politics on the crowd at the wake, that Ted hadn't made as much of an ass of himself as she had feared, and that there had been no major confrontations with Beth, a near miracle given past incidents and her own feelings.

Isabella had called after she arrived home late the previous evening to inform her of the terrible practical joke that had been played on Frank; the poor girl hoped Lillian would not hold it against the funeral home. Lillian assured her that it wasn't a problem, as long as she fixed him up before transporting him to Arlington.

Lillian did not take any pleasure in the aftermath concerning her late husband's particulars, but she had enjoyed Sam's indecorous verbal blunder and the excuse it provided for their private chat and the long overdue reconciliation it created. Her prior episodes with Sam, which were brief but crucial interludes in the course of their separate lives, had both ended badly, the first with her blaming him unfairly for not terminating her pregnancy, resulting in the first and worst of her bad marriages. But their second run-in had had an even worse conclusion; she had dumped New Haven on him, killed a potential renewal of their friendship through her absurd affair with Ted, and then compounded that by marrying Frank. Sam had more or less steered her into both relationships, but they were his best friends and he couldn't have felt good about it, given their own history. That had all happened over twenty-five years ago, a long time to leave such matters unresolved.

Since she was never made aware of the horsehair incident, Sam's outburst had come as something of a shock, rather like sticking a barbeque fork in a European electrical outlet. However, when she hauled Sam over to the corner and he blurted it out, she knew immediately that it was true, no doubt the source of the obscure stud farm references that would send Frank's Air America buddies into torrents of laughter. At that realization, she could only laugh herself. "Christ, what a moron," she had exclaimed to Sam, but he had immediately came to Frank's defense. No one gave anyone more second chances than Sam. Thank God for that.

As the viewers slowly arrived from the cemetery, Ted approached Lillian to express his condolences again and to apologize for any embarrassment he may have caused at the wake by joking around or harassing Beth. She laughed and reassured him that Sam had more than covered for him, and besides she knew that neither he nor Sam had pulled down Frank's pants; she did. "But why?"

248

"Ted, dear, I slept with the man for a quarter of a century and never noticed anything. How could I not check it out? I intended to rearrange his uniform, but that girl, Isabella, kept shutting down lights and I couldn't see anything. Hell, I don't see that well these days in broad daylight. Anyway, I just had to leave him as he was and send everyone off. I figured no one but the funeral home staff would know."

"And?"

"And what?"

"Did he have a hole in his dick?"

Some questions being a little too personal, Lillian blushed and did not reply, but that itself was a sufficient answer. Ted was satisfied that while Frank had gotten away with the prize, as he considered Lillian, the man did have his blemishes, so to speak.

The Arlington Cemetery services had been dignified and moving. Almost everyone from the wake was there, including Frank's ex-wife, whom Lillian had cornered at the end of the previous evening and invited. It hadn't been difficult to figure out. How many Chinese women in trench coats was she supposed to think her husband hung out with, anyway? And she identified Triana in much the same manner, Ted and Sam scurrying around overprotectively to make sure the young woman was feeling well, not to mention Rick hovering around her. Honestly, they must think she was senile already.

The only people who did not appear at the cemetery were her daughters and Beth's friend Jennifer. Tikki, she suspected, simply could not bring herself to more than one cursory appearance. There was still bad blood between Lillian and her youngest and there probably always would be. That was unfortunate, but there was nothing to be done about it. At least, Tikki and Dom both grew up with strong wills, perhaps her only real achievement as a parent, and Lillian was happy that at least her eldest acknowledged that.

As for Dom and Jennifer, they had gone home together the night before and were probably still snuggled up in Dom's cabin, a couple of lonely lesbians approaching fifty. Dom was a much better match for Jennifer than Beth, Lillian thought, and Frank would have loved this development. Lillian had been aware of Dom's proclivities for some time and was happy for them, as they eliminated their old jealousies and enabled them to resume a decent mother daughter relationship.

Lillian expected, however, that Beth would be upset with Jennifer's defection and probably vindictive, given that Beth detested her anyway. To her surprise, that did not occur. In fact, Beth singled her out at the hotel reception for a long chat, very friendly, filled with condolences, treating her as if they had a special connection because of their many years of living in New Orleans. Beth, it seemed, was to be honored in New Orleans the next day with a number of celebrities along the lines of Oprah, Clooney and Streisand, all charitable donors to the city. Beth's love of the city was real and she had given more money to local charities than most of the honorees, save Oprah, and if you counted investments as well as pure donations, she was in that league, as well.

Beth told Lillian that in her speech the next day she would honor Frank for his work in helicopter rescues and would note his heroic passing. He had come through for her during Katrina and she owed him for that. Lillian thanked her for her kindness, but added, "You won't say anything about High Noon or body piercings, will you?" Beth laughed a little defensively and promised she wouldn't, kissing Lillian on both cheeks. The Irish, Ted once said, honored their heroes only after they were safely dead and buried, and that seemed to be how Beth felt about relationships. Still, Lillian accepted the gesture.

Beth then worked her way to the exit to catch a taxi to Reagan National, hugging Ted on the way and asking Sam if he forgave her. "No, Beth, of course not," he replied jovially. He meant what he said, but Beth could take it any way she wanted and obviously accepted the opposite meaning as a working hypothesis. Sam was generous in forgiveness, but when forgiveness wore thin for those who injured his friends, telling the truth with a smile was the next best option. She'd reach the proper interpretation eventually.

Sam looked around the room for Inga. He had a few words to say about being a "cut-out" that wouldn't have been prudent to say the previous night, when she was trying to fade into the woodwork.

Now that the charade had failed, he could confront the woman and intended to do so. He found her at the complimentary bar, sipping Grey Goose vodka on the rocks. He confronted her aggressively. Sadly, however, a decade of resentment for Inga playing a double game, manipulating his assignments with Fran, could not overcome the cold rationality of the case officer. Madame Inga was a professional, always had been, always the queen of MICE, the intelligence agency guidelines for recruiting agents and defectors. In a corner of the reception room, she quietly reminded him that he had enjoyed the money for his assignments, had shared her anti-Soviet ideology, was compromised in his own way by sleeping with an agent—Fran—and certainly had his ego stroked by seeing himself as a valuable asset. In fact, his only problem since he found out about Fran's higher status was his bruised ego. She was happy he blamed her rather than his wife.

Everything she said was true. Sam did enjoy the financial, patriotic, and personal satisfaction rewards of playing spy, but he couldn't have gotten through Rome and Leningrad without Fran. Accepting Inga's logic, he had no gripe. So, they put the animosity aside and "caught up," to the extent it is possible to do so with a CIA case officer when one's security clearance expired ten years ago. Had she remarried? Yes, but she couldn't say to whom. Was she about to retire? No, but never say never. Where was she working? Same old...same old. Her focus? Couldn't say, but she would always be known as the woman from Macao. Had she kept in touch with Frank? Yes, because of the kids, of course; they were both proud of them. And Frank knew quite a lot about her work, so she needed to know about Lillian, Ari, and Triana, as well. New Haven? Naturally, not a problem, Lillian got lucky. Suluhu? Yes, not a problem, he's one of the good guys. Can Ted consult with you on this book he plans to write? "Of course," she smiled, "but it might be more than he really wants to know; we had to check out him and his wife as well."

"Uh, what do you know about the graffiti in the men's room outside the Barrington offices, in say, 1980?"

Inga smiled enigmatically. Then Sam asked a question that he had wanted an answer to for quite a while:

"Exactly how deadly is my wife with a Glock 23 or SIG-Sauer P225, anyway?"

"There are things you don't want to know, Sam. Trust me."

The reception went smoothly, the awkwardness of the wake having worn off the prior evening with the realization that those you had thought about over the intervening years—some with resentment, some with yearning, others with curiosity—had been frozen in your mind, and your images of them were no longer valid. They were older; you were older.

By the time of the reception, most of the attendees were comfortable with the changes, although the interactions varied greatly between those who had seen each other often and those whose last meeting had taken place more than a decade before. Ben, for example, took for granted Rafi's frailty and mental decline and Rafi accepted Ben's increasing paternalism without question. Sam, on the other hand, spoke to Rafi as if it were still 1985 and Rafi did his best to respond in kind, expounding on the latest technology and how he had contributed to it. Rafi would leave the reception feeling revived and really pissed at Ben for the first time in years. That was good for both of them.

It was that way for Ted, as well. He had been in touch with Sam, not too often, but relatively recently and easily related to Sam and Fran as retirees; they, in turn, respected his devotion to his sons and were unsurprised by his retirement announcement. Ted, however, could only respond to Lillian as he had that long time before. They flirted and, beyond that, challenged each other to respond to the moment as the current reality, rather than reacting to one another in some routine pattern determined by the past. It was stimulating. The disruption of easy habits over the two days affected all those present, but perhaps Ted the most.

———

The gathering broke up by late afternoon, necessitated by travel arrangements and Lillian's limited claim on hotel space. Driving up I-95 to Manhattan after the reception, Ted thought back on the two days, concluding that his was a strange generation, indeed. The Greatest Generation had their war heroes, and Rick and Ilsa always had Paris with the *La Marseillaise* playing in the background. His mostly had stalemates and defeats, and he and Lillian made love in a portable toilet to a really bad rendition of *Don't Worry Baby*. Still, just because it was gross didn't mean it wasn't real, and, still, the country came to dominate the world in their time, as enemies collapsed or became more and more like them. There must have been something of value in there somewhere. Of course, the boomers eventually screwed it up, destroyed the economy, and turned politics into partisan squabbles among crackpots. *Damn, the young will soon be seeking the wisdom of the elders among that bunch. We should warn them. No, if they haven't figured it out by now, they never will.*

For the first forty miles driving north, Ted mulled over the music of his generation, concluding, with all due respect to Frank's preference for the Doors, that the signature tune must be "American Pie" and not just because people his age grew up with the ill-fated musicians before the day their music died. It was unfair, he thought, that some accused Don McLean of not reaching his potential just because his inspiration was concentrated so strongly in that one song and one or two others. That seemed to be the curse of the times for his friends at the wake and reception, for the generation as a whole, the generation lost in space; to be judged by what they had *not* done, not what they achieved. They made progress in gender and racial equality, but sexual preference and religious divisions seemed as unresolved as ever, among his contemporaries as much as those who came later. Why didn't they take on those issues? Why didn't they do more to stave off the now threatening economic collapse? Why didn't any of them rise up to lead the country? And so they existed as silent placeholders between the last defenders of the republic and its traditional values and the squabbling beneficiaries of an over-expanded empire. Well, screw the next generations if they can't take a joke. Only unsolved problems make life worth living anyway. He wouldn't take that away from them even if he could.

He passed Baltimore, thinking Lillian would be home by now, at peace with the thought that the reunions were not a complete disaster. He smiled and let his mind drift back to the song. He loved it, he admitted, not because it *was* profound but because the lyrics *seemed* both profound and obscure. Just like his ad campaigns. Why should the levies being dry be a bad thing? They wouldn't agree with that in New Orleans. How does moss grow on a rolling stone? What quartet did Lenin listen to while reading Marx? The answers didn't really matter, but the questions were somehow symbolic of his contemporaries' dilemmas, allowing in good will for a multitude of interpretations. He could never bring himself to corrupt the song by using it in advertising designed to achieve a fixed commercial result.

The song was about enduring premature losses. Members of his generation experienced its share of them: leaders who inspired them cut short, JFK, King and Bobby and others; many of their cohorts, now names inscribed on that wall near the reflecting pool with those of the boomers they fought alongside or, worse, led into battle only to risk being fragged for doing so; worst of all, their lost bards and minstrels, Buddy, Richie, the Bopper, Morrison, Janice and the rest of the endless list. The lyrics allowed you to mourn those you missed in your own way and not think about the others. That said, however, he was still waiting for a girl who sang the blues to bring some happy news.

Despite Ted's melancholy, he took pride that it was *his* generation, more than the one before, or the boomers, who confronted the changing relationships between men and women. By 1967, when the first boomers had just turned twenty-one, the post-war sexual revolution and its less frivolous sister, the feminist movement, were already irreversible, birth control had been accepted, and the legal and social foundations for equal rights in the workplace were established, displacing the traditional bifurcation of male and female roles. By the 1970s, the turmoil of this transition was beginning to slow from the rapid boil of the sixties to a less active simmer, tapering to the luke-warm eighties. You could see it in the music, his music, the rough edges of rock and roll displacing the ballads of the fifties, then diversifying to speak more clearly to the multiple subcultures the upheaval created. It seemed like they were killing romance, groups like the Doors or Stones, but in reality they were merely struggling obdurately for our right to redefine it on our own terms.

Sam, he thought, had gotten swept up in trying to make sense of it all, trying to place himself in the heads of these women, not realizing that they were just as confused, just as torn apart by the disintegration of comfortable, well-defined roles as he was. Frank, he thought, may have been a sexual opportunist, gathering the low-hanging fruit that was so plentiful back in the day. Still, Lillian aside, he didn't hold that against him. Frank did not so much exploit women as go with the flow, part of that flow being that many women didn't really want men to understand them until they worked it out for themselves. Frank was good with that, but Sam never got it through his skull. It was ironic that despite all that desire to understand women, he didn't have a clue to what his own wife was up to while Frank, through his ex-wife, undoubtedly did. Still, Frank and Sam were each unrepentant in the course he chose, each tolerant of the other.

Ted felt battered enough by women and didn't really want to know any more about any of them, especially Beth, who maybe was more complicated than all the rest. She was, from what he'd been told by Beth's social friends, a very good person outside of the office; but if you worked with her you had to watch your back unless you were a dead Irishman. How in hell did we create that? Then he thought of the odd floral arrangement Beth sent to Barrington's funeral. They were not flowers of sympathy; Ben's description was clear on that. Something had happened there. And perhaps other things had happened to her long before she joined the Ward. So, let it go. She had her reasons.

Like Sam, Ted adored Ari nearly all his adult life. He resented that Ari had dumped all her troubles on Sam back at Harvard and that, despite his continuing correspondence with her, she chose to consult Sam about the baby, not him. He felt the same about Lillian confessing her troubles to Sam. It didn't seem right, even though he almost certainly was better off without those dubious favors. In the end, a vague empathy may be better than an in-depth understanding.

Ari defiantly made the biggest decision a woman could make about the irrelevance of race, made it in a society that was not yet ready to accept that conclusion, even in the midst of the most liberal bastion of enlightenment in the country, if you believed those academic hypocrites. She paid for her decision with a life of emotional isolation, rescuing others, but never herself. Sam was right, it was courageous, but it was a fire that could consume you if you came too close. He had thought he had wanted to know everything about Ari, and then about Rebecca, who was having the somewhat same struggles about religion. But by the time he had reached middle age he concluded that was stupid and he didn't regret it now. In the end, Ari proved a good friend and he was able to achieve a reasonable peace with Rebecca. He and Ben were the only inmates of the Ward not to be divorced and that counted for something. Thirty-five years of marriage before she died. He shook his head in disbelief at that fact and pulled through the first booth of the Jersey Turnpike, allowing the scanner to collect his toll.

Yes, he thought, his generation bore the brunt of the sexual revolution, feminism and their intermingling with race and religion, attempting to untangle the tangled ball of twine it inherited and rewind it with less snarls and fewer broken strings. It couldn't be done perfectly, of course, you had to tie a lot of knots and make a lot of splices. It wasn't a thing of beauty, but it was serviceable. No apologies.

As he approached New York, beginning to remember the coming tenth anniversary of nine-eleven, he recalled the story of the hijackers being enticed by the promise of eternity with seventy-two virgins. True or not, the primary meaning of that story was simply *you idiots don't know anything about women*. The prospect of spending eternity with seventy-two women sounded like hell to him.

Even at seventy, however, Ted was not quite done with women. Lillian had let him know that it was going to be a little lonely without Frank blustering around the house, noting that Dom had her own life and wouldn't be around much, especially after she met Jennifer at the wake and hit it off so well. Perhaps he would like to come down for a few days of sailing on the Chesapeake or even go

down to the islands, now that he was retiring. He accepted immediately. Lillian wasn't singing the blues now and was still pretty hot
for seventy.

The first graffiti appeared as he drove into the city, triggering
a nearly automatic reaction. The Duke don't dance, he thought,
Dux a non ducendo, the Duke don't dance. *But that should never stop
you from dancing yourself.* Words of the prophets, baby. Words of the
prophets.

CPSIA information can be obtained at www.ICGtesting.com
Printed in the USA
LVOW121739050712

288897LV00019B/122/P